Sh⋯ **Flint** lives in Singapore with her husband and two ch⋯⋯n. She began her career in law in Malaysia and also wo⋯⋯ at an international law firm in Singapore. She tra⋯⋯d extensively around Asia for her work, before res⋯⋯g to be a stay-at-home mum, writer, part-time lec⋯⋯ and environmental activist.

Sh⋯⋯i also writes children's books with cultural and en⋯⋯mental themes, including *Ten* and *The Seeds of Time*, as ⋯⋯ as the Sasha series of children's books.

Vi⋯⋯amini's website at www.shaminiflint.com

Inspector Singh Investigates: A Curious Indian Cadaver

Shamini Flint

piatkus

PIATKUS

First published in Great Britain as a paperback original in 2012 by Piatkus
Reprinted 2012

A CIP catalogue record for this book
is available from the British Library.

ISBN 978-0-7499-5342-3

Typeset in Caslon by M Rules
Printed and bound in Great Britain by
Clays Ltd, St Ives plc

Papers used by Piatkus are from well-managed forests
and other responsible sources.

MIX
Paper from
responsible sources
FSC® C104740

Piatkus
An imprint of
Little, Brown Book Group
100 Victoria Embankment
London EC4Y 0DY

An Hachette UK Company
www.hachette.co.uk

www.piatkus.co.uk

For Subash and Qrissya

Reporter: What do you think of Western civilisation?
Gandhi: I think it would be a good idea.

'Khoon ka badla khoon se lenge!'
We shall avenge blood with blood.

Prologue

31 October 1984.

In India, word of disaster spreads like head lice. Eyewitnesses and police officers whisper news to family, family members talk to friends and neighbours, they gossip with the servants, coolies, drivers and with the boys over a whisky at the cricket club. And not forgetting, of course, the cross-wired, long-distance, static-filled trunk calls to relatives. Soon, all is known, some of it true, some of it mistaken, some of it made up for effect – different accounts believed by different people. But the story has a life of its own. Eventually, careful versions of events appear on television and radio – but nobody trusts Doordarshan for the truth. Theirs is just one version, the official version, the one the government wants you to believe. Usually, it means that people believe the opposite. What is it that they say about India? If something is true in India, then the equal and opposite is true as well.

When Indira Gandhi was killed, we heard it first from the

1

milkman. He was shouting and angry, spilling his milk out of the steel pots attached to his bicycle, waving his arms and threatening retribution against whoever had done it.

'Indira Amma is dead! Indira Amma has been killed!'

They called her that – Indira Amma – the Mother of India. Not the Sikhs, of course, but the rest, especially the Hindus and the Congress supporters.

'Was it the Moslems?' demanded the milkman of no one in particular although he'd gathered quite an audience of anxious housewives. They are troublemakers, he said. Nothing has changed since Partition. If they have spilled Nehru-Gandhi blood, theirs will flow like the great rivers of India, like the Ganges and the Brahmaputra.

Mata shushed the milkman and said it was all wild talk and nothing was known except that Indira was dead, and maybe even that wasn't true. Certainly, no one knew who had killed her. Remember, she said, in that schoolteacher's voice, people assumed that Moslems killed Mahatma Gandhi and it turned out to be a radical Hindu.

But in case there was to be trouble, *Mata* asked the cook to check the food stocks and told us that there was no need to go to school that day. It wasn't safe. You see, when Indians get het up, crowds gather as quickly as flash floods during the rains, mobs form, shops are barricaded by terrified owners and traffic grinds to a standstill while a sea of people flows past, shouting and chanting and punching their fists in the air. If Indira Amma had been assassinated, said *Mata*, it was better to stay at home, stay away from crowds, stay out of trouble.

It was difficult for us kids to feel sorry about her death. Not when the death of a prime minister meant a holiday from school; from Mr. Arun with the cane and Mrs. Janaki with the 'spot tests' whenever she didn't feel like teaching.

We first heard it was the Sikh bodyguards later that evening. *Pita* came home from work early. He walked in from the main road and he was dusty, pale and worried. Her own bodyguards had murdered the prime minister, he told us. Satwant Singh and Beant Singh were their names. One had been killed on the spot and the other was in custody.

Mata cried when she heard the news.

'But is it true?' she asked. 'Perhaps there has been some mistake. You know as well as I do that there are always rumours ...'

'I think not,' said father, shaking his head. 'It is revenge for Amritsar. Some say she was shot sixteen times. A defenceless, elderly woman.' He clasped his hands together as if praying for deliverance. 'A price will be paid for this.'

Pita was a middle-ranking civil servant in Delhi. He was a quiet man, small-sized, unlike the vast majority of Sikhs. His turban always looked too big for him, sitting on his head like a wild mushroom. He was a disappointment to Tara Baba, my grandfather, but I didn't know why. Perhaps it was because he wasn't ambitious. I heard Tara Baba ask him once, in an angry tone, whether he planned to spend the rest of his life stamping documents in triplicate in a musty office. *Pita* had smiled a little and said, 'We value different things. I respect your choices. Why can't you respect mine?'

Mata was adamant. 'Gandhi should never have sent the army into the Golden Temple. Sikh hearts have turned to stone. And now see the result.'

'I'm not sure she had a choice,' replied *Pita*. 'Temples are

3

places of worship, not war. We should never have let separatists hole up in our *gurdwaras*.'

Pita always looked at both sides of an argument. It was one of his tricks that really annoyed me. I liked things to be certain; right and wrong, black and white. For *Pita*, everything was a point of view. Surely there were some truths that could not be turned on their head? Maybe the Prime Minister's bodyguards shouldn't have killed her. But Tara Baba said thousands of innocent Sikhs had died in Amritsar and the government was covering it up.

That night, no one felt like sleeping. I could hear *Mata* and *Pita* whispering together until a cotton-candy, pink dawn broke outside. I stood in the garden and took a deep breath. Early morning is the only time that the air in Delhi is crisp and fresh, like cold milk. And then *Mata* called me in.

There was no telephone at home so we didn't know that mobs had rampaged through Trilokpuri in West Delhi, attacking Sikh households and businesses. The leaders said that Sikhs had been celebrating the assassination, that we had handed out sweets to the neighbours and *gurdwaras* all over the country were lit up as if it was Diwali. But none of it was true. Not in our area anyway. Some of the neighbours came to ask my father's advice because he was a civil servant and they thought he might know what was going on. Where are the police? they asked him. Is the army to be deployed? *Pita* said that the soldiers would arrive soon to keep the peace and things would return to normal. It was best to just stay indoors and lock up tight and wait for the curfew to be announced.

'Should we remove our turbans, cut our hair?' suggested a broad-shouldered bear of a man, staring at his feet and not meeting the eyes of the others. 'Just temporary, you understand?'

'It is part of our Sikh identity handed down by the gurus,' insisted one of the neighbours. 'I will not take it off at the first sign of trouble!'

Pita raised a hand and touched his turban with thin fingers as if faintly surprised that he was encumbered with one too.

Later, I noticed that father had changed his dark turban to one of pure ivory. I knew from funerals that white was a sign of mourning. What was he mourning? I wondered. Indira? Sikhs? The future?

'Khoon ka badla khoon se lenge!' We heard the chants later that day just down the road from our Sikh colony in West Delhi. *We shall avenge blood with blood.* The sun was so intense overhead that it was like standing too close to the stove when mother was flipping chapattis.

I was badly scared by then. I could see that *Mata* was stealing glances at us children from time to time. *Pita*'s face had hollowed and his pepper beard looked like poison ivy climbing up his cheeks.

A thin figure ran up to our front gate – and to my surprise, I recognised the milkman. He had a can of paint and he marked our front gate with a great red splash. It looked like blood, streaked against the gate, splattered on the walls, dripping onto the pavement.

'What is he doing?' I asked.

'Marking the Sikh homes,' answered *Pita* quietly. I don't think he really meant for me to hear that. He was just speaking his thoughts aloud. I suddenly realised how easy it was to identify Sikhs because of the *dastaar*, our turban. No wonder that burly fellow had wanted to take his off. Mind you, it wouldn't have helped. The milkman would know every Sikh household in the colony – hadn't he been delivering our milk for years?

'The police, the army. Where are they?' asked *Mata*, her voice a whisper, barely louder than the chants that were getting closer.

'There is no one.'

The mob reached our gate. They were screaming for us to come out, hungry hands rattling the gates. We cowered indoors like mice. Finally, one of them lit a huge kerosene torch and held it high so that the air around his head shimmered and I feared him as if he was a spirit creature come up from the bowels of hell to torment us.

'Come out now or we will burn the house down and all the Sikh traitors within it.'

My father shouted, 'There are women and children here. I beg you to leave us.'

'You come out and we will consider sparing the rest,' hollered a large, well-fed man. He looked like one of those dignitaries who always sat in a front row armchair at cricket matches.

'That is Anil Gupta – from the Congress party,' said *Pita* and his tone was cracked and parched like a patch of earth without rain. I was too young to understand but later I realised that it meant that the violence against Sikhs had been instigated by powerful figures. It explained why there was no sign of the police or military. We were on our own.

'Come out now,' screamed one of the others and there were howls and jeers from the rest.

Pita walked to the door. 'I have to go,' he said, 'or we will all be killed.'

'*Naa*,' whispered *Mata*.

'You try and escape out of the back door,' he insisted.

I was sobbing now. Why was there no way to show despair except through the same tears which I used when *Mata* would not buy me sweetmeats from a street vendor?

Pita put his hand on my head. 'You will be the man of the house when I am gone, son. Take care of your mother and siblings.' He smiled a little. 'Especially little Ashu.'

I turned to look at my young sister. She was in *Mata*'s arms, wide-eyed but not crying. Not really understanding what was going on.

Pita walked out to the gate.

'Come, *bhai*. Come and tell us why you killed our Mother!'

I recognised the mocking tone of a school bully who'd cornered the bookworm behind the toilets. Father kept walking, his pace never faltering. I would never have guessed that he had that kind of courage. He was such a quiet, gentle man, unable to raise his voice in anger even when I played truant from school. He reached the front gate, unlocked it, opened it a crack and stepped through. Later, when I revisited the scene in my head as I did through most of my childhood, I realised that he was trying to shift the focus from the house, from us.

A mob is more than the sum of individuals. It is more like a single creature with many arms and legs, hydra-headed but working with one idea. This creature grabbed *Pita* with its many hands and tied his own behind his back. The many mouths jeered and spat. Suddenly, it produced a tyre and put it around my father's neck. The man with the torch held the burning end to the tyre and it caught fire. *Pita* writhed and screamed. I was about to run to him when *Mata* grabbed my arm and then wrapped her arms around my skinny struggling frame.

'Tanvir, *naa*. We must leave him. Come now.'

I hesitated and she screeched at me, 'You heard what your father said. You are the man of the house now!'

Ashu began to cry. She didn't like it when *Mata* was upset.

I turned around to have one last look. *Pita* had fallen to the ground. They were kicking him as he lay. His head and turban were on fire, like a human torch.

'Khoon ka badla khoon se lenge!' We shall avenge blood with blood.

One

Mrs. Singh had recently stumbled upon the Internet. This was a source of enormous aggravation to her husband, Inspector Singh of the Singapore Police Force. Especially as he was still on medical leave from his job as Singapore's most successful and least appreciated murder cop. The inspector felt quite well enough to return to work after his mishap in Cambodia but his bosses were adamant that he adhere to the letter of his medical leave certificate and not return a day, an hour or even a minute too soon. This supposed concern for his health was a thin disguise. Superintendent Chen had merely seized a golden opportunity to keep him out of the way for a while. Singh had to admit that there was a certain irony in his desperate desire to return to the office. Usually, when ensconsed behind his big and pathologically orderly desk, his foremost desire was to slip out for a long lunch, ideally accompanied by a cold beer and followed by an afternoon nap.

'Eighty per cent of doctors in the United States are of Indian origin,' snapped Mrs. Singh, looking up from the computer for a moment to ensure that he was paying attention.

'That can't possibly be right,' protested Singh.

'It says so right here,' said his wife, pointing a bony finger at the screen and basking in the blue light like an acolyte before a high priest.

'Not everything you read on the Internet is true,' muttered Singh, addressing his remark to the skinny back in the flamboyant pink caftan.

A slight stiffening of the muscles along her spine and an aggressive jabbing of the 'Page Down' key indicated her resistance to this notion but she did not deign to respond.

Mrs. Singh didn't have a modicum of cynicism when it came to the Internet. She'd been brought up to believe that the print news was always accurate and not even the suspicious lack of bad news in the Singapore papers had taught her caution. She had now transferred this blind faith to the musings of various self-proclaimed pundits on the Web. And her current all-encompassing favourite subject was India.

Perhaps, mused Singh, still contemplating his wife's back, it was a reaction to the Singapore government's constant lauding of China's economic success, industrial might and abundance of culture. Non-Chinese Singaporeans like his wife were forced to look elsewhere for inspiration or accept this Chinese hegemony. And India, the 'world's largest democracy' (as Mrs. Singh had informed him complacently, and slightly more accurately than usual, over breakfast), was the natural choice.

Singh sighed and wondered if he dared sneak out for a smoke. His various doctors had been adamant that he needed to give up cigarettes, at least during his recuperation. Singh had agreed, his sudden brush with mortality having made him more cooperative than normal. But he was fast discovering that the flesh was indeed weaker than the spirit. And while he would have happily succumbed to the temptation to light up, Mrs. Singh, as his guardian – more like prison warden – was keeping a close eye on him. Except, of course, when she was immersed in her absorption of propaganda.

Singh, realising quickly that one person's obsession was another's opportunity, heaved himself out of his chair, trying not to gasp for air like a stranded fish. He was barefoot, his pristine white sneakers sitting neatly by the front door as if inviting him to wander further afield than his living room. It was a new pair. The previous pair had not survived his Cambodian adventure. The inspector knew he had a packet of cigarettes hidden on top of the spare bedroom wardrobe but he would need a stool to reach it. He was not much taller than Mrs. Singh and his turban, although it appended useful inches to his stature, did not add reach to his arms. He was just clambering onto a chair with that degree of care shared by invalids and the overweight, when an impatient tut-tutting by the door informed him that he'd been caught red-handed.

His wife's expression was not cordial. 'Can't you even just for once follow the doctor's advice?'

'I'm trying,' said Singh, despising the plaintive note in his voice. 'But . . . I'm so fed up that they won't let me go back to work.'

'I suppose you're worried about all the killers escaping while you're resting at home?'

He ignored the snide tone and answered the substance. 'Yes, I am. My colleagues will just "round up the usual suspects" and throw them in jail.'

'I'm sure they must have done *something* – the police only lock up the criminals.'

Singh wondered whether to discuss the presumption of innocence with his wife and decided that he didn't have the energy. Women like her, conservative and narrow-minded, were quite willing to believe that someone arrested for pilfering was congenitally pre-disposed to commit more serious crimes, eventually and naturally culminating in murder. In her view, fixating on the evidence for an individual crime was just pedantic. Mind you, Singh had met high court judges with the same attitude. He wondered for a moment why his wife had such faith in the police force in the abstract and so little confidence in his role in it.

'Actually, the problem is that you have nothing to do.'

Singh was forced to concede that she had a point. He wasn't really filled with righteous anger over uncaught killers and unsolved crimes. He had just watched his fill of cricket – who would have thought such a thing was possible? – on television. Plus, he missed aggravating the higher echelons of the police force.

'And you're getting fat,' she continued. 'Fatter,' she amended, running a critical eye over his rotund form.

Why didn't she just laminate a list of his flaws and hand it to him at pre-arranged times during the day? 'What do you expect when I'm home for three meals a day and you serve so much food?' It wasn't fair to blame his wife, an excellent cook, for his own lack of self-discipline when it came to her culinary offerings but he was in no mood to be reasonable.

'You don't have to eat everything – you wipe up the last drop of curry with your naan. I'm surprised you don't lick the plate!'

This was not the time to confess that he was sometimes tempted to do just that.

'Well? What do you suggest I do?' he continued. 'They won't let me go back to the office.' He wrinkled his broad nose in disgust at his prolonged isolation and stuck his full pink lower lip out in a full pout. 'Superintendent Chen is going to keep me at home for as long as possible while pretending he's just concerned about my health! And *you* won't even let me have a smoke.'

His wife gazed at him thoughtfully.

'What is it?' he asked suspiciously. She looked smug, like Tendulkar needing a mere four runs with three overs to go.

'My cousin in India – Jesvinder?'

He didn't know – was quite unable to identify individuals amongst the massed hordes of his wife's relatives – but decided not to interrupt.

'Her daughter is getting married in Mumbai. I think we should go for the wedding.'

The *choora* ceremony was just ridiculous, decided Ashu. She tried to keep any expression that reflected her thoughts from showing on her face. It was bound to provoke questions. Or, more likely, a lecture. One of those 'you're such an ungrateful child, you don't know how lucky you are' refrains.

'You're such a lucky girl,' coo-ed a toothless old crone on cue. Ashu thought the wizened creature was some sort of great-aunt but she wasn't sure. Who could remember the details of every family member who had crawled out of the woodwork on the news of her impending nuptials? No day passed without her mother introducing her to yet another relative who would clasp her hands and kiss her cheeks and congratulate her on her astonishing good fortune.

'*Achha*, why such a glum face? Maybe you can't wait for the wedding day?'

This was the air-headed interjection of one of her air-headed cousins. To be fair, the girl was usually a sensible creature who got good grades in school but there was nothing like a family wedding to turn everyone under the age of seventy-five into a moron. Especially the girls, all dreaming of meeting Mr. Right. Or to be more precise, all dreaming that one of the officious community matchmakers would find Mr. Right and be able to convince him that she, the girl, was docile, fair, had child-bearing hips, was from a family that usually only produced sons and was an excellent homemaker.

Ashu glanced down at her clothes. Such finery. She felt like a Barbie doll – a politically correct, dark-haired, dusky-skinned Indian version – in a hot pink *salwar kameez*. She wriggled her shoulders. The outfit was so rich with embroidery and embellishments that it was actually weighing her down. Or maybe it was just the sure and certain knowledge of what the future held that constituted the burden on her shoulders.

'I got a call today – even your aunty and uncle from Singapore are coming.' Her mother, Jesvinder, had seen the warning signs – pursed lips and stormy eyes – and was intervening to distract her daughter.

This piqued Ashu's interest. 'From Singapore? I didn't even know we had relations there.'

'My cousin – mother's brother's daughter who married that policeman.'

'Policeman?'

'Inspector Singh from Singapore police. *Verrry* high up in the Force.'

Ashu nodded thoughtfully. He might be useful, this senior policeman. Someone she could consult on this matter that was keeping her awake at nights – as if she didn't have enough on her mind to provoke insomnia a thousand times over. She glanced in the mirror. They'd painted her face carefully but the discerning would spot the hint of dark shadows under her eyes. She saw her best friend, Farzana, watching her anxiously and essayed a weak smile.

'What sort of policeman?' she asked.

'Murder.' The younger of her two brothers, only a year older than her, used the word with relish.

She scowled at him. Ranjit lived his life in some sort of Bollywood parallel universe where he was a swashbuckling hero who always got the girl and not a pimply twenty-seven year old with the family nose and an Adam's apple that protruded further than his chin.

Ashu hadn't inherited the family nose with its distinct

bridge which was a shame because if she had, that paragon of all desirable traits in a husband, Kirpal Singh, might have been persuaded to look elsewhere for a bride. In the end, her family pedigree, educational achievements and indubitable beauty, not to mention the dowry promised by her grandfather, had outweighed her taciturn demeanour on their formal introduction. She'd been told later by Aunty Harjeet that Kirpal had interpreted her silence and monosyllabic answers as a perfectly understandable shyness. So much for scaring away a few suitors. It seemed that her husband-to-be was not a great reader of character.

She turned her attention back to the mysterious uncle from Singapore. 'What do you mean "murder"?'

'He's a murder investigator,' explained Ranjit. 'Tracks down murderers,' he added as if she was some sort of half-wit.

'Actually he could have been even more senior in the Force – but he doesn't want to be promoted. He likes his work.' This explanation from Aunty Harjeet was greeted with melancholy headshakes all around. It struck Ashu as a commendable independence of spirit but she knew it was precisely the sort of eccentric behaviour frowned upon by her family.

'He sounds like an interesting man,' offered Ashu, in defence of this unknown uncle. She should have known better.

'Very difficult for the wife – your Aunty, my cousin sister,' continued Aunty Harjeet, reaching for her thick long single plait of hair and coiling it around her neck and over her shoulder. It looked like she was in the grip of an ebony boa

16

constrictor. 'All his cohorts are much more senior than him now.'

Headshakes greeted this loss of face.

'And,' inserted the old crone who seemed to have a very firm handle on the family gossip, 'I have heard that this Singapore inspector of police smokes tobacco.'

There were gasps and shudders. 'It is shocking that a Sikh gentleman should have a fondness for cigarettes,' agreed an uncle. 'It is banned by our religion – by Guru Nanak Singh himself.'

'So is alcohol,' said Ashu pointedly. The men of her family were never averse to a thimbleful of Johnnie Walker – and then some. It was typical of the hypocrisy that so annoyed her about her relatives. Once again she was ignored although shocked murmurs still echoed through the room as the conversation was relayed to those in the further reaches who might have missed the gossip first-hand. Ashu took a moment away from her own troubles to feel sorry for this unknown uncle, Inspector Singh. If he was hoping to be welcomed warmly into the bosom of the family when he got to India, he was in for a rude surprise. She wondered what, or who, had persuaded him to put in an appearance. He didn't sound like the sort to attend the faraway weddings of unknown nieces as a matter of courtesy. Probably hen-pecked, she concluded.

The bangle ceremony was reaching its zenith. Her maternal uncle produced a beautiful wooden casket with intricate mirror work on the lid. Probably made by some poor village artisan who hadn't been paid enough to feed his family for a week, she thought dismissively. He opened it slowly and with a flourish. There were 'oohs' and 'ahhhs' from the gathered clan. A row of red and white bangles, glinting and gleaming, were nestled in red satin.

He took them out reverently and she extended her wrist, noting the complex patterns of henna that had been painted on a few days ago. The henna was a dark brown hue, the colour of old blood. Ashu suppressed a shudder. It was bad enough to have been turned into a piece of installation art without imagining that the graceful lines had been etched into her flesh with a sharp knife.

The family took turns to slip the bangles on her wrist. Ranjit slung one on, grinning broadly as he did so. She had to smile in response to his delight. Her eldest brother was last and she realised that he'd been silent and distracted during the ceremony. It was not like him, he much preferred to dominate conversations, expressing his views loudly and with authority. Ashu wondered what was bothering him – and then decided she didn't care. Tanvir was part of the reason she was in this predicament and she could not forgive him for it. She'd asked him if she had to go through with the wedding, begging him to see her point of view. A single raised eyebrow had expressed his surprise and disapproval at the question. 'Will you break your grandfather's heart?' he'd asked and she had found that the answer to that question, even if it was at the expense of her own freedom and happiness, was 'no'. And then the final straw – he'd gripped her upper arm hard enough to bruise and said in that ugly voice, 'Be careful, Ashu. I will not allow anyone to bring dishonour to the family.'

When she was laden down with bangles – twenty-one of

them – Ashu wagged her fingers experimentally and they jangled merrily in complete contrast to her dour frame of mind.

'Forty days you must be wearing them now,' cackled the old crone. 'And only your husband is the one allowed to remove them.'

'How am I supposed to get any work done?'

'That is the origin of the tradition,' explained her mother. 'The bride is allowed to rest for her big day because she cannot do housework, cleaning and cooking, with all these heavy, noisy bangles.'

'I wasn't thinking of housework exactly,' said Ashu dryly and was met with gales of laughter. It was always the same, realised Ashu. Whenever she was at her most serious, her relations assumed she was joking. Well, they would be none the wiser if she slipped the unwieldy accoutrements into her handbag and snuck out of the house. Matters were too important to be left as they were while she indulged in long-winded preparations for her society wedding.

'And now we can look forward to the Anand Karaj,' said Aunty Harjeet, fixing her wandering eye on her niece with disconcerting intensity. 'It will be the talk of Mumbai. Your grandfather has spared no expense for his favourite grand-daughter.'

'You should be very grateful,' chuckled the old witch.

Anand Karaj – the wedding ceremony. She knew it meant a 'blessed union of souls'. Ashu fought back the sudden tears, overwhelmed by events that were unfolding with the speed of a Mumbai taxi. She didn't doubt that there *could* be such a thing – a blessed union of souls. She, after all, had been fortunate enough to find just such a person, to feel just such a bond.

Unfortunately, it wasn't with that paragon of all Sikh virtues, Kirpal Singh – her husband-to-be.

Later that week, Tanvir sat at a corner table in Leopold's, peering at the menus that were under the clear plastic table top. There had been some hesitation about the choice of location. Was it necessary to choose a Mumbai landmark to meet? his guest had asked. Even he, a foreigner, had heard of the café. Surely that was the best way to ensure that they were spotted? Tanvir had patiently explained his thinking. He was a wealthy, well-known man-about-town. Everyone knew his antecedents and his connections and most importantly, thanks to his grandfather, his prospects.

So if they planned their meeting in some hole-in-the-wall tea shop where the vendors still sold *chai* in disposable clay cups, and he was spotted, there would be eyebrows raised and questions asked.

He mimicked the tone. '*Yaar*, you won't be believing who I saw hanging around a real *goonda* place!'

But Leopold's, even since the attacks, especially since the attacks, was where he and his ilk belonged: the young of Mumbai, the future of India with their imported cars, Italian shoes, tailored Nehru jackets and, in his case, matching turban. Religious trappings as a fashion accessory. It was a strange world whichever way you looked at it.

Tanvir glanced at his watch. He'd been waiting half an hour now. Jaswant was running late. Surely, Canadians – even Canadian Sikhs – didn't follow Indian time where 'ek' minute actually meant twenty? He contemplated his new friend. So far he'd proved himself reliable. Most likely he had underestimated Mumbai traffic and was stuck in a taxi somewhere inhaling exhaust fumes. He shook his head – Jaswant had told him there were areas in Canada where turbans outnumbered baseball hats. Mind you, Canadian Sikhs hadn't always made themselves popular. They had downed an Air India flight en route to Canada in 1985 in revenge for the storming of the Golden Temple. The authorities referred to them as 'homegrown terrorists'. Tanvir smiled. It sounded so wholesome. Like organic vegetables.

There was a steady stream of people coming in and Leopold's was filling up as it always did. A mixture of expats, tourists – there was a macabre edge to their presence now, since the bombings – and locals. Like *kichiri*, this aspect of Mumbai. Many random ingredients thrown in to season a single dish. Some added spice and sweetness but many of the ingredients left a bitter aftertaste.

A voice at his shoulder said, '*Arrei, bhai,*' and he turned around, smiling with pleasure. Jaswant pulled up a chair and sat down.

A groups of acquaintances wandered over. Mumbai was just a big bloody village, decided Tanvir. He restrained himself with difficulty from telling them to get lost. He knew what was coming – useless chitchat, some backslapping, sarcastic remarks about his tailor or his love life. But the chance meeting would be quickly forgotten unless he behaved out of character. So he would have to bite his tongue and grin and appear as delighted to see them as they were to see him.

'Tanvir, you're too important nowadays to make time for your old buddies, eh?'

He shrugged at the overweight thirty-something advertising executive. 'Busy, man. You know how it is.' He winked broadly. 'Got to make time for the girls.'

The group turned as one to look at Jaswant, curiosity awakened by a stranger in their midst. 'Who's your partner in crime?'

Unfortunate choice of words. 'My cousin down from Canada,' Tanvir said untruthfully and then grinned. 'Looking for an Indian bride.'

Jaswant clasped a few extended hands, adding, 'The Canadian girls, they don't know how to cook like my mother any more!'

There was loud laughter but also understanding.

'My sister is the best cook in Mumbai,' said one of the men, propping his expensive shades on his thick mass of oily hair.

'Well, then – email us a photo and proposed dowry,' said Tanvir. 'But you need to know, *bhai* – it's gonna take a lot of zeros to prise my cousin away from his mother!'

His friends looked suitably impressed. They knew he, Tanvir, was worth a lot. Rumours were already flying about how many *lakhs* were being demanded in the marriage mart for him. Even more than had been paid for his sister – the family was going to turn a profit. Not for Tanvir and Ashu, grandchildren of Tara Singh, the desperate adverts in the 'personal' sections of the daily papers. He'd had a few giggles just that morning over some of the classifieds. Homely. Fair. High moral values. Apparently, 'homely' meant having home-making skills as opposed to being pug ugly. It was just as well he didn't have to trawl through the thousands of pages of 'fun-loving girls who loved cooking', all of whom seemed to have extensive educational qualifications but were described as being 'at home'. Was all that education just to add column inches to the adverts in pursuit of a husband?

'Yes, if my cousin says it's OK, I'll be round to sample her wares,' said Jaswant to more loud laughter although the brother of the girl looked offended.

'Why don't you lazy bastards find something to do?' asked Tanvir. 'My cousin and I have things to discuss.'

'Like which clubs you're hitting this evening?'

'Exactly,' said Tanvir, high-fiving the guy and wishing that he could punch him instead for forcing him to play this ridiculous role when he had more important things on his mind.

The group took the hint and wandered away to pounce on some other acquaintances and Tanvir turned to Jaswant, temper restored. 'So, "cousin" – time to make a plan.'

'Well, we have the goods,' said Jaswant, smiling.

'I saw the newspapers – the "audacious raid", "inside job" – good work.'

'Money makes all things possible,' explained his friend.

'Well, *bhai*, that's why I'm here.' Worried creases suddenly slashed his cheeks. 'But are you sure we're in the clear?'

'The authorities think it was the Pakistani intelligence services – ISI. To cause trouble in Kashmir.'

For some reason this amused Tanvir and he began to chuckle. In a moment his companion had joined in too.

*

The plane was coming in to land. The wheels had been cranked out with some clanking and juddering. Singh felt a wave of apprehension. His wife sensed his tension and looked up from her reading material.

'I don't like flying, especially the taking off and landing bits,' he explained, more to distract himself than anything. His wife knew very well his dislike of being airborne.

'Nothing to be afraid of. Many new private airlines in India because country is a huge economic success, even bigger than China,' said his wife, self-appointed oracle of India.

Inspector Singh was always suspicious of exponential growth in any industry but particularly the gravity-defying ones. Did they have the pilots for the rapid expansion? Did all the new employees know what they were doing or were they dancing through the skies with the insouciance of mosquitoes? The policeman glanced out of the window nervously although there wasn't much he could do if a careless jet was bearing down on them.

'Jet Airways, Kingfisher, Sahara . . .' she added.

'Kingfisher? But that's an Indian beer!' He might not be an expert on birds or airlines but he certainly knew his beer.

'Also airline,' she replied.

'Well, I hope they're not sampling the wares,' he grumbled. The policeman very much regretted agreeing to visit India for the wedding of his wife's niece. But there was no going back. Mrs. Singh was adamant. They would both attend the celebrations and it would give him a chance to catch up with that branch of the family which had not fled India for greener pastures. There was no point explaining to his wife that avoiding her relatives was one of his main ambitions in life and he'd always been grateful that at least some of the pack remained in India.

Still, the food was bound to be good, spicy curries galore, if he could avoid getting ill with 'Mumbai belly' or 'Delhi belly' or 'whichever part of India you happened to be' belly. He would avoid her relatives in the same way he'd always done – by sitting irascibly in a corner and allowing their waves of curiosity to wash over him.

The sound of the flaps caused Singh to clutch his seat in sudden terror. He peered out of the window, trying to gauge the distance to the ground, and was astonished and momentarily distracted by what he saw. In every direction, punctuated randomly with crumbling concrete structures, spread a vast shanty town, the predominant colours of which were rust and festive patches of blue. He suddenly realised that the blue was industrial tarpaulin, used like Scotch tape to plug holes, drape gaps and cover leaking roofs. In another world, like Singapore, the flashes of blue would have been the swimming pools of rich men.

As they descended, Singh spotted piles of empty bottles on roofs and clothes flapping on lines. Were they actually going to land on these shacks? Just as he considered adopting the brace position of his own free will, he saw the boundary fence of the airport. The slum reached right up to the perimeter. In fact, the policeman saw clothes drying on the fence itself, flapping in the wind and the engine blowback.

Singh was distracted by a strong and unpleasant smell that suddenly pervaded the airplane. He sniffed cautiously, protruding nostril hairs quivering. It didn't smell like burning fuel or melting plastic or any of those olfactory sensations that would have caused him to make a dash for the exits.

He turned to Mrs. Singh who was reading the in-flight magazine with the disdain of one who preferred to Google her subjects rather than have them pre-selected by an editor.

'What's that stink?' he whispered.

'India,' she answered succinctly and then turned her attention back to a gleaming picture of the Taj Mahal resplendent in its manicured gardens, its reflection shimmering in a lake, not a blue tarp in sight.

Two

'Sardarji, porter?'

'Taxi?'

'Cheap, fast? We go now!'

'I am taking your bags, Sardarji.'

'Aapka shubh naam kya hai? What is your good name? Can I be of extreme help to you?'

'I can recommend very good hotel.'

'Special price for you, Sardarji. Not tourist price!'

Singh gripped the trolley on which his small bag and Mrs. Singh's ample suitcase were perched with both hands and tried to look like a native of India. After all, he had the props for the part – the turban, the beard, the gut – except that the genuine article seemed able to peg him for a foreigner immediately. Perhaps it was the fear in his eyes that was visible to the observant. How else to explain the various solicitations being shouted at him as he used his trolley as a barricade? He would soon have to use it as a weapon. Maybe if he ran one of these fellows over the rest would give up trying to attract his attention with loud shouts and shirt tugs.

The inspector took a deep breath – and regretted it immediately. The stench rested on the intense humidity as if it was a pedestal. Singh, waiting outside the Chhatrapati Shivaji International Airport – he didn't think the name had much hope of becoming common parlance – decided that it was noxious enough to kill. He looked around and noticed that the residents of Mumbai seemed indifferent, or at least accustomed, to the odour. Foreign tourists were holding their hands over their mouths and noses. Most looked shell-shocked although that might have been the aggressive attentions of porters and taxi drivers all jostling for custom; poking, prodding, negotiating, discounting and generally harassing visitors. Singh noticed an intrepid fellow make off with a selection of bags over the protests of the owner, one under each arm, a third on one shoulder and two perched on his head. As he went, he was still able to waggle his fingers in a beckoning gesture. His would-be customer, faced with the prospect of losing his luggage completely, gave it up as a bad job and hurried after his self-appointed porter.

Singh looked around and spotted a poster that read, 'Do not spit. Spiting person will be fined.' Well, he could refrain from gobbing saliva all over the place but he was filled with spiteful feelings towards his wife who had left him to fend for himself in this alien land. Mrs. Singh had decided, much to her husband's irritation, to visit the toilet – 'What were you doing on the plane for seven hours?'

Singh wiped his brow with the large handkerchief he kept

for that purpose and felt the familiar sensation of sweat trickling from under the rim of his turban and down to his chin. His beard would soon reach saturation point and then the perspiration would drip like a leaky faucet.

Mrs. Singh finally hove into view.

'About bloody time,' he muttered. 'These fellows have been trying to take our passports, our bags, our trolley – they'd have walked off with me balanced on their heads if you'd taken any longer.'

'Strong but not that strong,' remarked Mrs. Singh, leading the way to the taxi rank.

The inspector looked down at the pavement and stumbled backwards in fright.

'What are you doing?' demanded his wife. He'd stepped on her toes with a heavy foot.

'Bloodstains,' he whispered. '*Every*where. Must have been a massacre!'

'Don't be silly,' said his wife.

'Then what is it?'

'*Paan.*'

'What?'

'*Paan* – betel nut juice. Indians always chewing and spitting.'

Singh stepped forward gingerly and peered myopically at the rusty stains. He supposed she was right. Now that he was paying attention, he noticed that the jaws of the people around him were moving with the measured rhythm of masticating cows.

'Cool car?'

'What?'

'Cool car or non-AC?' demanded the gentleman at the booth for pre-paid taxis.

'Err – cool car,' said Mrs. Singh, her usual *sang froid* shaken by this choice between two incomprehensible options.

Singh glowered at her but followed meekly in her footsteps. She was the old India hand, not him, prone to making a visit every few years to see her relatives and stock up on *salwar kameez*. Their driver was a swarthy, pock-marked fellow. He wore a formerly white shirt stained with unidentifiable fluids. The henna red hair dye didn't improve matters either in the policeman's considered opinion. He hoped at least that their taxi would be the famous Ambassador that had plied Indian streets for decades. That would cheer him up. Black and yellow with the rounded curves of a beautiful woman. He was keen to meet that old stalwart of Indian transport. He was to be disappointed.

The 'cool car' turned out to be a pint-sized brand new blue and white Maruti Suzuki.

'I'm not sure I'm going to fit,' he complained. 'And what about the luggage?'

'Must just be squeezing a little. Tata Nano is even smaller, Sardarji!'

'No Ambassador?' he asked plaintively.

'Phased out, *saar*.'

Singh grunted his disappointment. All this industrialisation and development that his wife kept harping on about apparently meant that the famous old vehicle had been consigned to the scrapheap. What else had India lost in its desire to impress Mrs. Singh?

'What sort of car is that?' he asked, pointing at the masses of black and yellow taxis plying the same route. They were ramshackle but at least had a bit of character.

'Fiat Padmini. But not AC cab.' He continued proudly, 'This is AC cab, *saar*' – which his wife whispered, although he'd worked it out, meant that it had air conditioning so the scent of Mumbai was excluded for the most part.

To distract himself from the driver and the drive – they were now weaving between cars, trucks and auto rickshaws – he said, 'So, tell me again – whose wedding are we attending?'

He had to repeat the question, a few decibels louder. The driver was leaning on his horn with the intensity of a musician in the trumpet section of an orchestra. Singh noted that many of the trucks had the words 'horn, please, horn' painted on the rear. And Indian drivers, unwilling to spurn such a polite request, were indeed horning and tooting with gusto.

'I told you, my cousin's daughter. Very smart girl. A scientist working for some big company here in Mumbai. And now they've found her a good boy.'

A smart girl and a good boy. A match made in heaven. It was a curious element of Indian culture than men and women were still 'boys' and 'girls' until they had achieved the state of matrimony. So much for driving licences, the right to buy cigarettes or vote. None of these were sufficient indication of a graduation into adulthood. Only holy matrimony would do.

'Who is he?' asked Singh, determined to keep his eyes on his wife and not the road which had narrowed from highway to backstreet. Stray dogs darted across at random intervals and the driver weaved cheerfully between piles of construction debris like a slalom skier. And to think, thought Singh bitterly, that he complained about the erratic habits of Singapore taxi drivers. The truth of the matter was that he was spoilt.

'Whoa, man,' he yelled as the taxi swerved to avoid a placid but skinny cow and missed an auto, laden with an entire family, by a whisker.

'Must not hit cow in Mumbai,' explained the driver, grinning and exposing red-stained teeth sprouting like weeds in his mouth.

'Because the cow is sacred?' demanded Singh. He was concerned about the man's priorities.

'Yes, yes – you're right, Sardarji – cow is sacred to Hindus. But also if we hit cow then riot will be starting and crowd will certainly kill us all.'

Singh pinched the bridge of his nose and hoped fervently that the driver was exaggerating. He didn't want to think that they had been millimetres away, not just from the cow, but from a lynch mob.

They were suddenly transported from the carnage of the airport surrounds onto a twenty-first century bridge. Singh felt as if he'd slipped through an extra-large rabbit hole.

'Worli Sea Bridge,' explained the driver.

'You see how modern India is?' demanded his wife proudly.

Hadn't she noticed the first half-hour of their drive? The policeman kept his mouth shut. He didn't want to provoke an argument in the narrow confines of their 'cool car'.

Singh's eye was drawn to a beautiful white dome and minaret that appeared to be floating in the sea.

He tapped the driver on the shoulder and then regretted the physical contact. 'What's that?' he asked.

'Haji Ali mosque,' explained the driver. 'Can only go there when is low tide, *saar*.'

That didn't sound very convenient to Singh. What happened if one got it wrong? Was death by drowning the largest killer amongst unsuspecting pilgrims?

Mrs. Singh, who had been ignoring this interchange, now said, 'An MBA.'

'What?'

'The boy is an MBA.'

'What in the world are you talking about?'

'You asked me about the boy my niece is marrying. Well, he's an MBA – from a US university.'

Singh could feel a headache coming on from the combination of the stress, smell and now his wife's ability to define a prospective groom by his educational qualifications. It could be worse, he supposed. The girl would probably have been described by her skin colour, 'fairness' being an Indian obsession.

'I meant what sort of *person* is he?'

'How would I know that?' asked Mrs. Singh, sounding astonished. 'I've never met him before.'

'The girl then – what about her?'

'My niece – Ashu Kaur.' She paused for a moment. 'Very fair girl.'

'If I get caught, my relatives will have me flayed alive.'

'Why? What do you mean?'

'A few days before the wedding, the bride's not allowed to leave the house. I snuck out.'

The girl with the long hair, dressed in jeans and a long-sleeved T-shirt, looked profoundly disgusted. She shook her arm and the bangles, hidden by her sleeves, jangled noisily. 'The *choora* ceremony is over, you see. They gave me the bangles.' She snorted. 'Might as well be handcuffs, you know?'

'I'm glad you came,' whispered the young man.

'I just hope none of the servants saw me.' Ashu's mind was still on her escape.

'I've been waiting here, walking up and down ... I had to see you,' he continued urgently.

Sameer was a tall young man with swept-back dark hair and a slightly dissipated air, the consequence of a failure to shave and the dark shadows under his eyes. Ashu sat down next to him on the low wall that ran the length of Marine Drive. She reached out a hand and touched his cheek. The profoundly affectionate gesture was interrupted by the sound of her bangles rattling.

'I wore a long-sleeved blouse just to cover these damned things – otherwise every Sikh busybody on the street will know that I'm betrothed. But now I sound like a street vendor. Kids will be asking me for ice cream next.'

The man flung himself down on the rampart and stared moodily out to a sea which was choppy and almost grey, reflecting the turbulent winds and steel-coloured, rain-laden sky. Ashu followed his gaze and picked out a few fishing boats almost hidden in the mist and spray. The fishermen were desperate to haul in a catch for the avaricious buyers at Sassoon Docks regardless of the weather. Across the water, at an angle, she could see the fishing village with its upturned, gaily painted boats and reams of nets spread out across every available surface. It looked picturesque from a distance but she knew that up close it was almost indistinguishable from a slum.

Sameer turned to the girl and seized her hand. 'You can't do this to us – to me.'

'I'm sorry, Sameer – I have no choice.'

'We have our whole future ahead of us and you're destroying it.'

Ashu smiled a little. It was Sameer's passion for life – he was not a man for half-measures – that had first attracted her to him. That and, if she was honest, his astonishing good looks. But it hadn't taken long, working side by side with him in the lab, for a friendship to blossom. And then suddenly, unexpectedly, a love so strong that it had the contrary effect of making her feel weak-kneed in his presence.

She wondered whether she should tell Sameer that she'd sought help from Tanvir and decided against it. There was no point. He was already so resentful of the family that was keeping them apart – it would just make things worse. Nothing she could say would reconcile him to her decision to go through with the arranged marriage because she owed it to her mother and grandfather. How could she have anticipated that she would meet a colleague and fall in love with him?

The memory of their work together in the lab reminded her of her other worry, forgotten in those first few minutes of seeing her love again.

'Did you find out anything at the factory?' she asked.

He sighed and ran thin long fingers through his hair. 'Nothing yet. I'm still not convinced that you're right.'

She nodded. 'I know – it seems impossible. I can hardly believe it myself.'

'I'll keep looking. I promised you that and I'm not one to break my word.' There was a wealth of bitterness in his voice.

She added quickly, knowing he would be annoyed, 'Before I came here, I went in to the office and spoke to Tyler.'

'What? I asked you not to do that!'

She didn't respond, waiting for the flash of temper to subside. She knew him so well, knew exactly how long it would take for him to calm down again.

'What was the reaction?' asked Sameer, a few moments later.

'Not that happy.'

'What do you mean?'

'He said he would stop me talking at all costs – wouldn't let me destroy his reputation on a whim.'

'A bunch of sick people is not a *whim*.'

She smiled. 'That's what I said.'

'Do you think he meant it?'

She raised two shoulders in a careless shrug. 'What can he really do to stop me?' Far more of a concern was the other allegation Tyler had made – but that was something she was definitely not going to share with Sameer.

'I want you to be careful,' he warned, his eyes darting about as if trying to spot unseen dangers.

'I will.' She didn't really think there was anything to worry about. It was a gesture to reassure Sameer. The gusts of wind tugged at her hair like a young child. Marine Drive was a common lovers' rendezvous, in the public eye but with a sense of privacy. Hemmed in by the Arabian Sea – and the cement culverts that kept the water at bay – on one side and the fast-moving traffic on the other. It was late afternoon and uncomfortably warm so the 'queen's necklace', as the Drive was sometimes called, was almost deserted. There were still a few men in long shorts, white shoes and black socks panting along the path, trying to lose their enormous overhanging stomachs. Ashu shook her head ruefully. Mumbai was one of the few places in India where sections of the population had weight problems.

'Are you really going through with the wedding?' Sameer demanded, refusing to let the matter drop.

'I don't have any choice now.' She had meant to be distant, even cruel – to help this man that she loved forget about her. She'd told herself that she was coming to say goodbye – nothing more. But looking at him, drawn in by the intensity of his gaze, Ashu knew that she had been lying to herself. She dashed away teardrops with the back of an angry hand. She'd come out to see him because she couldn't bear to do anything else. There was no way she could let go so easily, consign their relationship to the past. Would she be able to do so after she was married to another man? She felt a moment of pity for her unsuspecting groom. Still, there was no question in her mind that it was her grandfather's wealth and status that had been uppermost in Kirpal's mind when he'd agreed to marry her. After all, she thought bitterly, she was quite a catch.

'You can't marry him,' insisted her boyfriend.

Suddenly, she was angry. 'Why are you making this my fault? You said that our marriage would break your mother's heart. What choice did I have – do I have?'

'We would have found a way,' he muttered uncertainly.

37

She looked up and noticed the worn poster for an old movie on a curve of the rampart. It was not difficult to guess the subject matter of the tale – star-crossed lovers, family misunderstandings, a brother gone bad and finally, after a few exuberantly choreographed dance numbers with much hip-shaking and breast-bouncing, a happy ending.

Her life had all the ingredients of a Bollywood movie except the happy ending.

She took Sameer's hands in hers and let the teardrops fall unchecked. 'I cannot break my mother's – or grandfather's – heart. It is better that we both learn to accept that.' As she said it, she wondered whether the accusation that Tyler had levelled against her grandfather changed anything. The bride-to-be shook her head and strands of hair whipped her cheeks. It was all too much to bear. Ashu was so engrossed in her own thoughts that she did not hear a car slow down on Marine Drive.

The taxi drew up in front of a most imposing building. The last time Singh had seen it, on television, the façade had been marred by scorch marks, black smoke billowed angrily from windows and heavily armed military and police personnel surrounded the place.

'The Taj hotel,' he breathed.

'Taj Mahal Palace hotel,' she corrected.

'What are we doing here?' He was suddenly irritable. 'Unless you are overestimating a police inspector's pay cheque?'

'I could never do that,' retorted his wife. She smiled suddenly, a rare occurrence in their interactions. 'This is a surprise for you. The girl's grandfather has arranged for all the overseas relations to stay here.'

Singh nodded thoughtfully. It was not an unheard-of custom, of course. His own wife's parents had housed the relatives who had descended on Singapore for their wedding all those uncountable years ago. But that had been at the YMCA.

The doors to the taxi were flung open by doormen in white gloves, silk shirts and turbans of immense size. Bellboys dressed like throwbacks to the Moghul era unloaded the boot. Singh eased himself out of the vehicle with relief and craned his neck to get a view of the hotel frontage. It had Moorish domes like the old railway stations in Kuala Lumpur, massive bay windows which reminded him of the Raffles in Singapore, and a hundred other exquisite details from balconies to spires that were all its own. The doorman ushered them into the foyer with a flourish. Singh looked up at the vaulted alabaster ceilings littered with crystal chandeliers. Underfoot, far too grand a base for his grubby sneakers, were plush carpets that shimmered and changed shade as he walked towards reception. How did one keep carpets clean in Mumbai?

An exquisite young lady in a silk printed turquoise sari did her best to slip a garland of jasmine flowers around his neck but he fought her off with vigour. Inspector Singh of the Singapore police did not wear flowers, however sweet-smelling. Mrs. Singh subjected herself to the floral welcome with more grace.

The inspector turned to his wife who was prosaically rifling in her handbag for their passports. 'So what does this grandfather do? I never knew you were from a wealthy family.' He made it sound like an accusation.

'Would I be married to you if my father had this money? No, her *other* grandfather is the rich one. He is the industrialist – Tara Singh.'

Singh looked blank so she continued accusingly, 'His name is always in the newspapers. He gives away a lot of money to charity and supports Sikh causes.'

'Maybe we could persuade him that I'm a Sikh cause.'

His wife ignored this interjection as not meriting a response and said, 'Ashu's father died when she was young so she was dependent on her grandfather for everything. They say he treats her like his own daughter.'

Their passports were discreetly examined, rooms assigned and they were magicked away by a bellhop who spent fifteen minutes showing them where the light switches, Internet connection and bathroom accessories were located. The inspector's eyes lit up when he was finally directed to the well-stocked mini-bar.

Singh felt in his pocket, found a few torn and stained rupees, handed them over and was thanked in a tone which carried so much disdain that he suspected that he'd failed to meet the minimum tipping threshold. Still, he wasn't a wealthy American tourist or even a successful Sikh entrepreneur like this Tara Singh. Singh kicked off his trainers, peeled off his socks and sauntered to the windows, curling his toes into the thick carpet as he went.

'Come and look at this,' he insisted to his wife who was unpacking the clothes and carefully arranging them in the immense wardrobe.

They both looked out at the churning sea, the harbour littered with small boats and large ferries. In the foreground, right on the waterfront, was a massive pastel yellow arch – the Gateway of India.

'It was built to welcome King George V when he visited India,' explained his well-briefed, Google-friendly wife.

'They didn't think a bunch of flowers would do?' asked Singh.

'Anyway, it was only completed twelve years after the visit.'

Singh grinned. That was the sort of managerial incompetence that he found amusing. He abandoned the view, picked up the newspapers and looked at the various headlines. A minister had been accused of corruption in a newspaper sting. There had been encroachments by Pakistani troops over the line of control in Kashmir. Editorials solemnly urged the government to adopt a firm stance. Right, thought Singh. Two nuclear powers adopting a 'firm' stance was definitely the right way forward.

Farmers had been committing suicide in large numbers as their crops failed because of a severe drought in the northern states. Global warming was to blame according to scientists and the government had promised tough climate goals. Next to the article was another one, lauding the Tata Nano, the 'one lakh' car. No one seemed inclined to point out the contradiction between reducing global warming and sticking a bunch of cheap cars on the road. Humanity was doomed, decided Singh, which made his job of hunting down individual murderers particularly pointless. He needed an arrest warrant for car manufacturers and government officials. Perhaps he would put in a request to Superintendent Chen when he got back.

Singh read on, oblivious to the newsprint ink on his

fingers. The army had confessed that a shipment of C4 had gone missing from a munitions depot but they were optimistic about recovering the explosives before the goods 'fell into the wrong hands'. Singh sighed. There was something to be said for the 'no news is good news' approach of the Singapore dailies. Certainly, an ordinary day's worth of news in the *Straits Times*, tucked in between the advertisements for supermarket chains, cheap holidays and miraculous slimming treatments, didn't look quite like this.

'Half the articles assume I know all the background already. And what's wrong with prepositions?'

'What are you talking about?'

'Listen to this – "Title judgment expected in second land dispute between mosque officials and temple priests in Maharashtra next week. Police urge all parties to be calm and respect judgment of court as in Babri Masjid case." What are they talking about?'

'Babri Masjid case is very famous.'

Singh ignored the implied criticism and nodded at his wife to carry on the tale.

'Mosque was built on a holy Hindu site during the Moghul period. Birthplace of Lord Ram.'

'Birthplace of a *god*? You're joking, right?'

'Many riots after Babri mosque was destroyed by Hindu activists in 1992. Thousands killed, especially in Gujarat. But now Allahabad high court has ordered that the land be shared between Hindu and Moslem parties.'

'Solomon's choice,' said Singh brightly.

His wife ignored him. 'In the end there was no violence when verdict came out.'

Singh looked at the newspapers. 'Well, that must have made a change.'

His wife didn't like the implied criticism of her beloved India. 'Lots of tensions in India between Hindus and Moslems,' she said, but whether by way of explanation or exculpation Singh wasn't sure. 'All that man's fault.'

'Who?' asked Singh genuinely puzzled that his wife had found a single party to blame for decades of violence.

'Jinnah!' she snapped, referring to one of the authors of partition and Pakistan's first prime minister.

'I think you'll find he had help.'

His wife ignored this heresy.

'Now another land dispute verdict is coming. This time mosque is in Maharashtra. Jama Masjid.'

The fat man shrugged his fleshy shoulders, retrieved a can of Kingfisher beer from the mini-bar and flung himself onto the bed that was made up with crisp white sheets and an embroidered brocade bedspread. He snapped open the can and let the bubbly gold liquid wet his parched throat. He wished Superintendent Chen could see him now and then changed his mind quickly. He wouldn't have put it past his superior officer to summon him back and assign him to a case if he saw his inspector nestled so comfortably in the lap of luxury. Singh wanted to get back to work, but not that desperately.

The *goondas* had chosen their ambush point well. The only creature watching proceedings was a glossy crow with its head on one side and an expression of indifference on its face. Sameer had been lost in his own worried thoughts, a maze with no escape route. But that had been a mental trap. Now he was in a physical one and he'd walked in without paying any attention to his surroundings, without sensing the danger. He could have kicked himself but knew he didn't need to bother. The three men in a semi-circle, all of them in the crouch that predicated an attack, were about to punish him well for his lapse of concentration. He backed away slowly until his back was against a wall, looked at the men, looked at the gaps between them. They had the angles covered. He wasn't going to be able to make a run for it. The man at the apex took a step forward and his sidekicks stepped in as if they were wired together.

'I don't want to fight,' said Sameer in an agreeable tone as if it was the most ordinary statement in the world. 'If you need money, I'll give you what I have. It's not much.' He gestured to his pocket, inviting permission to retrieve his wallet.

'We don't want your stinking money,' spat out one of the men who looked as if he'd been put together in a hurry by a blind bricklayer.

Great. This was personal. They weren't after his money, they were after him. Sameer was prepared to bet he knew who had sent them. He looked around, wondered whether to shout for help. Although it was still daylight, they were in a narrow road in the deep shadows of buildings. He could smell blocked drains and rotten fruit. The sides were like prison walls, high and stained with peeling paint, graffiti and the inevitable political posters and advertisements featuring Amitabh Bachchan. Didn't the old man have enough money already?

Sameer flexed his fingers and raised his hands palm up. It

gave him some protection from a sudden blow but didn't look aggressive. Truth be told, he doubted that he could turn these guys from their purpose. They looked as keen as mustard, spoiling for a fight, the *paan* stains on their lips like blood. They'd been well paid, he guessed. But they might under-estimate him if he looked suitably cowed.

'We've been sent to teach you a lesson,' said the leader.

'Your boss too afraid to do his own dirty work?' Sameer's tone was flippant. At this stage, it was worth annoying them. Anger might cloud their judgment, impair their reflexes.

'He doesn't want to soil his hands on rubbish like you, *bhai chod.*'

They'd been circling closer as they spoke. Sameer watched them carefully, rocking back slightly on the balls of his feet. He knew they'd come in together. Why ruin the odds? He looked for the signal from the leader, a wave of the hand, a nod of the head. Anything so that he would have that split-second warning – whatever good it was going to do him. Despite watching, he missed it. They rushed in as one.

He dodged, feinted, tried to strike, aiming somewhere soft like the lips or nose. Three against one. He wasn't even getting close. He air-punched in the best tradition of Bollywood – he could almost hear the 'dish, dish' soundtrack as his fist whis-tled past a cheek. Sameer tried to stay on his feet, lashed out some more. He wondered if they'd been given instructions to work him over or whether the family wanted him out of the picture – completely. Either way, he didn't want to rely on the restraint of these men. He dodged a blow that would have put him on the deck. Once he was down, he was dead. They were taunting him, he could see their lips move, ugly twisted mouths. But he couldn't hear past the blood pounding in his veins. A punch caught him on the side of the head. Sameer felt his neck snap to one side, his ear explode in pain. But he was still on his feet. He whirled around, arms raised to protect his head, tried a shoulder charge. The leader swept his legs from under him. His last thought as he fell was that it had been a smooth move, a trained move. Nothing but the best for his enemies it would seem. Then he was curled up on the patchwork road, feeling the blows rain down on his back and shoulders. The pain from each kick exploded in his brain like firecrackers. Colourful spots swam before his eyes. And then, mercifully, everything went black.

Three

'Enough sleeping. Time to go.'

'Go where?' muttered Singh, opening a heavy eyelid and reaching for the remote control.

'Visit the family, of course. Or why do you think we're here in Mumbai?'

Singh was not impressed with this energy. 'I've just found a cricket channel,' he pointed out, waving an arm in the general direction of the television. 'Mumbai Indians playing.'

'Mumbai Indians?' asked his wife.

'A bit oxymoronic,' he agreed, 'but a great team.'

'You can watch a replay later.'

How had he come to marry a woman who did not appreciate the difference between a 'live' game and a dull replay for which he would already know the result? The same way this Ashu Kaur was marrying 'an MBA', he supposed: with eyes closed and fingers crossed and very little information about their soon-to-be spouse save for skin colour and educational qualifications. The inspector sighed, a gentle rolling sound. He should have insisted all those years ago that the matchmakers found him a wife with a fondness for cricket. On the other hand, Mrs. Singh was already a formidable creature – was placing a heavy willow bat in her hands really a good idea? Singh, chewing on his bottom lip, decided that he preferred a wife who could cook over one who could bat.

He clambered out of bed, huffing and puffing like a mountaineer tackling the last ascent on Everest. 'I need a cigarette,' he said wistfully.

'In *this* hotel?'

Singh eyed the smoke alarms discreetly tucked into the ceiling. After their terrifying encounter with terrorists who had invaded the hotel, murdered indiscriminately and holed themselves up in a corner before fighting a last stand with the police, the hotel probably had a 'shoot to kill' policy if anyone set off an alarm.

'Anyway, you cannot have a cigarette in front of the family.'

Singh nodded. Even he, with his disregard for protocol, wouldn't dare light up in a Sikh home in Mumbai. He'd heard horror stories from his wife of Sikh men, foolish enough to smoke in public in India, being harangued by strangers. It was quite possible that Mrs. Singh had made up these tales to frighten him – he wouldn't put such underhand tactics past her – but he wasn't taking any chances.

'Where is their place, anyway?'

'Not that far – Colaba district.'

'How do we get there?'

He had his answer soon enough. Standing together on the

road outside the hotel, they were bombarded with the usual offers of transport.

'Let's take an auto rickshaw,' said Singh, feeling a sudden intrepidity in an alien land. It was probably the beer talking. 'We'll see more of Mumbai.'

Again he was disappointed. 'No autos in city, *saar*,' said one of the solicitous drivers. 'Phased out. Only in Bandra.'

'This effort to clean up Mumbai has removed all the adventure,' complained Singh petulantly as he stared after two young men, in stone-washed jeans and polyester long-sleeved shirts, walking along with their arms draped affectionately over each other's shoulders. Homosexuality was largely ignored or denied in Indian society. But apparently, friendly physical contact between heterosexual men was completely acceptable. Perhaps it was because contact with women was frowned upon. Maybe young unmarried men had no choice but to walk around arm in arm or hug their mothers if they desired physical human contact. He nudged his wife, hoping to draw her attention to the pair, but she was still considering their transport needs.

'No autos but you want adventure? OK, then – we'll try non-AC.'

Singh, having belated second thoughts, nodded dubiously and demanded of the nearest fellow, 'How much – Colaba.'

'Three hundred rupees, *saar*.'

'I checked in the hotel,' whispered his wife. 'It shouldn't be more than one hundred rupees to get there.'

'It's still a pittance,' argued Singh. Were they really going to haggle about a few dollars? He'd rather get on with it. He might be back in time to watch the second half of the cricket if they hurried.

'If you're not careful, everyone will cheat you,' said his wife, shooing away the driver with a firm hand.

The next fellow demanded two hundred rupees but Mrs. Singh was determined to stand her ground.

'*Sat sri akal, bhai*. Good day to you. I will be taking you with great pleasure.'

Both Inspector Singh and his wife turned around to see who had greeted them in Punjabi instead of Hindi or Marathi.

An enormous Sikh man in a grey turban that brushed the roof of his taxi continued loudly in English, 'Come, come. Nothing to wait for here. You can trust me. The Sikh must take care of the Sikh and I am your brother. *Tua-day naal mil ke khushi hoi hai.*'

Mrs. Singh, not so easily swayed by this appeal to Sikh brotherhood demanded abruptly, 'So, how much to Colaba?'

The man climbed out of his Fiat and gestured with open palms. '*Arrei*, sister. How can it be more than one hundred rupees for such a distance?'

'You see,' whispered Mrs. Singh triumphantly, 'we just had to find someone trustworthy.' She continued darkly, 'In India, you can only trust your own kind. Blood calls to blood.'

One friendly Sikh and suddenly they were all part of the Sikh brotherhood. Singh was always impressed at his wife's ability to draw large conclusions from infinestimal pieces of evidence. She'd fit right into the Singapore police murder squad.

In a few minutes, they were whizzing past small boys who had the latest cricket scores written on bits of cardboard. They held up the information for passing traffic and the drivers exclaimed at the news – Sachin Tendulkar had scored a fifty – and threw coins at them in thanks. So much for avoiding the result of the game, thought Singh. This system was more efficient than subscribing for updates on a mobile phone.

The dust flung up from the dry roads caused Singh's eyes to water and throat to hurt. There were hardly any trees en route. A few straggly sugar palms and the odd clump of coconut trees looked as miserable, grey and dusty as he felt. At the next light, the car was surrounded by thin hands as small children held their open palms up to him. Some had books and flowers to sell, most were empty-handed. All the kids had the hollow cheeks and thin limbs of chronic hunger. Singh remembered the overweight children in Singapore supermarkets shouting at their Filipina minders and reached into his pocket, determined to give away all the cash he carried.

'*Naa! Bhai*, you mustn't do that,' shouted the driver and set off at such a speed that Singh was flung back against the seat.

'Why not?' demanded Singh, enraged by the thwarted attempt to salve his conscience.

'If you give, more will come. Very bad idea to fall for their tricks.'

'Tricks?'

'Waiting for foreigners to be feeling sorry for them. Others will steal the money anyway.'

Singh didn't doubt that there were adults ready to filch the collection but that didn't make him feel any better about leaving the kids empty-handed.

By dint of weaving through traffic and running lights they arrived at the apartment building that matched the address in Mrs. Singh's notebook.

Singh reached into his wallet, retrieved a hundred rupees and handed it to the driver.

There was a sorrowful shake of the head. 'No, no, *bhai*. You are misunderstanding me. One hundred rupees *each*.'

Inspector Singh paid up without hesitation. The expression on his wife's face was worth every penny. So much for the Sikh brotherhood.

The apartment building was tall and modern and would not have looked out of place in Singapore. In Singh's view, it was extremely dull. 'I thought that these rich Indians lived in mansions with one lot of stairs going up and another coming down and dancing girls everywhere?'

'You watch too much TV.'

A guard made them print their names in a thick notebook which he'd carefully ruled into sections with a blunt pencil. He licked the tip, initialled the entry – the inspector noted that he was the eleventh Singh to visit the building that day – placed the pencil behind his ear and waved them in. They took the lift and rode up in the company of a thin man with an enormous bundle of washed and pressed clothes tied in string on his head and a grimy *lunghi* wrapped around his waist and pulled up between his legs to form a pair of baggy shorts.

'*Dhobi wallah*,' explained Mrs. Singh and was rewarded with a toothless grin from the laundryman.

The inspector nodded and wondered why a man who clearly took pride in his handiwork didn't bother to wash his own outfit.

Outside the apartment door, Mrs. Singh adjusted her resplendent *salwar kameez*, purchased at Mustafa's in

Singapore for just this occasion, smoothed her *dupatta* and patted the bun on the back of her head. She gave Singh a look that combined disgust with resignation – she'd never been a fan of his uniform of dark trousers, white shirt and white shoes, let alone the surfeit of pens in his breast pocket – and rang the doorbell.

The door was flung open immediately and a young Sikh man with a large nose, an Impressionist-style splash of acne, scraggly beard and large turban stared at them with an expression of bewilderment on his face.

'Who are you? What do you want?'

The inspector's wife took a step back at the belligerent tone. Her husband was made of sterner stuff but he too was puzzled. Who was this scowling whippersnapper? Surely not the MBA? This was certainly not the welcome – *chai*, sweetmeats and gratitude – they had expected.

A high voice could be heard calling in the background, 'Ranjit, who is it? Is there any news?'

In Singh's professional opinion there was a note of fear running through the words.

A small woman in a vivid yellow cotton *salwar kameez* hurried forward and peered anxiously over the young man's shoulder. Wispy grey hair poked out from under the *dupatta* that she wore wound tightly around her head. When she saw Mrs. Singh, her plump-cheeked, apple-shaped face creased in recognition and into a welcoming smile.

'You are here!' she exclaimed. 'We forgot you were coming this afternoon. Come, come.'

'*Mata*, this is not a good time,' said the stripling urgently.

'This is family,' said the old woman, ushering them in and waving the youth away when he seemed about to barricade the entrance. In an apologetic voice, she said, 'My youngest son, Ranjit.'

Further introductions were hurriedly made and the inspector was not surprised to discover that this was Jesvinder Kaur, widow, mother of the bride, cousin of Mrs. Singh and dependant on her father-in-law's generosity. After the initial greeting which had been genuinely affectionate – did his wife really provoke genuine affection amongst her relatives? – the tension in the room returned immediately. Fine lines of stress and fear radiated from the woman and her son like invisible trip wires. Inspector Singh was not a senior policeman for no reason. He had finely honed instincts of which he was inordinately proud and he was quite sure that they had stumbled upon some family crisis. He also knew that he wanted no part of it. He'd seen it before – crisis in the midst of a large family was always accompanied by high drama. Whatever the root cause, and it was usually trivial, matters would inevitably deteriorate into tears, raised voices and a failure to serve meals on time. It was time to make himself scarce.

His wife had other ideas. She followed the other woman across the threshold hastily, her skinny frame in marked contrast to the ample outline of her cousin.

They were barely seated on a sticky leather sofa in the front room when his wife began her cross-examination.

'What is it? What's the matter?'

Singh, scrutinising Jesvinder, noted the dark panda rings around her eyes and a redness about her irises that suggested recent tears. Her youngest son, angular collarbones visible at the neck of his cotton *kurta*, sat next to her. The room, although crowded with furniture and knick knacks, was otherwise empty. But Singh had a distinct feeling that they were not alone in the apartment.

The doorbell rang.

'It must be him, *Mata*.' The boy's knee was bouncing up and down like a see-saw, a physical manifestation of immense stress. He added, 'Is there a way we can keep him out?'

Singh was impressed. There was someone at the door who was even less welcome than they had been? What was the Indian equivalent of a Jehovah's witness? One of those emaciated, naked, dusty fakirs with matted hair and wild eyes who wandered the streets?

The bell rang again.

'There is no way. I must go to him,' said Jesvinder.

She didn't have to – a middle-aged woman with broad hips, jet-black hair in a single plait, eggshell-smooth skin and a rather disconcerting wandering eye ushered an elderly gentleman into the room.

'Tara Baba is here,' she said unnecessarily and then stood quietly by the door. The wandering eye gave her the appearance of an ultra-competent security guard, who could look in all directions at once.

Singh stared at the elderly dapper creature in the neat turban and snowy beard who walked in with small slow steps, leaning on a polished, ivory-handled cane. So this was Tara Singh – Tara Baba to his family – the font of generosity who was sparing no expense over his granddaughter's wedding including putting up motley relatives at the Taj. His suit, with the Nehru collar preferred by Indian businessmen, was clearly expensive. There was a certain gravitas about his demeanour that might have been intimidating in a boardroom. Tara Singh's gaze flickered over the assembled group, hesitated for a puzzled second when confronted with a rotund fellow Sikh and then quickly dismissed him as irrelevant. He focused his gaze on his daughter-in-law and the inspector recognised that this slight old man was a force to be reckoned with. The unblinking black eyes, under the sparse eyebrows, held the attention of the woman like a basilisk.

'What's going on?'

Silence greeted his question – this was the quietest family gathering he'd ever attended, decided Singh. Usually, an occasion involving his wife's relatives resembled a riot in a henhouse.

'Where is she?' The quiet voice had the contrary effect, in the pin-drop silence, of suggesting that he'd screamed the query at the top of his voice.

The inspector noticed for the first time that Tara Singh's left hand, the one that did not have the cane head in a white-knuckled grip, was trembling. The old man feared the answer to his question.

He continued, 'Where is Ashu? What have you done with my granddaughter?'

Four

The rat was behaving oddly.

Mahesh, squatting next to a ditch, peered at the creature. It was huge, all the rats in the slum were. They always seemed to have ample food, unlike the people. It had grey-brown slick fur, the long hairless tail of its kind and fevered eyes like bright currants. Instead of foraging for food in the garbage-strewn area or travelling in a sea of fur with the other rats, this one was turning round and round as if it was a puppy chasing its tail. Once, every few seconds, it would run madly in one direction, stop suddenly and rush back the opposite way as if it was surrounded by terrors on all sides. Mahesh shuffled back a little while maintaining his squatting position. The scene was making him uneasy. He knew very well the dangers of rat bite. It was easy to catch some nasty rat-borne disease. Doctor Amma, who came almost every morning to tend to their ills, always warned the kids to stay away from the horrid creatures. But this situation was different. The rodent acted as if it was possessed by demons. Mahesh wondered whether he should bring it up with anyone and then decided that none of the elders would take kindly to the introduction of a conversation about rats.

It was at moments like this, when he needed to consult a grown-up, that he missed his mother. Not his father, of course. The wiry man with muscles like rope knots drank himself into a stupor every night but had always used his last conscious moments to thrash Mahesh. The boy remembered his mother's worn, tired face and that last evening when she'd taken a blow to the side of the head trying to defend him. Still watching the rat, Mahesh hugged his knees close to his chest and blinked hard. She'd been all right once he had helped her to the pallet on the floor that was her bed, wiped the blood away with a clean rag and brought her some water to sip. But he'd made up his mind then, as he maintained his bedside vigil, one wary eye on his snoring father.

In the morning, just as first light was breaking, he wrapped his spare shirt into a bundle, tied it around his waist with twine and walked two miles in bare feet. When he reached the railway line, Mahesh snuck on board the slow goods train bound for Mumbai. In the end, his escape had been easy and he wondered why he'd not done it years ago.

Arriving at Victoria Terminus – renamed the Chhatrapati Shivaji Terminus but always referred to as 'VT' by the natives of Mumbai – had been a shock, a blow as hard as any of his father's. The enormous cavern, the locomotives, the jostling crowds, the flashing boards with train timetables, the shoeshine men, the porters with bags piled high on their heads and the gangs of youths selling bottled water and defending turf from newcomers. Mahesh lived on rotting food from the bins until he'd learnt to stand up for himself against the big boys, to sleep on the platform so lightly that he could sense trouble before it found him and to run away as fast as his legs would carry him when the police came to clear the homeless away.

He'd even made a friend. A boy just like him with a village home left far behind and the survival instincts of a ferret. Eventually, Mahesh had fallen in with a gang who controlled a small but sufficient corner of the station. They appreciated his quick wit and his quick feet and the wide smile that caused the women in the 'ladies only' carriages to reach into their purses for a few rupees to buy a bottle of water they didn't need. Mahesh smiled a little at the memories. He'd been hungry, tired and dirty but almost happy as well. He'd picked up English so he could con tourists. He'd saved money so he could rescue his mother except for when he purchased a bright orange shirt with buttons and pockets, the first time he'd ever bought something for himself. He'd been genuinely amused to discover that the words on the mucky torn poster of Gandhiji on the subway wall read, 'Cleanliness is next to Godliness.'

Life had been all right until those men came with their guns and bombs and blood was splattered and pooled on the VT station floor and his best friend lay dead with his arms blown off and a hole in his chest the size of a young coconut. The gang leader moved Mahesh to a slum outside the city. 'You can come back when you're ready,' he'd said and there had been just a hint of warning that the boy was not to get ideas into his head about moving out of VT permanently.

A voice interrupted his contemplation. 'Nice shirt, Mahesh. You think you're Shah Rukh Khan?'

The boy grinned. He was indeed wearing his favourite orange shirt, newly washed and dried by the post-monsoon sun that penetrated the slum and lit up the pools of oily water with rainbow colours.

'What are you looking at?' the other boy asked.

'Dancing rat.'

His friend came over quickly and peered into the drain. 'Another one? I saw a rat doing this earlier today.'

'Auditioning for Bollywood, maybe!' said Mahesh and then laughed uproariously at his own wit.

'We don't know, Tara Baba,' whispered Jesvinder, the girl's mother.

'What?'

'We don't know where Ashu has gone.' It was Harjeet, the aunt, speaking from the doorway and providing corroboration.

The old man swayed as if subject to invisible conflicting forces. Singh realised for the first time how frail Tara Singh was. He wondered whether he was unwell or merely old. It was impossible to gauge his age from his face. Despite his snowy beard which was almost two fistfuls long, his face was unlined and his eyes were clear. Jesvinder suddenly gave up the battle to be calm and gave full rein to her fear. She fell to her knees at Tara's feet and clutched him around the shins, weeping with the abandon of someone grieving the dead.

Inspector Singh, completely nonplussed by this display of

emotion, averted his eyes while trying to process the information he'd received so far. *Ashu* was gone? Wasn't that the bride?

Mrs. Singh hurried over to her cousin and tried to help her to her feet but the woman was distraught and beating the ground with heavy fists. Her son, galvanised into action by Mrs. Singh's attempt to help, managed to drag his mother to the sofa where she slumped back and half-disappeared into the cushions, still sobbing wildly.

'Tara Baba, you must sit down. This news is a great shock to you,' said Harjeet.

The old man nodded and lowered himself slowly into an armchair, using his cane for support. When he spoke again, Singh noticed that his voice was crisp and resonant, the expensive English accent of the very wealthy in India softened around the edges with a lilt from the sub-continent. 'Stop howling, woman,' he barked at his daughter-in-law, 'and tell me what has happened.'

When there was no answer, Tara turned to his grandson and said, 'What about you, Ranjit? Will you make a contribution for a change?'

Ranjit flushed and his acne stood out like a rash. This gawky young man was not a favoured grandchild then. Was the girl the only one who had garnered a spot in the useful affections of the wealthy entrepreneur?

'I'm sure she's all right, Tara Baba.'

'I need more than your convictions.'

A deep voice from the door said, 'Tara Baba, there is not much we can tell you. I have just returned from looking for Ashu.'

The inspector guessed that this was another brother to the missing girl, an older one from the self-confidence he wore like a comfortable suit.

Tara Singh's shoulders became more rounded and his jaw slackened. 'Tell me what you can, Tanvir. I trust you.'

It seemed that Tanvir too was a favoured grandchild. Looking at him, it was not entirely a surprise. The good fairies had been present in large numbers at his birth, bestowing height, good looks and an aquiline nose.

'She disappeared some time yesterday or early this morning,' explained Tanvir, 'although she was not supposed to leave the house because the *choora* ceremony was complete. We all thought she was in bed resting. She claimed to have a headache.'

'I'm so sorry, it is my fault. I should have watched her.' The mother wiped her face so vigorously with her *dupatta* that she left a furrow of red streaks down her cheeks. Tanvir walked over and placed a comforting hand – or was it a warning hand, wondered Singh – on her shoulder. Ranjit, officially excluded now, huddled at the end of the sofa looking more resentful than concerned.

'*No* one can blame you, Jesvinder. You're her mother, not her prison warden,' said Harjeet.

'Was there any sign of forced entry or a struggle?'

Singh's detective instincts had overcome his reluctance to get involved.

His wife looked daggers at him, displeased at his sudden metamorphosis from bystander to participant.

'And who might you be?' asked Tara with old-fashioned courtesy.

Jesvinder interrupted before Singh could fashion his own response.

'This is my cousin from Singapore,' she said, nodding in the direction of Mrs. Singh with a small smile, 'and her husband, Inspector Singh who is the head of the Singapore police.'

Singh wished that Superintendent Chen was present to witness this unexpected promotion.

Jesvinder added, tears welling up again, 'They're here for the wedding. Staying at the Taj.'

'Well then, if he's a policeman, he knows what's he's talking about. Answer his question.'

If he's a policeman? Singh didn't like the overt scepticism from Tara.

Every member of the immediate family, Tanvir, Ranjit and the mother, shook their heads in unison but again it was Tanvir who acted as spokesman for the family.

'No – the apartment was as usual today. I checked with the houseboy who opens things up in the morning – he said everything was locked up from the night before. Nothing is missing.'

They all digested the implications of this. From the expressions on their faces, the reality was unpalatable in the extreme.

Singh articulated their thoughts. 'So the girl left of her own accord.'

'But why?' The question from Tara Singh was impassioned. 'The wedding is in a few days. Why has she left without telling anyone?'

'The obvious inference is that she didn't want to go through with it,' remarked Singh.

His wife's eyes warned him that this was dangerous

ground. Tanvir stood up and strode over until he was towering over the seated inspector.

'What are you trying to say?'

'Well, she's due to get married and she runs away from home . . . what else is one supposed to think?'

'Are the Singapore police trained to leap to conclusions, Inspector?'

Tanvir's ironic remark was a little too close to the bone. Still, one did have to examine the obvious before indulging in colourful speculation.

'Embellish your theory, Inspector,' said Tara Singh. His voice was as sharp as the knives with stiletto points that Singh sometimes found embedded in the chests of victims.

'Is there a boyfriend?'

There was a hiss of sound, like air leaking out of a car tyre.

'Of course not,' said Aunty Harjeet in a definite tone, twisting and pulling at her plait as she spoke. 'Ashu's a good girl. Anyway, we would have known if there was such a thing going on. If not me, then her mother at least.'

Singh caught himself before he smiled at this convoluted defence. Ashu was a good girl and they trusted her but in any event she was watched. He noted that the brothers had not been so quick to leap to her defence. A more modern outlook or inside knowledge? The inspector stood up and walked to a mantelpiece which was decorated with ceramic cherubic figurines. Singh identified a cow, a dog and a milkmaid. It was like stepping back in time – to his own youth – when such collectibles were prized. There was also a silver-framed studio portrait of a girl at her graduation. She wore a hat and gown and smiled self-consciously and rather reluctantly at the camera. She had a firm chin with a mild cleft and hazel eyes light enough to have a greenish tinge. Her hair was tucked behind one ear but cascaded over the other.

'Is this Ashu?' asked Singh, picking up the portrait with two beefy hands.

There were brief, guarded nods.

'A beautiful and intelligent woman. Would it be so odd if she had a boyfriend and preferred him to the MBA?'

'It is completely out of the question,' said Tanvir, as if daring Singh to pursue the subject. 'Ashu fully understood her responsibilities to the family. She would never run away.'

Out of the corner of his eye, Singh noted that the younger brother looked scared. There were secrets within this family. But was there anything odd in that? All families had something to hide, a sin that loomed large in the household although trivial in the greater scheme of things. A quarrel between members, feuding factions, perhaps an affair. It didn't necessarily have anything to do with the missing woman.

'You will not be familiar with *Indian* culture, Inspector,' explained Tara Singh in a patronising tone, 'but I can assure you that a well-brought-up Sikh girl like Ashu understood that her family would arrange a suitable marriage for her.' He continued, 'And we would appreciate it if you did not make any further suggestion to the contrary as her reputation might be damaged beyond repair – even if we prevent word of this escapade getting out.'

Tara Singh had gone from a state of near panic to treating the disappearance as an 'escapade'. What had reassured him? wondered Singh. The knowledge that she must have left the house of her own free will? The inspector was not so sanguine.

'You might keep her disappearance a secret for a few days – but she'll be missed at the wedding.'

There were angry glares directed at Singh but no one protested his logic.

'Do you know where she might have gone? Friends, family? A hideout?' he asked. He turned to Tanvir. 'You said you were looking for her – where did you go?'

He shrugged. 'The park where she goes for her morning walk, a friend's house, the coffee place not far from here where she sometimes stops.'

'No sign of her?'

'No sign of her,' he agreed.

'No one – not friends or family – would keep her presence a secret – not from me.' There was confidence in Tara's voice.

Was it justified? If the old man was right, then where had Ashu gone? Mumbai was not the sort of place where an un-accompanied single woman would feel comfortable. What was the euphemism for bothering women in India – Eve teasing? It made the practice sound benign but a man of his experience of the darker side of life knew that such behaviour was the pinnacle of a slippery slope.

'Are any of her clothes missing?' he asked.

'I didn't think about that. I haven't checked.' The mother answered slowly, understanding dawning in her large brown eyes.

'What are you waiting for then?' snapped Tara Singh.

Jesvinder hurried out of the room with Mrs. Singh hard on her heels, whether to lend a hand, provide some emotional support or ferret out more information, Singh couldn't guess.

*

Mrs. Singh stood at the door while her cousin sporadically pulled open drawers in a tall wooden chest.

'Policeman *bhai* doesn't know my daughter or he wouldn't say that she has a boyfriend,' said Jesvinder defensively as she rifled through drawers like a light-fingered thief looking for the hidden stash of family jewels. The article of furniture was ancient and the drawers were sticky and uncooperative.

Mrs. Singh nodded. 'Yes, he only sees modern girls in Singapore – Chinese, you know – so he thinks that our girls might behave the same. With boyfriends and *what not*.'

There was a silence while they both contemplated the decadence of other races and cultures and sheered away from the details of 'what not'.

'India too is getting more modern,' said Jesvinder tearfully and the inspector's wife wondered whether a *mea culpa* was in the offing. It was true what her cousin said about modern manners though. Just that morning, she'd spotted two girls with bare arms from shoulder to wrist. That would have been a sight to provoke whispers and jeers just a few years ago.

'She was happy about the marriage?' asked Mrs. Singh.

'Of course,' was the defiant response. 'Kirpal is from a very good family.' She added, as if determined to make a clean breast of everything, 'But not much money any more.'

A man as wealthy as Tara Singh was probably looking for pedigree rather than wealth, guessed Mrs. Singh.

No further confidences were forthcoming so Mrs. Singh looked around the bedroom with a beady eye. It was small and crammed. A bookshelf was laden with chemistry texts. Where were the novels of romance and suspense? The bed was neatly made, the orange cotton handloom bedspread a bright spot of colour in the otherwise drab room.

'Her bed is made,' she said.

'Yes, Ashu is always tidy.'

Did girls who were about to run away from home make their beds first? Mrs. Singh didn't know. She tried to imagine what she would do in similar circumstances but her mind balked at contemplating such independent behaviour as to leave home in the run-up to a marriage, jangling bangles announcing this perfidy to the world.

'What were her hobbies?' asked Mrs. Singh.

'Always she was reading a book – and mostly books about the work she did at the factory. She is a research scientist, you know?' This was said with a proud lift of the head although Mrs. Singh suspected she had no idea what Ashu's job actually involved. In similar circumstances, she would have been clueless and Mrs. Singh was not one to attribute superior powers to her female relatives than she possessed herself.

'What about your sons?'

'Tanvir works for his grandfather in the office. Ranjit is still studying. He wanted to do literature at Mumbai uni but Tara Baba says he will not waste his money on such useless pursuits. So now he is studying for a marketing degree. Already doing a Masters. Much better. Easier to get a good job.' She sounded as if she was rehashing old arguments that had been put to her by Tara Singh.

'So only Ashu is ... ermmm ... independent?'

'Actually, the factory where she works belongs to Tara Baba.'

The family were well and truly caught up in the tentacles

of their benefactor, realised Mrs. Singh. Had it been too much? Was that why the girl had run away? Jesvinder stood up slowly and the creak in her knees was audible to her cousin. She walked over to a cupboard and flung the doors open as if determined to confront whatever she might find head-on. Mrs. Singh, standing next to her, was struck by the simplicity of the cloth and hues, so unlike the primary colours favoured by many Indian girls.

Jesvinder's next words were mildly apologetic. 'I do not mean to criticise Tara Baba. He knows best in these matters. And we owe him everything. Things were very bad for us when my husband died.'

The missing girl's mother looked around the room as if seeing it for the first time through the eyes of a stranger. 'Tara Baba helps us with schools and jobs but he says it would not be right for us to live more grandly than my husband could have provided.'

Mrs. Singh's eyebrows shot up. His generosity had limits then.

'We are very very grateful for all he has done for us,' continued Jesvinder and she sounded as if she really meant it. 'Especially for Ashu.'

'Do you think she has run away?' asked Mrs. Singh.

'I don't know,' said Jesvinder. 'I don't know what to think. But none of her clothes are missing.'

Singh looked around the room, noted the simple furnishings; wooden framed chairs with square cushions, the two sofas and a carpet with loud geometric designs. A small picture of Guru Nanak Singh, founder of the Sikh religion, a gold leaf halo around his head and a snowy white beard down to his chest, was on the wall. He looked a little like Tara Singh, realised the inspector. The guru's finger was raised in admonishment so Singh looked away and gazed instead at a small glass-topped table in the centre of the room. The apartment was certainly not luxurious or ostentatious. Tara Singh might be the family benefactor but this apparently did not imply unlimited largesse.

Singh decided to continue in the vein of a policeman rather than contemplate the furnishings in silence. 'Where did Ashu work?' he asked.

'She was a chemist,' replied Tanvir. 'At Bharat Chemicals. They have a factory in Mumbai.'

'That would be a good place to begin a search although it might be difficult to be discreet.'

'They will be silent on the matter if I tell them so,' said Tara Singh.

'My grandfather owns a majority shareholding in the company,' explained Tanvir. 'It is a joint venture with the Americans.'

'I don't believe that Indian entrepreneurship should be limited to call-centres,' said Tara with the air of a man who had made the same point on many previous occasions to people more worthy of his insights.

Singh remembered the taxi drivers and porters – and especially their recent encounter with the self-proclaimed Sikh brother. 'You're quite right,' he agreed. 'There is no shortage of entrepreneurial spirit here.'

Tara Singh appeared to belatedly remember his manners. 'Are you enjoying your stay at the Taj, Inspector?'

'Yes, very much. I must thank you for your generosity.'

'Nothing is too good for my Ashu.'

Mention of Ashu reminded everyone present that the bride had gone missing. Glum silence reigned once more and not even the policeman had the heart to break it.

The door opened and Jesvinder waddled back in. Mrs. Singh had a hand on her elbow to steady her progress.

'What is it?' demanded Tanvir.

'Nothing is missing – all her clothes except what she was wearing are still here.'

'Maybe she planned to buy herself new ones,' suggested the inspector.

'Her handbag is in the room too with her wallet and credit cards. The only thing that is gone is her small purse – which she used when she was just popping out for a short while and needed a few rupees only for taxis.' She added, 'It's easier because there is a lot of bag snatching in Mumbai.'

Mrs. Singh's gripped her own handbag more tightly.

'What does this mean?' asked Ranjit, finding his voice for the first time since being belittled by his grandfather. 'Why would she run away without any clothes?'

Singh noted that the younger brother at least was not so adamant that Ashu would 'never run away' as Tanvir had asserted earlier. 'It appears that your sister did not intend to stay away for very long,' said Singh. Deep frown lines appeared on his forehead. Ashu had not intended to remain absent. And if that was the case, where was she? Somewhere in Mumbai without a change of clothes or much money.

'Does she have a mobile phone?'

'She left it charging here,' said Ranjit.

'She was always forgetting it . . .' added the mother quietly.

'Inspector Singh, what do you think we should do?'

The policeman looked at Tara Singh, who had gone from supercilious to desiring his advice in a few short moments. Needs must, it would seem.

'Call the police,' he answered abruptly.

'That's out of the question,' barked Tanvir.

Tara Singh cocked his head to one side as if he was thinking. At last, he said, 'Not yet. We should make our own inquiries first.'

'How will you do that?' demanded Singh. It was a ridiculous notion – this was definitely a job for the police with their extensive resources.

Tara Singh raised his cane and pointed it at the policeman from Singapore. 'I won't be doing it, Inspector Singh – you will.'

Five

'As a favour to me, you will look into this mystery of my granddaughter's whereabouts.' Tara Singh's tone was clipped. A man used to having people dance to his tune. Well, he'd found himself a fat man with two left feet and no rhythm.

'You need professionals,' insisted Singh. 'The Indian police.'

'And are you not a professional then, Inspector Singh?'

'I'm a professional in my own country,' he said stiffly, hackles raised. 'Here, I am a stranger.'

His wife added quickly, 'And he investigates murders, not missing persons. He would have no idea what to do, Tara Baba.'

The inspector scowled at his better half. She was right – he would have no idea what to do – but surely a good Sikh wife should be blindly supportive? Even when she was on his side she could only achieve their mutual ends by undermining him.

'I cannot go to the police – not yet,' said Tara. 'Trying to keep a secret within the wider Mumbai police force is like trying to hold water with a sieve.'

Singh rubbed his eyes with thumb and forefinger. Missing persons often came home in boxes and that was the truth. But not the whole truth. Not always. Singh glanced at the picture on the mantelpiece and hazel eyes met his without blinking. He really hoped this girl had developed a case of cold feet and made a run for it. He would hate to think of such a young life snuffed out – whether by accident or design.

'My sniffing around will raise questions too.'

'You will have to be discreet.'

Singh scratched his tummy with thick short fingers. 'How can I be discreet when I am asking whether anyone has seen a missing bride?'

'I'll leave that to you,' said Tara. 'But perhaps you could make your inquiries more general – pretend to be from the groom's family checking her antecedents. That would not be uncommon before a marriage.'

'A few days before the wedding?'

Tara Singh shrugged.

The timing was not perfect but, to give the old man due credit, it was almost plausible, decided Singh. And although he was a murder cop, tracking down the girl should not be that different from a murder investigation. Understanding the victim was still key to any resolution of the mystery. Once he got to know this Ashu Kaur, albeit vicariously, through her family, friends and workmates, he might be in a position to deduce where she'd gone. Indeed, *why* she had gone. And here, for a change, there was even the possibility of a happy ending. Or, at least, an ending where the protagonist was alive which would make a change from his usual diet of dead bodies. Singh was tempted. He knew it was a ridiculous assignment. The family should go to the police and that was that. A freelance private investigator looking for a missing person amongst the twenty million people living cheek by jowl in Mumbai? He would have a better chance of success looking for the proverbial needle. On the other hand, this girl was not one of the nameless, homeless millions who poured into Mumbai looking for a better life only to find themselves sleeping on sidewalks or crammed into slums. Ashu Kaur was *somebody*. She was Tara Singh's granddaughter.

Tanvir had been quiet and still, listening to the unfolding conversation. Now he said, 'Tara Baba, I respect your decisions in all things, but I do not think this is a good idea.'

Sycophantic little tosser, thought Singh, protecting his inheritance with a bit of brown-nosing. He looked at Tara Singh. Weren't these big-time industrialists supposed to be good judges of character? Surely he could see through the boy? And why was the brother reluctant to have Singh involved anyway? Didn't he want to find his sister?

Out of the corner of his eye, Singh noticed that his wife was nodding in agreement with Tanvir. Typical. There seemed to be a general disbelief that the short inspector with the pot belly and holed socks was the man for the job.

'Let me search for my sister,' continued Tanvir. 'It is *my* responsibility.'

'More trips to the coffee place?' asked Singh. These people needed to understand that it wasn't amateur hour.

'Maybe, she will just come back . . .' whispered Jesvinder.

'She must have just been confused or worried. It is not easy for a young girl to leave her home to be married.'

Singh caught the sudden memory, throbbing through her faint words, of a bride's first journey into the married state with a man she barely knew.

'What about the husband-to-be?'

'He must not in any way be informed of this situation,' stated Tanvir.

The inspector looked across at Tara and saw a firm nod of agreement.

'He will not be expecting to see her – she should not be leaving the house,' pointed out Aunty Harjeet. Singh nodded his approval at her words. Unlike the rest of them with their testosterone-fuelled assertions, this woman was thinking.

It was certainly a plus that tradition dictated that Ashu be secluded prior to the wedding. It meant that her absence from her usual haunts would not be thought of as out of the ordinary.

Singh remembered that he was on enforced medical leave. It might be ages before he had a juicy murder to deal with if Superintendent Chen had his way. This case – a missing person, a secretive family, a powerful scion, a city of contrasts and a wedding deadline – was certainly not for the faint-hearted. But wasn't he Inspector Singh, leading criminal investigator in Singapore, at least in his own estimation? He looked around at the family members of the missing girl. Two brothers, the mother, grandfather and an aunt all staring at him with different degrees of hostility and hope. The older brother was the angriest, the mother, the most hopeful. That fitted in with his assessment of their characters.

'I'll do it!' he said, slapping his thigh with an open palm for emphasis and was rewarded with matching horrified expressions on the faces of Tanvir Singh and his own dear wife.

Tanvir Singh hurried to his bedroom. It was clean and functional. Plain white sheets, a cream bedspread, bare walls and a small television with a DVD player attached – but without an untidy stack of movies to hint at his tastes. Only the bookshelf provided some insights – a few histories, Indian and Sikh, and a stack of biographies ranging from Gandhi to Malcolm X. Yellow 'Post-it' notes stuck up from the pages like gelled blonde hair.

He reached for his mobile phone and quickly stabbed the green key. He needed his 'last dialled' number and he needed it quick. He tapped his foot, keeping time with the rings.

'What is it?' asked the man at the other end. 'I thought we were going to limit calls? I still have a lot of preparation to do.'

'This is important,' said Tanvir, succinct and bitter.

'What do you mean?'

'My sister – Ashu Kaur . . .'

'The one who is to be married? I heard about that. You gonna get me an invite? Sounds like it's going to be a great party. I'll be able to show you my *bhangra*. Some people say I'm the best dancer in Canada!' The tone was jocular, not yet worried by Tanvir's ominous tone.

'Well, there's not much chance of that right now. She's . . . disappeared.'

'What?'

'Yes – and there's talk of calling the police.'

'That would not be helpful.'

'I realise that, Jaswant.' Tanvir's tone was cold. He hadn't called so that they could repeat the obvious to each other. The call was a warning about a developing problem. A potential deal-breaker. He felt a surge of anger and had to take a few deep, calming breaths, focus on the process, not the outcome. He knew his own temperament best although there were family members – like his foolish brother, Ranjit – who would argue that only those at the receiving end could truly know a temper.

In any event, this was not the time to let anger cloud his judgment. They had worked too hard to get to this point.

'What do you think has happened to her?' asked Jaswant.

'That's the least of our concerns right now.'

There was silence at the other end. Shock perhaps at a brother's callousness. More likely an acknowledgement that the time for small talk was over.

'What should we do? We have to keep the police out of it. There's only a few days to go to judgment! We might have to wait years for another such opportunity.' Jaswant, although the older, was turning to the natural leader between the two of them, looking for guidance.

'Leave it to me,' said Tanvir. 'I'll figure something out.'

'Like what?'

'I don't know yet.'

'Jesus, Tanvir! Your sister isn't a nobody – she's the granddaughter of Tara Singh. If she's disappeared there's going to be a huge manhunt. Police, press, politicians – the whole shebang.'

'Do you think I don't know that?'

'Most likely she's been in an accident or something like that ...'

'Or got cold feet about the wedding and headed for the hills.' Tanvir made the suggestion tentatively.

'You're right,' agreed Jaswant. 'But she couldn't have picked a worse time, that's for sure.'

Tanvir fell silent, turning options around in his mind. Nothing seemed viable. Jaswant was right when he said that a girl like Ashu could not disappear without creating a city-wide stir. He felt his anger begin to boil over again. Trust his idiotic family to create yet more trouble for him. There were times when he would gladly have admitted to being adopted, a genetic stranger to his do-gooder sister, Ashu, and poet brother, Ranjit. How was it that he was the only one who had inherited Tara Baba's drive and purpose? The rest of them were weak – like his father had been.

'If we have to postpone, it is better than outright failure,' warned Jaswant.

'That's coward's talk,' was the response. 'I haven't come this far to let some family crisis get in the way.'

'Talk is easy, *bhai*, and talk is free,' said Jaswant, 'but you're going to have to make this problem go away and I don't know how you're going to do it.'

'Leave it to me – I'll buy us some time until judgment,' snapped Tanvir. 'After that they can turn Mumbai upside down looking for my sister, I don't care. I'll find a way to keep the police at bay – and anyone else with a long nose for sticking into other people's affairs.' An image of the fat policeman from Singapore was front and centre in his thoughts as he uttered the last line.

Tara Singh nodded his head now to acknowledge the inspector's willingness to investigate but he'd not expected him to do anything else. He was used to other men doing his bidding. Wasn't that the advantage of power and money? He wielded them with a light touch for the most part, but he knew how to get his own way. He eyed the policeman sitting pensively like the Buddha with his hands folded over his ample stomach. He looked ridiculous but he'd asked the right questions so far. Tara sniffed the air and then wrinkled his nose fastidiously. Did he smell tobacco on the inspector from Singapore?

That was the problem with the Sikh diaspora – they maintained those practices of the faith and culture that were convenient and dumped anything that was mildly inconsistent with their inclinations. The old man sighed and felt a twinge of arthritis in his fingers, especially the hand gripping the ivory handle of his cane. He was not in a position to choose his tools. The fat policeman from Singapore would have to do.

Tanvir might have been able to handle the job; he had a good head on his shoulders. But he would not be sufficiently discreet. In his personal and often expressed opinion, the younger brother Ranjit was a waste of time, a skinny bookworm tied to his mother's apron springs. That's what happened sometimes when boys did not have a father figure. Not that the boy's father had been an exemplar of a warrior race. Tara Singh reminded himself that his son had faced death bravely. What was the quote – *nothing became him so much in life as the leaving of it?* That summed up his son. All in all, Ashu was the best of them and now she was gone.

His attention was drawn to the policeman who had straightened up with difficulty on the soft sofa and then hauled himself to his feet, his efforts reminiscent of a bug on its back trying desperately, with flailing limbs, to right itself.

'I will need a free hand,' said Singh.

'Of course,' he replied.

'I will need to question each of you individually. You might not enjoy the experience.'

'My granddaughter is more important to me than my pride, Inspector.'

The policeman nodded but a faintly raised eyebrow conveyed his scepticism.

'I need access to her workplace.'

'It will be as you wish.'

There was silence.

'Is there anything else, Inspector Singh? The hours are passing and time is not on our side.'

Inspector Singh cracked his knuckles and looked uncomfortable. 'There is one thing ...'

'Well, spit it out, man.'

'She left the house for some reason or another but if the clothes and handbag left behind are any indicator, she did not intend to be out for long.'

'Yes.'

'She might have met with some mishap. She wasn't carrying any identification ...'

The inspector trailed off and Tara Singh nodded his head, ignoring the quiet weeping of his daughter-in-law. It was out in the open now, the possibility that Ashu had been the victim of some sort of accident.

'I realise that. I have a few friends in high places and I have already asked them to make discreet inquiries.'

'With the police and the hospitals,' suggested Singh carefully, not looking at the girl's mother.

'Yes. They will call me if there are any ... possibilities. It might take some time. In India, Inspector Singh, life is sometimes very cheap.' He could have added that many bodies went unclaimed because relatives could not afford a funeral. Men and women left their villages to find work in the cities and were far from loved ones when some accident carried them away. And of course, there were those who were killed in the sudden outbreaks of communal violence – it was difficult to find the family of these victims, many of whom might have died at the same time, escaped to their villages or be too traumatised to search for the missing.

His own son might have been one of the uncountable if the violence visited upon him had happened somewhere other than his own front gate. Tara had been the one to visit the morgue to identify his son. It had been a futile effort. The size and shape of the corpse had been similar but the creature he looked at had been burnt beyond recognition from the neck up, melted rubber from the tyre forming a thick layer, like an oil slick, around his neck and shoulders. He had finally been convinced – been forced to believe the horror story that Jesvinder had narrated – that the corpse was his only son when he'd seen the crescent shaped scar on his knee.

He looked up and saw that the Sikh inspector was looking at him quizzically.

'Well, what is your first step to find my granddaughter?' he asked, a nip in his tone suggesting impatience.

The policeman had opened his mouth to answer when Tara Singh's mobile rang. The old man raised the phone to his ear with a shaking hand.

'Are you sure?' he asked. There was a silence while he listened to the answer carefully. 'I will come now.'

He would not meet the eyes of his family members when he turned to speak to them. 'That was the minister. A ... a body of a young woman has been brought in to the police. He thinks I should have a look.'

'I will go, Tara Baba. It is not fitting that you should have to do this – again.' Tanvir Singh's beard was coal black against his light skin.

'No, this is something I must do.'

He used his cane as a support and rose to his feet. He swayed there for a moment and Singh was the first to see his eyes lose focus. 'He's going to faint,' he shouted and, moving quickly for a fat man, was just in time to catch Tara Singh before he fell to the ground.

The two men sat in the back of the limousine as far away from each other as possible. Tara Singh had been left behind. He'd recovered consciousness but his appearance was of someone who'd been subject to the ageing process in fast forward. He'd ordered the inspector to go along with Tanvir and to take his car. Singh, feeling sorry for the old man, bit his lip at being ordered about like a servant and fell in with his wishes.

'Where are we going?' asked Singh, glancing over at Tanvir.

'Worli – a police station,' replied the other man.

Singh stared out of the window and noted that Mumbai vehicle number plates contained enough letters to write a novel. Was that an indication of the number of cars on the road or the bureaucratic nature of the car registration department?

The silence was broken by Tanvir. 'I don't know why Tara Baba has asked you to help us.'

'I don't know either. Maybe because I'm a policeman.'

'Why should that matter? This is not a criminal case!'

'We don't know what sort of case it is.'

The macabre nature of their errand might go some way towards clearing up that particular question but he couldn't help but hope that the body was not that of Ashu. He liked the look of the girl in the photograph – the bright eyes and strong chin, cleft like a man's. Singh scratched his beard under his chin. It always itched when he was troubled. The fact of the matter was that a young woman lay dead. Was it right to wish away the trauma from his own family? If it was not Ashu, it meant that someone else would suffer the pain of sudden loss.

He reverted to staring out of the window. At night, Mumbai looked like every other big city. Skyscrapers reached upwards, lit from within like a Christmas tree. Shopping complexes and small hole-in-the-wall tea shops competed for business. Modern apartment buildings housed the affluent. Billboards lined the roads advertising the latest Bollywood films. Traffic ebbed and flowed around them but Singh was cocooned in the luxurious interior of his limousine. Was this how the rich insulated themselves from the reality of Mumbai? The road snaked forward, puddles of visibility from street lights appearing at regular intervals. In each puddle of light, like a morality play, the homeless lay on carefully laid out bits of cardboard or blanket. The 'new middle class' of Mumbai, spoken of in hushed tones by economists, stepped over the sleeping forms or skirted around them without breaking stride as they headed for the nearest Starbucks to fulfil their destiny as the engine of Indian economic growth.

The car drew up outside an old building. Red-brick arches invited visitors within and there were flowering plants in the compound. It was less sterile by a long way than Singh's Singapore station. Tanvir led the way, his firm stride belying any nervousness or hesitation. Was he confident that this unfortunate creature was not his sister? Quite likely, he was merely trying to show up the inspector from Singapore. Look at me, his stride proclaimed, I am man enough to do my duty, however unpalatable. My grandfather doesn't need you prancing all over our personal affairs in your silly shoes.

The officer who came out to meet them was deferential to the point of obsequious. 'The minister called,' he explained quickly. 'You are the brother of Ashu Kaur – grandson of Tara Singh?'

Tanvir nodded once.

'I am Assistant Commissioner of Police, Patel, at your good service.'

Singh did not bother to mention that he too was a policeman although not one who took as much pride in his uniform as ACP Patel. The Indian's khaki uniform was starched stiff and the crease lines had been created by an expert. His belt was pulled in tight and created a mass of flesh on either side although in this respect, at least, Singh had the edge. Patel had bags under his eyes that sagged in concert with his jowls as if his face suffered an exaggerated gravitational pull compared with the rest of humanity. He wore a peaked hat and had shoulder flashes with three stars and the letters 'IPS' on them. Indian Police Service, surmised Singh.

'And you are also relative of missing girl?'

'Yes,' agreed Singh amicably.

'A very senior policeman from Singapore,' said Tanvir. 'My grandfather has asked for his help.'

The inspector was interested to note that Tanvir was willing to use his position to garner some advantage even if he personally objected to Singh's role.

The effect of the statement on the Indian policeman was electric. He clasped Singh's hand in both of his and shook it vigorously. 'Such a pleasure and an honour to be meeting you.'

'Perhaps we can view the girl?' demanded Tanvir.

'I'm afraid you will not be finding this easy. Body is not at all in good shape,' explained Patel.

'Cause of death?' asked Singh.

'Body is very burnt. Our first understanding was that this incident was related to riots last night in Haji Ali mosque area.'

'That's nonsense!' said Tanvir, incredulous at the idea that his sister might have been caught up in such an unsavoury incident.

'Cadaver was found in vicinity.'

'And now?' demanded Singh. 'You said that was your "first understanding"?'

'Now we are not so sure.'

'What do you mean?'

'Rest of bodies caught up in blaze, there was no trace of kerosene. Not like this one – you can be smelling kerosene even from across room.'

'Suicide?' asked Tanvir.

There was a nod.

'Surely not – it would be such a horrible way to die,' insisted Singh, revolted by the idea.

'You are saying that,' said the Indian policeman, his expression lugubrious, 'but actually it is quite a common method of suicide here in India.'

Singh scowled. He was tired. He smelt bad. He was in a police station in India in the company of an arrogant young man. The last thing he needed was cultural variations in suicide methods.

'Let us see the body,' he said abruptly. 'If it's not Ashu, we are just wasting our time speculating as to what might have happened.'

The ACP shrugged a burly shoulder as if to suggest that the body would have been his first port of call but who was he to argue with members of Tara Singh's family let alone a senior policeman from Singapore? He led the way through a maze of narrow corridors until they came to a room at the back.

A body lay on a steel trestle, covered in a thin cotton sheet. Two blackened stumps, which Singh assumed must once have been feet, stuck out from the bottom. The stink of kerosene and burnt flesh was strong enough to make his eyes water. ACP Patel was fastidiously holding a spotless handkerchief across his nose and mouth. Tanvir looked as if he was about to throw up but when Patel asked him if he needed more time in a solicitous tone, he shook his head.

The ACP walked over to the corpse and flicked back the sheet with the flair of a conjurer. Singh shut his eyes for a moment. Tanvir was made of sterner stuff. He walked closer to the table and looked down at the body. The face was blackened; lips burnt away exposing teeth in a wild grimace. One eye had been incinerated but the other was open and staring. Patches of hair remained on the scalp but most had been destroyed by the flames. An ear remained intact and untouched and was devastating in its incongruity. A small gold earring with a red stone glimmered on the lobe.

ACP Patel cleared his throat. 'Are you able to identify body?'

Tanvir nodded once and then cleared his throat and spoke. 'Yes, this is my sister, Ashu Kaur.'

'Are you sure?' asked Patel, looking at the grotesque parody of a human being on the table.

'Yes, those were her favourite earrings, you see.'

Six

Singh, trying to spare Tanvir further unpleasant details, whispered his questions to the ACP while the brother was in the washroom – as if the stench of death could be erased through the application of soap and water.

'A death in unusual circumstances – there will have to be an autopsy.' Patel's tone was apologetic and his intention clear. Singh was to convey the regret of the police to Tara Singh that his granddaughter would not be coming home yet.

'But please tell Sardarji Tara that it is a formality only and we will release the body for burial as soon as possible.'

'Will you investigate the death?'

'Of course! But between us it is quite clear the girl is killing herself to avoid marriage. We will close file as soon as possible to avoid further embarrassment to family.'

'You know about the marriage?'

'Who doesn't, Sardarji? Everyone in Mumbai is invited.

This will be causing a huge scandal.' He shook his head.

'You don't think it could be foul play?'

ACP Patel looked shocked, his jowls dragged upwards by his arched eyebrows. '*Naa, naa!* She just had frozen feet, you know? We will soon be finding evidence of an unsuitable boyfriend, I am quite sure of this. I just hope he hasn't been killing himself too. Perhaps they were thinking that they were like Romeo and Juliet?'

'Call me if you find anything,' suggested Singh, eager to avoid any further Shakespearean parallels, and scribbled his Indian mobile number on a piece of paper.

'It will be my great pleasure,' said ACP Patel and sounded as if he meant it.

The sound of footsteps signalled the return of Tanvir and both men dropped the subject with tacit agreement.

In the car, he agreed with Tanvir that they would not reveal the extent of the damage to the body. 'My mother and grandfather are not strong enough for such knowledge,' Tanvir muttered and Singh had nodded his great head in acknowledgement. No close relative should have to go through such an ordeal. Singh had taken a strong dislike to the deceased's eldest brother quite early on in their acquaintance but he had to admit that the man had courage.

'Any idea why your sister would have done such a thing?' he asked.

'None whatsoever,' replied Tanvir, 'but this is going to break Tara Baba's heart.'

*

Indian families tend to respond to death, even that of the old, with uncontrolled exhibitions of grief. Even Sikhs, who are taught to view death as an opportunity for a soul to reunite with its maker, are not averse to a little loud mourning.

It was not surprising therefore that the death of a beautiful young woman just before her wedding provoked scenes that would usually have caused the inspector to seek refuge elsewhere. His wife, however, insisted that they stay at the apartment even if it turned into an all-night vigil. This wasn't exactly the rest-cure his doctors had recommended, dashing around Mumbai identifying burnt-out corpses. But when Singh saw the upright posture of Tara Singh as he sat quietly in a chair accepting condolences, he felt that he owed it to the old man to stick around for a while. His mission to find the girl had not lasted very long. She'd been found. Not hiding out with some boyfriend to avoid the upcoming nuptials but a ravaged creature on a steel trestle table. In his mind's eye, he could see the twinkling ruby in her ear.

Lost in thought, the inspector hadn't noticed Tara Singh walk over to him. Now he looked up and met the tired eyes of a grieving old man.

'Walk with me for a moment,' said Tara and the inspector nodded his head in acquiescence.

Tara Singh led the way onto a small balcony with ornate balustrades painted a light blue. They both looked out over a fairyland of lights. Mumbai was as awake at night as during the day. Silhouettes of buildings and cranes framed the horizon. A full yellow moon hung low in the sky like a Chinese lantern. Faint sounds of laughter, sirens and traffic drifted upwards from the streets. All cities had the same rhythm at their heart, decided Singh. Under the blanket of night, one could feel at home in any metropolis in the world. Especially one like Mumbai where, at this time of the year, the humidity wrapped itself around his shoulders like one of his wife's shawls and reminded him of Singapore.

'I cannot believe that she killed herself.'

Singh had expected this opening gambit so he was not surprised. The intentional taking of life was hardest on the bereaved. They had to acknowledge that all the love and affection and material goods showered on the victim had not been sufficient to tether that person to life. Suicide was like an accusation of failure to those left behind. A kick in the gut or the teeth.

'It wasn't your fault,' said the policeman automatically. He didn't think that Tara Singh would find comfort in platitudes but it was all he had to offer. It might even be true. Who could comprehend the state of mind of someone who'd committed suicide? Singh, who loved life despite his constant grumbling and saw it curtailed by violence far too often, knew that he did not have the imagination to place himself in Ashu's shoes.

'I'm telling you that I knew Ashu. She was like a daughter to me. There is no way she would have killed herself – and in *such* a way.'

'The police seem quite sure,' he replied.

'The police in India are like a river, Inspector Singh, always taking the path of least resistance.'

Singh decided to save the metaphor for an occasion when he could use it on Superintendent Chen.

'She was a scientist,' continued Tara. 'She was always very rude about what she called the Indian fondness for drama. I can imagine that, if she had a terminal disease, she might take a practical way out, with sleeping pills. But this self-immolation? It's completely out of character.'

Singh didn't answer because he could not agree but his silence spoke volumes.

'You don't believe me? You didn't know Ashu so I can't blame you. But I'm determined to get to the bottom of this.'

'I can understand that.'

'Will you look into it for me? Exactly what I asked you to do when we thought she was missing, investigate? But this time you're looking for an explanation of what happened.'

'Will it really make you feel better to know why she did it?'

Tara Singh raised his cane and pointed it at Singh's chest. 'I have never shirked from the truth and I will not do so now.'

Singh, who had taken a prudent step backwards when Tara Singh wielded his cane like a weapon, now watched the old man smash it down on the balcony railings. It shattered into pieces, fine jagged splinters visible at the breaks.

Tara Singh tried a small smile but his heart wasn't in it. 'I'm sorry. I don't know what came over me.'

The inspector found his voice as he knelt down on the floor and picked up the larger pieces. 'Anger is just one small part of grief,' he said and then wished he hadn't sounded like someone on the Oprah Winfrey show.

'So, will you do it?'

'I'll need access to family, friends and workplace. The husband-to-be as well.'

Tara Singh drew his hand across his eyes but nodded once more.

'And you may not like what I find,' he added.

'I see that.'

Did he? wondered the inspector. After all, all roads might lead to a tyrannical grandfather.

'All right then,' said Singh reluctantly. 'I'll investigate Ashu's death.'

'Have you gone mad?' demanded Mrs. Singh.

His wife's voice had the incisiveness of a scalpel when she was on the warpath.

'Bad enough you agreed to look for that girl when we thought she was alive – but *now* what are you hoping to find?'

'The truth?' he suggested and immediately regretted engaging in conversation.

'The truth? How will you find the truth?'

It was a good question, thought Singh, although he suspected that his wife had uttered it in a purely rhetorical, quite possibly metaphysical, manner.

'Anyway,' she continued, pacing the floor of their hotel, 'we all know the truth. The silly girl killed herself. I can't believe that anyone in my family would do such a thing. After they found her such a good husband as well.' Mrs. Singh wrenched her hair into a bun with such force that he suspected she had pulled some hair out at the roots. It explained the sudden tears in her eyes.

'Tara Singh doesn't believe it was suicide.'

'What does he know?'

'He knows Ashu . . .'

'So also the brother – but when I spoke to Tanvir he thought Ashu must have done it.'

The inspector looked up with interest. 'Really?'

Mrs. Singh nodded curtly, reluctant to be drawn into a

discussion on the merits. Her husband knew from experience that she much preferred to harangue than to converse. 'He doesn't know why – maybe she got second thoughts about the wedding and was too afraid to tell the family.'

'What about the mother and younger brother? What do they think?'

'Too upset to say. But I am telling you it was suicide.'

Singh remembered the stubborn chin and sighed.

Mrs. Singh was getting into her stride. 'The problem with you is that you like showing off. Always thinking you should investigate this murder, that murder. Then suddenly missing persons also you want to find and now suicide you want to investigate!'

'I thought you'd appreciate my trying to help your family.'

There was a loud snort in response. 'What is the *use* of finding out why she did it? It won't make anyone feel better! Better to forget as soon as possible.'

Singh had a sudden clear memory of Tara Singh's stricken face when Tanvir had broken the news of Ashu's death. 'I don't think there will be much forgetting in that household.'

'Yes, they are very unlucky. Probably the sons will struggle to make good marriages now. Even the handsome one.'

The inspector assumed that it was Tanvir's looks which had won her approval. The pimply, skinny Ranjit would never have qualified for the epithet.

'Why would that be?' he asked.

'What for pay a big dowry if the family is cursed?'

'That's a bit extreme, isn't it?'

'First the father, now the daughter. It's too much.'

'What happened to the father?'

Mrs. Singh looked faintly pleased that she had the inside scoop on the family history and, more importantly, her husband was showing some interest in her gossip for a change.

'Killed!' she said dramatically.

'What do you mean, woman?'

'In the riots in Delhi after Indira Gandhi was shot. Gangs attacked their colony because there were a lot of Sikh families there.'

Mrs. Singh sat down on the plush chair by the window and gazed out at the Gateway. Her tone was troubled as she continued. 'They doused him in petrol and put a burning tyre around his neck. The whole family saw it. Tanvir was about seven and for a long time he would not speak. Ashu and the youngest boy were too young to remember . . .'

Singh switched off the television. His appetite for cricket and room service had diminished in the face of these latest revelations.

Perhaps the daughter had chosen this particular method to kill herself because of her memories of the past. Had it been some sort of bizarre homage to her long-dead father?

It seemed a most unlikely choice for a modern Mumbai woman with a good job and an MBA waiting in the wings.

'If Tara Singh had not rescued them, the family would have been finished.'

'It's not exactly the lap of luxury, that apartment.'

'He didn't want to spoil them – make them forget their roots. But he did pay for all their education. And they all work for him except that youngest boy who is still in university.'

The policeman nodded. He was being churlish to suggest that the old man had been anything but generous.

Mrs. Singh's voice took on a conspiratorial note. 'They say he agreed a big dowry with the boy's family – for Ashu.'

'Do people still pay dowries in this day and age?'

'Of course they do. Even Sikhs who are not supposed to by the teachings of the gurus. Nowadays the boys are asking for more and more. They want money and jewellery and property and washing machines.'

'Washing machines?' Singh was baffled.

'Any electrical item. Everyone is wanting one to show off. Even if they still give the clothes to the *dhobi wallah*. He irons also, you see,' she said, making a vigorous motion with her right hand. Mrs. Singh – the method actor.

So technology had not yet mastered all the skills of that wiry man in the dirty *lunghi* with a pile of clothes on his head. Singh was suddenly glad. To his surprise, he realised that India was getting under his skin. Already, he was feeling defensive about the old way of doing things.

'I guess Tara Singh can afford a big dowry,' said Singh, looking around at his opulent hotel surroundings.

'Yes, but some of the fathers are taking loans from money-lenders, losing their homes, anything to get the girls married.'

'I don't remember getting anything from your family,' complained Singh.

'What you get depends on *who you are* and *what you have*,' said Mrs. Singh tartly.

Singh retreated from the argument hastily. He tried to imagine a world where sons were auctioned off to the highest bidder, prime ministers were assassinated, men were murdered in front of their families by angry mobs and young girls killed themselves in dramatic fashion to avoid arranged marriages.

He suddenly felt guilty that his own father had left the Punjab looking for a better life so many decades ago. Singh had grown up in Malaysia and then Singapore. A quiet existence without the vicissitudes of life in India. Singh Senior had settled down to serve his colonial masters with genuine enthusiasm, sent his children to English schools and made it quite clear that their future would have to be forged in this new world. And Singh had done reasonably well for himself. He had a job which suited him down to the ground. Not even Superintendent Chen could deprive him of the satisfaction of a killer tracked down and a victim avenged. It was true that he was not wealthy like many Sikhs of the diaspora including his own brothers-in-law. They had become professionals, husbanded their earnings, invested in property and were now busy cultivating expensive habits and speaking of their Indian heritage with the pride of those who did not have to deal with the bureaucracy, corruption and grinding poverty on a daily basis.

Did he feel any vicarious pride in India? It was difficult to say. He wore his turban out of habit. It was more security blanket than religious symbol. He ignored all the teachings of the various gurus and avoided the *gurdwaras*. He was not the tall warrior of Sikh legend but a short stout man with a limited wardrobe who struggled to reach his shoelaces in the morning. Indeed, it was quite possible that he adopted the turban as an exercise in irony. On the other hand, especially in Singapore, he'd always been aware that he was not part of the homogenous majority seeking after the status symbols of life: cars, condominiums and club memberships.

But he didn't belong in India either. As far as the

population of Mumbai was concerned, he was just another tourist to be fleeced, a foreigner without the necessary survival skills for the big city. Which raised the question – why had he allowed himself to be bullied into taking this case of the suspicious suicide of the beautiful bride? Perhaps it would give him some insight into India, a sense of belonging or at least an understanding of the family history. He grinned, causing his wife to look at him in surprise. That was a rather ambitious proposition. Failing any insights into India, there was still the Taj, the food, the cricket and unexpected sightings of well-preserved Ambassadors. Quite likely, that would have to do, decided Singh, and reached again for the room service menu and the television remote control. In the absence of cigarettes, these would have to be his emotional crutch.

The next morning, Inspector Singh decided that, as the girl was dead and the wedding was off, there was no need to ignore breakfast in pursuit of answers. His appetite was sharp and the reasons were twofold. One, he'd missed dinner while traipsing around looking at corpses. And two, his wife had elicited the information that breakfast was part of the generous package sponsored by Tara Singh.

The inspector was firmly convinced that his high standards would not be compromised and in this, he was right. The coffee was piping hot as was the milk. The beverage options included *chai* and other spiced concoctions. The spread had every conceivable type of Indian bread from roti to naan, and thosai to idly. Each came with a varied assortment of curries and chutneys. And, as if that was not sufficient, there was a vast Western spread: eggs scrambled, poached or fried, sausages, bacon and ham, baked beans and hash browns as well as a Japanese corner which smelt to Singh like rotting fish. Beef – holy cow – was not on the breakfast menu but the hotel had decided to ignore the demands of the other major religions. Just as well when considering the diversity of religious opinion in India – he'd have been reduced to eating boiled rice otherwise.

'Are you really going to eat that much?'

He didn't bother to answer his wife and opened the newspaper instead. There was a cholera outbreak in the slums, more nuclear sabre-rattling from the governments of India and Pakistan and a riot because a Bollywood film had gone too far. Apparently, Indian morals were being compromised. Singh smiled happily. They just didn't make the newspapers like this in Singapore.

'What are you going to do first in this "investigation"?' asked Mrs. Singh, managing to incorporate verbal inverted commas around the word.

'Talk to the family.'

'You're going to offend everyone.'

'A girl is dead.'

There was a sudden round-shouldered slump from Mrs. Singh.

'What's the matter?' Surely his lack of manners wasn't sufficient to provoke this fit of despondency from his usually invincible wife?

'I was looking forward to the wedding.'

He nodded sympathetically. He'd stumbled on her discussing what to wear with her sisters on at least three separate occasions in Singapore.

'What are you going to do?'

'Sit with the family.'

The inspector winced. He knew the drill. A death was always greeted with a gathering of the community. Mostly womenfolk but men would also be present, especially those who were retired. The mourners would sit on borrowed chairs along the walls of the home or in huddles around tables rented for the occasion and speak in low tones about the departed if there was family within hearing range or about the cricket results if there wasn't. Sometimes there would be an outbreak of loud wailing when a close relative, probably hurrying back from some far country, walked in exhausted.

'Not a great way to spend the day,' he said.

'Will the body be there?'

'I doubt it. There will have to be some sort of post-mortem for a death like this.'

'That will be difficult for the family. They will want to bring Ashu home, wash and dress her and organise the funeral.'

'I think you'll find that this is a closed-coffin situation.'

Mrs. Singh sighed. 'She was such a pretty girl.'

'After the cremation, it won't matter anyway,' muttered Singh and then realised that this was probably very cold comfort to the family members of Ashu Kaur.

As they walked past the chandelier-lit lobby of the Taj, Singh noticed a turban protruding over the back of one of the low sofas. He skirted the paisley artwork on the floor; it seemed rude to step on it – why did they have art on the floor anyway? – and lumbered towards the turban on a hunch. He found Ranjit gazing at an antique horse on a glass table as if he was eyeing it up to auction at Sotheby's. On closer perusal it was possible to see that his gaze was blank, like the stare of the blind.

'What are you doing here?' Singh asked in a gentler tone than had been his first instinct. After all, this skinny boy had just lost a sister. He looked like a man in shock as well, hands trembling and shoulders hunched as if exposed to a chill wind.

'Tara Baba told me to come here and see you in case you had questions for me.'

Singh scowled. He didn't like the mechanics of his investigation being dictated by anyone, whether it was Superintendent Chen, faraway and unmissed, or the wealthy grandfather of a dead bride.

'But you were at breakfast,' continued Ranjit in an accusing tone. 'I've been sitting here for ages.'

Singh wasn't about to apologise for enjoying his morning repast.

'Just you?' he asked.

'Tanvir will be here soon. My mother is unwell but she will come when she is better.'

Great. Apparently the entire membership of this grieving family was going to parade through the hotel. That wouldn't be good for business if the lugubrious face in front of him was any indication. Besides, the Taj lobby was a place to see and be seen – not exactly a private venue. Singh made a quick decision. 'Let's find out if there's a room we can use for interviews,' he said and walked over to the front desk where a smiling young thing in a blue sari suggested that one of the small conference rooms at the business centre could be leased for a few days.

Singh nodded at the woman with what he hoped was a rich man's insouciance about cost. 'Put it on my bill.' If Tara Singh wanted him to investigate, he would have to absorb incidental expenses.

In a short while, they were ensconced in a room with a large window overlooking the Gateway. Singh noticed that his witness was gnawing his fingernails hungrily. Perhaps he had eschewed breakfast.

'Why does Tara Baba want us to see you?' asked Ranjit.

'He didn't explain?'

'Tara Baba doesn't explain – he only gives orders.' A hint of a smile played around his lips only to be chased away by memories. 'And I follow them.'

'He wants me to look into your sister's death.'

'Oh – I see,' he responded in a voice that suggested he didn't see it at all. 'You mean, like find out why she did this?'

'I guess so,' said Singh, acknowledging to himself that this was the reality despite the grandfather's suspicion of foul play.

'So, what do you have to tell me?' continued Singh.

'What do you mean? I thought you were going to ask me questions ...'

'All right. Tell me about Ashu.'

'What sort of thing do you want to know?'

'Anything – I'm a stranger, you're her brother – I expect you know more about her than me!'

'Well,' Ranjit stared at the older man helplessly, 'she was just, you know, Ashu.'

'That's very helpful,' remarked Singh, his words so laden with sarcasm that the boy turned pale and his acne glowed like traffic lights.

'She was smart,' he said at last. 'She loved her work at the chemical factory.' He added with greater conviction, 'And she was Tara Baba's favourite, of course.'

Singh nodded his approval, a reward for effort. 'What about your family?'

'There's just my mother and the three of us. Tanvir is the oldest and I am the youngest. And Tara Baba, of course.'

'Your father?'

'He died when I was still a child.'

Singh remembered what his wife had said about the father's death, that it had been during the anti-Sikh riots after the assassination of Indira Gandhi.

'That must have been difficult for you,' he said.

'I don't remember much. It bothers Tanvir much more than me, what happened to our father.'

That made sense. Tanvir had been old enough to be badly scarred by what he had seen.

Ranjit added, meeting Singh's eyes, '*This* is much worse for me.' There were tears in his eyes that lent an air of truth to his words. Singh remembered him confidently telling his grandfather that he was sure the girl was all right. He'd been quite wrong about that.

'OK, so why did your sister kill herself?'

Ranjit shivered suddenly as if he'd been at the receiving end of a cold blast from the air conditioning. 'I don't know.'

'You must have some idea.'

He shook his head and Singh wondered again why he affected such a huge turban for a young man. It was disproportionate and slightly comic. Was it a rather sad attempt to give himself stature? And if so, was he as lacking in self-confidence and self-awareness as that suggested?

'But you're sure it must have been suicide?'

'What else could it be?'

'Did she have any enemies?'

'Of course not,' said Ranjit. He added almost resentfully, 'Everyone liked Ashu.'

'Was Ashu happy about the impending marriage?'

'Tara Baba said that Kirpal was a good Sikh boy from a good family.'

'That's not an answer.'

'I think so. I mean, why wouldn't she be?'

'But did she have a young man? Aside from the MBA, I mean.'

There was a firm shake of the head but also a quick glance to see if Singh had been convinced by the air of certainty.

'Are you sure? It seems to me that you had your suspicions.'

'No, no. I didn't.'

Singh raised a single eyebrow.

'Well, it's nothing really.' The boy became garrulous and Singh wondered if it was to hide the truth in a flood of words. 'It's just that once, when we went to see a film together, at the Regal – I said something about the story which was one of those typical boy-meets-girl type of thing ...'

'Well, spit it out!' snapped Singh.

'I said that I liked happy endings.'

'And what did she say?'

'She sounded angry, you know? She said that a couple like that – there was no chance of a happy ending and I was a naive young fool.'

'What sort of couple was it?'

'I can't remember. Mixed religion, I think. He was Hindu and she was Moslem.'

'Is that true?'

'What do you mean?'

'Would it have been a problem if Ashu had found someone different?'

'Not a Sikh, you mean?'

'Yes – or poor, or Moslem, or Hindu, or handicapped, or with unfortunate personal hygiene! I mean, how would your family feel if she had branched out from the *good Sikh boy from a good family*?'

Ranjit was struggling for words, his large Adam's apple bobbing about like a boat on a stormy sea. 'Tara Baba would not like it,' he muttered finally.

'Would not like it but would grit his teeth and dance at the wedding because he loved his granddaughter?'

'Would not like it and would put a stop to it immediately!'

Seven

Singh kicked his heels in the hotel lobby for a good half an hour before he realised that Tanvir Singh, unlike his younger brother, had no intention of pandering to the convenience of his grandfather's recently appointed private investigator. However, he was pleasantly surprised to discover, on exiting the hotel in search of some form of transport, that Tara Singh had sent a car around to wait for him.

'*Wearewudyouliketobegoingsar?*'

Singh shook his head, nonplussed. 'I'm afraid I only speak a bit of Punjabi and no Hindi,' he explained, momentarily distracted as a horse and ornate silver carriage clip-clopped past. He assumed it was a tourist gimmick. They'd have been better off preserving the Ambassadors.

'For tourists,' explained the driver, following his gaze and confirming his suspicion. He reverted to his original question. 'Yes – *but wearewudyouliketobegoingsar?*'

The penny dropped with a loud clank. The chauffeur was

actually speaking English. It was a combination of the enthusiastically rolled 'r's and the curious choice of tenses that had thrown Singh off the scent. Great. He was supposed to investigate a death and he didn't even understand the natives when they spoke English.

'What's your name?' he asked.

'Kuldeep, *saar*.'

'Take me to the office where Ashu used to work,' he said.

'*Verrywellsar* – the chemical works.'

The drive was innocuous by Indian standards. They spent an hour and a half in traffic. Singh insisted on winding down the glass and handing a fistful of rupees to a man in a loin-cloth who appeared to be holding a seething mass of intestines in his arms while still having a few fingers free to clasp his collection cup.

'If you give him money, the rest will be cutting stomachs too,' warned the driver.

'What?'

'Always they are trying to have worst injuries to get money from foreigners. Sometimes, they are putting acid in eyes or cutting hand or leg ... or both legs and then wheel around in cart.'

Singh immediately spotted just such a contraption. Was it really possible that some of these were self-inflicted injuries? In such a culture was it that surprising that Ashu had killed herself in so dramatic a fashion? Mind you, these were the poor and destitute seeking the largesse of tourists, not the relations of Tara Singh.

He continued to stare out of the window, fascinated by the chaos and confusion of Mumbai. They passed pavement dwellings where whole families cooked over a portable gas stove, a sturdy mosque that was situated right square in the middle of the road causing the asphalt road to fork around it – Singh couldn't imagine the Singapore government showing such restraint in wielding its powers of compulsory land acquisition – and dozens of bright red buses packed to the brim with commuters. He'd soon completely lost his bearings.

'Where are we?' he asked, nonplussed by the length of time spent on crowded roads without lane markings that seemed to allow for seven vehicles abreast.

'North of Santa Cruz,' explained Kuldeep.

Singh looked out over the usual expanse of rust-coloured shanties draped at irregular intervals in the ubiquitous bright blue tarpaulins. It didn't look like California.

The chemical works' offices and factory were housed in a reasonably modern building with air-conditioning units attached to the exterior at regular intervals. A high wall around the perimeter was the main structural support of an ocean of flapping canvas and rusty corrugated iron which formed the residential area of yet another uncountable mass of humanity. It really wasn't difficult to believe that Mumbai was the most heavily populated city in the world.

A security guard stood by the steel gate and insisted on examining Singh's passport at length, staring at him and then at the photo with an air of great suspicion. How one could distinguish between one turbaned, bearded Sikh and another was a mystery to the inspector but the guard seemed to be making a serious effort.

At last, they were waved through.

'Lot of security,' remarked Singh for lack of anything better to say.

'This is very important factory.'

Singh got out of the car, stretched carefully – his breakfast was resting rather heavily in his stomach – walked into the cool interior with relief, and asked to speak to the boss.

The boss turned out to be an American gentleman named John Tyler Jr. whose office was modern, furnished in light pine and smelt of disinfectant.

'So you're the PI that Tara hired. How would I know why that girl killed herself? I just got to this hellhole.'

'By which you mean Mumbai?'

'Of course, whaddya think I meant? New York?'

'When did you get here?'

'Three months ago – and only nine more until my retirement to sunny Florida.' He sounded as if he was counting the seconds, let alone the minutes and days.

'Where were you before this?' Singh asked, seeking to prolong the conversation but not entirely sure what to ask this ornery character.

'Guangzhou.' The American stroked a long grey moustache. 'They said this is the other economic powerhouse of Asia.' He snorted his derision. 'In China things work.'

'But this is the world's largest democracy,' protested Singh. 'You're not going to get the same kind of order as China.' The fat man closed his eyes for a moment – he couldn't believe he was getting defensive about India and sounding like his wife to boot.

'I don't think much of the democracy they got over here.' Singh doubted that John Tyler Junior – how lacking in imagination had John Tyler Senior been that he couldn't even come up with a fresh name for his own son? – would be so keen to sacrifice his vote for cleaner streets in Florida.

'So you're not happy?' asked Singh, somewhat unnecessarily.

'It's impossible to run a business in this town. Corruption, nepotism, cronyism – you name it, it's here.'

'So was Ashu Kaur an example of nepotism?'

'Because she was Tara Singh's granddaughter? Actually, she was a good worker, smart, knew her stuff. And she didn't mind getting her hands dirty.'

'What does that mean?'

'You're not from India, are you?'

'Singapore.'

The American calmed down immediately. 'Now there's a place I like to do business. Clean, organised, honest, efficient and *no* slums on the doorstep.'

'Well, I guess those people have nowhere to go,' suggested Singh, his turban pointing in the direction of the adjacent slums, the guilt that he'd not been able to shake since getting to India overwhelming him once more. He tried his latest theory. 'It shows the tolerance within Indian society. There's no restriction on people moving into the cities to seek a better life even if it means greater discomfort all around.'

'In China, when the work dries up in the cities, they ship the migrants back to the villages,' was the American's response. He continued, 'Look, it's a safety issue, isn't it? This factory should be built away from population centres. Instead, we've got most of Mumbai trying to move into the compound.'

'Is it dangerous here?'

Tyler grinned, exposing orthodontically perfect teeth. 'No, not really. But we manufacture a lot of chemical substances.'

'What was Ashu's role?'

'She worked in our research lab.'

'So what did you mean – about getting her hands dirty?'

'I'll give you an example. I went into the lab once. Someone had spilt coffee. No one bothered to wipe it up because that wasn't their job – they were waiting for the cleaner. There were track marks up and down the floor. The place looked like a pigsty.'

'Ashu?'

'She was late that day. First thing she did was get a bucket and a mop and clean up the mess ...'

'And that's unusual?'

'Unheard of.'

Tyler added unexpectedly, 'It's a real pity that she's gone and done this. She was a good kid.'

It was the first human emotion other than anger and disgust the man had shown and Singh warmed to him slightly.

'Any inkling that this was going to happen?'

'You're asking me if I knew Tara Singh's granddaughter was going to kill herself?'

Singh grimaced. It was a fair retort.

'What was her relationship with her co-workers?'

'How would I know?'

'She seemed happy?'

'Yes, actually she did. Whenever I saw her about the place she seemed to be in pretty good spirits.'

Singh rubbed his eyes tiredly. He'd been in the car for almost two hours to get here and there didn't seem to be any treasure trove of information to be found. Ashu Kaur had been a cheerful and willing employee – great. Hardly a boost to theories of murder or suicide. Was there a way to get accidentally doused in kerosene?

'Are there personnel files?' he asked at last.

'Yes, but we have hundreds of employees.'

'Just Ashu's and immediate co-workers will do to begin with.'

'And mine?' asked Tyler snidely.

'And yours, yes,' and was rewarded by the American appearing suddenly discomfited.

The boss shouted for his secretary who turned out to be a plump woman robed in a neat cotton sari who was introduced as Mrs. Bannerjee and agreed, after shooting a look of pure curiosity at the inspector, to access the online files for him.

'Does this death change anything?' Jaswant the Canadian was glum, his elbows on the table and his chin cupped in one hand. He stared at the window panes with the peacock design but it was clear he was not admiring the art.

'Why should it?' asked Tanvir roughly.

'I don't know – she was your sister! Are you all right?'

'She was my sister. What do you expect me to say?'

'I heard you identified the body.' Jaswant sounded uncomfortable at the proximity of death which was ironic in the circumstances.

'Yes, I did.'

'Look, man – we can wait for another opportunity.'

The other man turned on him like a feral beast. 'Don't be ridiculous!'

'We can't afford any mistakes.'

Did Jaswant think that he was so weak? 'Look, Ashu brought dishonour on the family and that I cannot forgive. She died for me when she did that – not when I identified the body.'

'What in the guru's name are you going on about, man?'

'It doesn't concern you.'

'That's where you're wrong. Anything that could jeopardise this deal is of enormous importance to me.'

'All you need to know is that the death of my sister will not sway me from our purpose.'

Tanvir leaned forward and sipped his Diet Coke through a straw, debating whether to say anything else to his friend. Enough of the truth to satisfy him but not sufficient to worry him or scare him off. It was a fine line indeed.

'Are the police involved?' demanded Jaswant.

'No, no. Why should they be? She killed herself – end of story.'

'That's what they believe?'

Tanvir nodded firmly, the turban making his gesture emphatic. 'Why – have you heard anything different?'

'I'm new in town – do you think I have any idea what's going on? It just seems like they've made up their minds pretty quickly.'

'This is India, not Canada,' said Tanvir. 'The police are not going to look for trouble.'

'And your grandfather is satisfied with this explanation?'

'Yes,' he answered, not meeting the other man's eyes. It was true that Tara Baba had not asked the police to look any further into the matter, happy to agree with their suicide theory. 'I don't want them stomping all over my grand-daughter's memory with their big boots,' he'd said. But he'd asked that pest of a policeman from Singapore to investigate the death and that had been an unanticipated turn of events.

Tanvir felt his face flush with anger when he remembered his grandfather's order that he cooperate with the policeman. Well, he'd stood the fat cop up instead. Unlike his younger brother who responded to every command as if it was a dog whistle. One of these days he would get up the courage to ask his mother whether she'd played his father false in the pro-duction of Ranjit. It was hard to find any other explanation for a creature who bore so faint an imprint from the family genetic stamp.

'What's the matter?' asked Jaswant, looking at the other man with concern.

'Nothing,' said Tanvir and he meant it. The fat copper's attempts to investigate would be derisory at best. He was just looking for a reason to extend his stay at the Taj. Tanvir would bet that policemen's salaries in Singapore didn't allow for such luxuries. Tara Baba, a man famous for his keen eye for character, was growing old and losing his judgment. And he, Tanvir Singh, had nothing to worry about from this half-baked investigation. The important thing was that the body had been found. There would be no city-wide manhunt for a missing girl. The urgency of any investigation into the death predicated on the whim of his grandfather would be minimal. The police were not interested – the self-serving bastards recognised a hot potato when they saw one. Tara

Baba would soon come around to the view that Ashu had killed herself.

He rapped the table with his knuckles. 'We have nothing to be concerned about and no reason to amend our plans.'

Singh sat in front of a screen glumly, occasionally scrolling down with one grubby finger on a key. He hated computers. He especially hated information presented to him in such an impersonal way. There was no human touch here. Whatever opinions might have been found scribbled in the margins of a hard copy were nowhere to be found online. There were only facts; facts about age, date of birth, family, education and attendance at work but not a single hint as to the character of the individuals who worked in the lab at Bharat Chemicals. Even the digital photos were low resolution and failed to capture any essence of personality. He looked at the one of Ashu Kaur and compared it in his mind's eye with the picture on the mantelpiece in her apartment. In this photo, there wasn't that hint of stubbornness in the set of the chin or the rebellious sparkle in the eye. Perhaps he'd imagined it all, he decided glumly, and Ashu Kaur was just a melodramatic youngster who'd killed herself to avoid an undesirable marriage. ACP Patel's Juliet although Romeo hadn't put in an appearance yet.

'Such a terrible thing about young Ashu,' said Mrs. Bannerjee, who had been watching Singh's growing unhappiness with an empathetic expression and now dabbed her eyes with a fistful of tissue paper to indicate a solidarity of emotion.

He looked up morosely. 'Yes, a terrible thing.'

'Is it true that she used kerosene?'

He nodded wearily, wishing that he was not in conversation with this bright-eyed voyeur but reluctant to turn back to the PC.

'I cannot imagine why she might be doing such a thing,' she continued. 'Not even for one *single* moment.'

The emphasis roused the inspector from his stupor.

He sat up straight and looked at Mrs. Bannerjee, noting the neat black hair parted in the middle and pulled back into a round shiny bun threaded through with small white fragrant flowers.

'Yes,' he said, feeling his way. 'Especially when she was just about to be married.'

The red lips of Mrs. Bannerjee pursed shut. He had been too direct.

'And she enjoyed her job, I understand?'

'Very much,' exclaimed Mrs. Bannerjee. 'Always the first one in and last one out. So busy all the time!'

'I see,' said Singh, who didn't see at all but was now trying to keep the conversation with this mysterious woman going.

'So she worked long hours?'

'Yes, but also did slum work.'

'What does that mean?'

'Helped out next door – did some first aid and medical things like that.' Her nose wrinkled in disapproval. 'Not good for a young girl, I said to her, but Ashu was quite the stubborn one sometimes.'

'I guess she had a good heart.'

'Very good heart,' agreed Mrs. Bannerjee. 'And so worried about those people, you know?'

Singh didn't know – he was still being led by the hand in the dark as far as this woman's hints and allegations were concerned.

'Did she seem upset recently?'

'Well, very angry with the boss earlier this week,' said Mrs. Bannerjee.

'The boss? You mean Tyler?'

'Who else would I be meaning excepting John Tyler Junior?'

'How do you know she was angry?'

'Lot of shouting in his office. I didn't listen, of course.'

'Didn't you?'

'Actually, couldn't hear very much because door is closed.'

'But you think it had something to do with the slum next door?'

She nodded so vigorously that a few petals fell off the flowers in her hair. 'Just before door is closing, I heard her say something about their health.'

'Maybe she thought the factory was too close to it,' he suggested, remembering what Tyler had said.

'Could be. Anyway, Ashu is coming out of the room with face like sky during monsoons. And boss is shouting – *you just remember to keep your mouth shut!*'

'Now that is very interesting,' agreed Singh, wondering what could have set the two at loggerheads and why Tyler had not seen fit to mention it. 'Which day was that exactly?'

Mrs. Bannerjee made a show of consulting her desktop calendar and muttering to herself in an undertone.

At last she said, 'Three days ago.'

'But that . . .' Singh trailed off. He'd been about to point out that the date coincided with the date of Ashu's disappearance but he didn't want to add inches to Mrs. Bannerjee's gossip column.

'Wasn't she supposed to be off work already?'

There was a chubby shrug and he feared that the sari blouse would give way at the seams. 'She didn't stay long.'

'Do you know if she told anyone else what was bothering her?'

'No idea, Sardarji. But if she did it would be to her *verrry* good friend here.'

'Her *verrry* good friend?' asked Singh and then gave himself a mental slap for parroting her accent. It was certainly catching. 'Who was that then?'

'Sameer Khan, of course,' she said with an air of astonishment at his apparent ignorance. And it was true that he was nowhere in the investigative stakes compared to this gift-wrapped creature with her ear to every door and her eye at every keyhole. He was too nice in his methods, decided Singh. He needed to steal a page from this woman's manual on poking her nose into other persons' affairs.

'This Sameer Khan works here?'

'Also stayed very late sometimes. Lot of work in the lab, I am telling you.'

Singh's stubby fingers became almost efficient as he pulled up the records of this Sameer Khan. A black and white photo of a young man stared at him truculently from the screen.

'Is this young man at work today?'

'Yes, very upset you understand about the loss of a *colleague* but still here.'

*

119

In a few moments, the real life version of the photo was also staring at him truculently although this edition had a black eye, a deep cut to his chin and a rainbow of bruises. A fighter, apparently.

'Sameer Khan?'

'What's it to you?'

'What happened to your face?'

'Slipped in the shower.'

Singh shrugged off the terse responses and said, 'We need to chat.'

'Why? What do you want?'

'To talk about Ashu Kaur.'

'I have nothing to say,' he insisted although the bruising around his eye darkened as his pallor increased.

'You knew Ashu?' he asked.

A quick shrug. 'She worked here.'

'Tara Singh asked me to look into the matter of her death. I just need to ask you a few questions.'

If he'd hoped that Tara Singh's name would operate its usual magic, he was disappointed.

'That old fool,' snapped Sameer.

There was a sudden collective intake of breath from the other young men in white coats around the lab but the irate young man did not notice or, more likely, did not care.

'Don't you see that it's too late?' continued Sameer.

It was disappointing to be in a profession where he was always too late, realised Singh. In at the death, not before.

'Too late to save her – not too late to find out what happened.'

Sameer hesitated and Singh pressed home his advantage. 'Don't you want to know? I do!'

'Follow me,' said the other man. Singh hurried after, feeling mildly resentful of the long-limbed stride and youth of the man in front. Sameer Khan looked like a doctor from one of those hospital dramas, the one whom all the nurses were in love with and who always saved the critically ill patient at the eleventh hour. Singh was more like that television doctor fellow with the cane and the surly attitude.

Sameer led the way to a small room that smelt heavily of smoke. Someone, thought Singh wistfully, had been using it as a private place for a cigarette.

'So, what do you want to know?'

'You knew Ashu well?'

'Quite well,' he said non-committally.

'I heard that you and she liked to work late together . . .'

'That spying old woman, Mrs. Bannerjee, I suppose?'

Singh wasn't going to rat out his source. He lowered himself into a chair and felt it give slightly under his weight. He paused for a moment to ensure its structural integrity and then pointed to the chair opposite invitingly. 'Why don't you sit down and tell me everything you know,' he suggested in a mild tone, like a kindly governess.

'How can I trust you? You work for Tara Singh!'

'Tara Singh asked me to look into Ashu's death. However, I'm not in his pay' – unless you counted the luxury hotel but Singh decided not to mention that – 'and I am not here to protect anyone. Just to find the truth.'

'Where're you from?'

'I'm a policeman from Singapore and a distant relative by marriage to Ashu's family,' replied Singh.

'I've been there – most boring place in the world, I think,' said Sameer.

Singh grinned. This was a different opinion from that of the American boss.

'What are you doing in India anyway?'

'My wife dragged me here for Ashu's wedding.'

At this piece of information, the young man buried his face in his hands. Singh stood up and wandered over to the window to give the fellow a chance to gather himself. To his immense pleasure, there was an old Ambassador, ivory white and in tiptop condition on the main road. The iconic car wasn't quite extinct in Mumbai yet.

'Tell me about you and Ashu,' he suggested. He suspected he already knew quite a lot about the couple from the blood-shot eyes and aggressive manner of the chemist.

He was met with a defiant gaze. 'I loved her.'

So the innuendo of Mrs. Bannerjee, greeted by Singh with some cynicism, was rooted in the truth. But had it been mutual? Was this the reason for the sudden stark choice made by the girl?

'I believe you,' said Singh. 'How did she feel about you?'

Sameer sat up straighter and looked down his long nose at the inspector. 'I believe our feelings were mutual. I wanted to marry her,' he said.

It might even be true, thought Singh. 'And when she was forced to marry the MBA, she killed herself rather than go through with it?'

A simple answer, after all, and the one that he'd suspected

from the moment he'd found out about her disappearance. It was not difficult to see why a young girl might kill herself over the romantic young hero sitting across from him.

'I can't believe that,' said Sameer.

'The family has no doubt it was suicide.' This was a slight exaggeration as Tara Singh had certainly been reluctant to believe such a thing.

'They would say that, wouldn't they?'

Singh had to admire the creature. He was a wonderful Brontë-style hero with his swept-back dark hair, restless eyes and chiselled bones. Not Romeo, Heathcliff.

'She said that she couldn't marry me, could never marry me ... she seemed resigned to going through with the wedding. There was no reason for her to do this thing.'

'Whaddaya mean?' asked Singh, unconsciously mimicking the tone of the American boss. 'Why couldn't she marry you?' He wondered whether the fellow was already married.

'I'm a Moslem,' he answered.

'So?' asked Singh.

Parallel lines appeared on Sameer's forehead. 'She said it would break her mother's – and her grandfather's – heart if she married someone of another religion, *especially* a Moslem.' He smiled suddenly. 'We're not that popular in the marriage market for non-Moslems, I'm afraid.'

'Was she so loyal to her family?'

'She loved her mother. And she believed that she owed Tara Singh because he rescued the family when the father died.' He looked up. 'You heard about that?'

'Yes, he was killed in the riots after Indira Gandhi was shot.'

'He brought them up, paid for their education, got her this job – but most of all she knew that the old fool really cared about her.'

'And he would have been upset if she'd agreed to marry you?'

'Gimme a break,' barked Sameer, suddenly more Hollywood than Bollywood. 'I don't believe that Indians in Singapore have become so liberal that you're surprised!'

Inspector Singh spared a reluctant thought for his wife and all the numerous prejudices based on race, class, creed and religion that she carefully stored away to be trotted out at convenient moments. He nodded at the young man. 'I see what you mean.'

'Her family are devout Sikhs. Ashu told me that her oldest brother was still upset because some of their gurus were killed by Moslem sultans.'

'But that was hundreds of years ago,' protested Singh, vaguely aware that the last Sikh guru, Guru Gobind Singh, had been killed by Wazir Khan.

'These fanatics are all the same,' said Sameer. 'Entitlement complexes and imaginary grievances. You can see why they weren't ready to welcome a Moslem into the family, anyway!' He touched his bruised cheek with a finger tip and winced. 'I'm pretty sure one of them was behind the attack on me.'

'Even so, if Ashu really cared about you . . . ?'

Wasn't his wife always insisting that young people did exactly what they liked nowadays without any thought of tradition and culture?

'Ashu had an enormous sense of responsibility.'

'But to go the extra mile and actually get engaged to someone *else*?'

'The marriage was already arranged, you see, when we met.'

Singh nodded. That made sense.

'Ashu always put other people first,' he said with a small sigh. 'Like you know the slums outside?'

'Yes. Your American boss isn't so keen on them.'

'Well, most people think they shouldn't be this close to a factory – but Ashu used to go in there and help. She had first aid training and she'd treat the kids for cuts and scrapes, rat bites – the usual things.'

Singh tried not to think of a childhood where rat bites were a common ailment.

Sameer was still talking. The inspector sensed it was a huge relief for him to speak of Ashu. Forbidden, secret love could be very taxing on the individual. Or so he'd been led to believe from the various murders he had investigated over the years. He didn't think he'd ever been in that position, not for a very long time anyway and certainly not in relation to Mrs. Singh. He tried to remember an episode in his life when he'd been in the throes of young love. His memory wasn't up to it.

'So you see, even if it wasn't the best thing for her,' explained Sameer earnestly, 'she'd do it if she thought it was the right thing.'

'You're saying that she was prepared to go ahead with this marriage to the MBA even though she wasn't happy about it?'

'Yes.' His head was bowed as he admitted that Ashu's affection for him was not sufficient to sway her on a matter of principle. 'That's what she said and I believe she meant it.'

'Then why is she dead?' asked Singh. 'What other reason

could there possibly be for a young woman like Ashu to commit suicide?'

'You just don't understand,' he said, 'because you didn't know my Ashu. There is no way she did this thing.'

'What are the alternatives?'

'She was murdered!'

'Don't be ridiculous,' said the policeman although he was feeling uncomfortable. Tara Singh's doubts, easy to dismiss as the grief of an old man, were now seconded by the other person who knew the girl well.

Sameer leaned forward and steepled long fingers. 'Well,' he said, 'what if I tell you I know who did it?'

Eight

'It's my fault, you see,' said Sameer.

'What do you mean?' asked Singh. Had this fellow killed the girl in a fit of jealous rage? Perhaps there had been a suicide pact between them. Would he think better of Sameer or worse that he'd decided not to go through with it? He eyed the battle wounds on the young man. They looked fresh. About two or three days old, by his estimate. Were these injuries sustained while murdering Ashu Kaur? How did one douse a healthy woman in kerosene and set her alight anyway? He wondered if the autopsy would show that she'd been drugged or murdered before the fire.

'I persuaded her to meet me. I thought I might be able to change her mind about marrying that guy.'

'A few days before the wedding?'

'I know – I didn't really have much hope. I guess I just wanted to see her again.'

'And . . . ?'

'We met at Marine Drive.'

The fat man squinted hard, trying to get the geography of Mumbai laid out in his head. He was sure that he'd been driven down that long curving road with crumbling apartments on one side and the choppy sea on the other, both looking somewhat grey and tired as if sick of the sight of each other after so many long years. Despite this he remembered the taxi driver saying, 'Only rich people living here, Sardarji.' He'd wondered at the time why the 'rich people' seemed so averse to a lick of paint.

'It was the first time I'd seen her … since she stopped coming to work.'

'Did you change her mind?'

'No.' He grinned suddenly as if a happier memory of Ashu had suddenly taken centre stage. 'She was very stubborn. Usually, I couldn't even persuade her which restaurant to go to for lunch.' His mood darkened. 'And I didn't like her going into the slums, but she insisted.'

'Why didn't you want her to go there?'

'For her health,' he explained. 'She didn't have the immunities that those people develop over time.'

The inspector wondered whether 'those people' really had immunity or just died at a higher rate than the wealthier denizens of the city. He suspected the latter.

'I went there today to explain that she was not coming back,' Sameer continued sombrely. 'They were devastated. They relied on her.'

'Did her family know about her moonlighting as a health care professional?'

'Yes, but I don't think they approved.'

'Go on, so what do you think happened to her?'

'She wasn't supposed to leave the house for a few days before the wedding ceremony. Some dumb tradition. But she snuck out to see me.'

Singh assumed that the tradition was to prevent young women getting second thoughts about their nuptials by fraternising with old boyfriends. Not so dumb, really.

'We spent some time together – just talking. It was probably for the last time, you see.'

'Did you sense that she was having second thoughts?'

'No, if anything she was more determined to go ahead.' He grimaced. 'In fact, she was more concerned about some research she was doing in the slums. She'd gone to see Tyler that morning but hadn't had much luck with him.'

Singh's ears pricked up. Was this the root of the altercation that Mrs. Bannerjee had alluded to between the American and the owner's granddaughter?

'What was it about, this research of hers?'

'She seemed to think that there was a high incidence of illness in the children. Higher than normal, I mean. Adults as well.'

It seemed that, unlike so many others, Ashu had not learnt to walk past the poverty and suffering in the city without a second glance. His wife had explained that it was not that the townsfolk had become callous. They were mostly convinced that the suffering of the poor was karma, the consequence of misconduct in a previous life. Such punishment, if borne stoically, would lead to a much improved situation in the next life. And quite likely, reverse the positions between the haves and the have-nots. Mrs. Singh had looked at her husband

129

meaningfully and added this last with a warning note in her voice.

Singh had a sudden vision of the twinkling earring in the undamaged lobe of the dead girl. He shut his eyes against the memory. Was that karma too? He would have to ask his wife.

'As she was about to leave, to sneak back home – she was really nervous that someone might notice her absence – we heard a car pull up. A man shouted her name. He was very angry.'

'Who was it?'

'I don't know – a Sikh man in a turban. There might have been someone else in the car – I couldn't see.'

'What sort of car?'

This drew a blank expression. 'I don't know. Something ordinary – light coloured. I wasn't really looking.'

'What did Ashu do?'

'She looked upset – but she told me to stay out of it, she would deal with it.'

'Was she upset – or afraid?'

Sameer paused for thought, replaying the scene in his mind's eye, looking for nuances he'd missed before. At last, he said, 'More upset than afraid, I think.'

Singh nodded for him to continue.

'She went to the car and climbed in. They drove off at top speed, like the driver was in a rage.'

'And you let her go?'

Sameer flushed at the accusing tone. 'I guessed it was someone from her family, you see. Maybe one of her brothers. I was secretly relieved that our relationship was out in the open. I thought they might provoke her to lose her temper – call off the wedding, something like that.'

'I see.' And he did see – Sameer had hoped that being found out would cause a rift in the family, that Ashu would choose him after all.

'For a short while, I had some hope. I was actually happy. And then the news came that she was dead.'

'What do you think happened?'

'Whoever it was who picked her up – I think he – or they – killed her.'

'And who do you think that was?'

'The impression I got was someone quite young, wearing a turban – I saw the silhouette in the car. Someone she knew.'

'The brothers or the husband-to-be, I suppose,' suggested Singh, almost to himself, and was rewarded with an emphatic nod for his *sotto voce* musings.

'Yes.'

'But why?'

'You need to ask that?'

'Errr – yes.' Did this fellow not understand the concept of a motive?

'When they saw her with me – discovered from her I was an outsider, a Moslem . . . '

'What are you driving at?'

'They would have killed her as a matter of honour.'

'A matter of honour?' Singh's voice was laced with doubt.

'You don't believe me?'

'It seems a fairly extreme response, surely. *Murdered* for having an inappropriate boyfriend?'

'You think they're not capable of violence? Who do you

131

think did this to me?' He gestured aggressively at his face and then winced as the sharp movement hurt him.

'Quite a bad beating,' noted Singh.

'Three against one,' was the brusque explanation.

'And it was Ashu's family?'

'Hired thugs – but the grandfather or the brothers must have hired them.'

'And you have proof?'

'No – I just know it.'

Singh leaned back in his plastic chair and sighed. If the identity of murderers and other unsavoury characters was determined solely by the opinion of others, regardless of evidence, there would be very few unsolved cases in the police files. In fact, if strong opinions were all that were required to determine guilt or innocence, his wife would make the perfect police officer.

'So your certainty that Ashu was murdered by her family despite the absence of any evidence is based on your certainty that they were behind the assault on you for which you don't have any evidence either?'

Sameer was undaunted by the sarcasm. 'It's *your* job to find evidence, Singh. I've just made it easy for you by identifying the murderers.'

'Where will you be going now, *saar*?' asked Kuldeep the driver.

The inspector held up a hand, deep in thought. They were at the factory gates. Singh walked over and gestured for one of the men to let him out. He stood outside, noting the cracked pavements, clogged drains and exposed wiring absent-mindedly. The public sphere in India was not a pretty sight and in marked contrast to the pristine conditions within the compound of the chemical factory.

Singh was thirsty; Sameer's hospitality hadn't extended to offering him a drink, merely baleful glances. He looked around. There was a man on the sidewalk squeezing juice out of long strips of sugar cane with a hand-operated press. Despite the queue of workers waiting for the thirst-quenching drink, Singh suspected it might be the death of him. The stench from the slum was overpowering from where he stood, causing his eyes to water. It was the odour of uncollected garbage. Singh had a suspicion that the municipality dump trucks didn't come this way very often. He could see that there were a couple of planks over a big drain leading into the warren of huts. Children skipped over the planks and a few were in the drain itself, legs straddling the sides, fishing as far as he could make out. He made up his mind and stepped gingerly onto the makeshift bridge. It gave slightly under his weight and he looked nervously into the murky water. He was pretty sure he wouldn't survive an immersion.

'Sardarji,' shouted a young wit, 'not many people having a belly like yours are crossing. Soon you will join us down here!'

It was a fair point, conceded Singh. No one on the other side of the drains looked as if they had enough to eat. The women were wiry with protruding blade-like cheekbones and the men seemed composed of stringy ropes of muscle with straggly hair along their upper lips. The inspector was being stared at, not rudely, not even with any particular curiosity, but with the blankness of disorientation. He didn't belong there and his presence was a rock in the rivers of life flowing around him. Singh already regretted his decision to have a look around the slum. He had followed a hunch, something that he'd learnt to do over the years because it produced unexpected insights. Ashu had helped the residents here and therefore they might have reason to feel grateful to her – and be honest with him as a result. And he certainly needed some insights into this mysterious woman, Ashu Kaur, who had killed herself days before her wedding or, if the Bollywood leading man was accurate, been murdered.

Singh felt the hair on his arms stand up. There was something in Sameer's theory. He found it difficult to reconcile himself to the idea that Ashu was the sort to commit suicide. She seemed, from all the evidence, to have the strength of character to walk away from a proposed marriage if she was unhappy. Or, indeed, to go through with it and make the best of a bad situation if she felt obliged to fall in with her grandfather's wishes out of duty and affection.

Sameer's story of the last-minute assignation would explain why she'd left the house with a few rupees and no extra clothes. She'd intended a brief visit to the office – he needed to ask Tyler about their quarrel – and then a final meeting with the boyfriend. If a killer had intervened, it would explain why she never made it home. But an honour killing? Did that really happen any more?

Or maybe Sameer had killed Ashu rather than see her in the arms of another man. Singh's eyes shut like heavy theatre curtains during an interval. Surely that was an unrealistically overdramatic explanation? Mind you, Sameer Khan was a wildly poetic figure. Just the sort to kill his girl in a fit of rage. The fat man knew from experience that a thwarted lover was one of nature's killers. And the man had been carrying the marks of a fight. Singh didn't see Sameer as a cold-blooded murderer. But if the couple had a quarrel which became violent, he might have accidentally killed her and then tried to cover up the crime by setting the body on fire. It was as good a way as any to obscure bruising and a fat lip.

Singh realised that while he'd been rooted to the spot, trying to think his way around the problem, he had gathered a small coterie of children. They stared at him as if he was the main exhibit at a zoo. Although they were of all ages, dressed in ill-fitting hand-me-downs and grubby sandals, there was a mesmerising quality to the various pairs of deep brown eyes that held his attention.

'Are you growing roots, old man?' asked a child. He recognised him as the smartmouth from the drain. He looked about nine but was probably closer to eleven. An urchin with a pointy chin, dark skin, gleaming teeth and a bright orange shirt that he wore with pride.

'Do you know your way around here, boy?'

'Yes, of course, Sardarji.' The tone was scornful. Despite the difference in their situations, Singh had a sudden flashback to when he was a child. He too had been master of his territory, knowing the back alleys, the short cuts and the gardens without dogs. This kid with the skinny limbs was a kindred spirit.

'I'm looking for a woman who used to work here.'

'Everyone works here, Sardarji.'

Singh glanced around and saw that this was true. Women were washing clothes in buckets and hanging them out to dry on thin wires running at roof level. Rows of trousers were hanging inside out with their white pockets flapping. A couple of children were sorting through a huge pile of garbage, separating the recyclable materials from the rest with their bare hands.

'This woman helped with the medical needs of the community,' explained Singh and was rewarded with a blank stare which he felt he thoroughly deserved. The boy's English was passable, surprisingly good really, but Singh had sounded like a brochure for an NGO.

'I mean she was sort of like a doctor.'

'Oh! You mean Doctor Amma?'

The boy's eyes which had brightened perceptibly at the mention of Ashu now clouded over.

'She is not coming here any more,' he continued and rubbed his eyes with his knuckles like a small child.

'What happened?' asked Singh, wondering what they knew.

'She had an accident. And now she is dead.'

'I heard about that.'

'Then why you are asking questions if you knew she is dead?'

Smart kid, thought the inspector ruefully. He took a step forward – gingerly. He had no desire to slip off the uneven slabs of rock and stone into the patches of mud fringed with bright green mould.

'I'm trying to find out what happened to her.'

'Are you a policeman?' The suspicion of the downtrodden was in his question.

'No, no,' said Singh quickly, reflecting that this was mostly true. He wasn't a policeman in India.

'Then why are you asking all the questions?'

'I'm trying to help the family. Please believe me. I just

want to find out what happened to Ashu – your Doctor Amma.'

He was rewarded with a sideways thoughtful glance and was impressed by the length of the boy's eyelashes. He would have women swooning one day. The attitude and the eyelashes were destined for greater things than slum dwelling and fishing in drains.

'What's your name?'

'Mahesh.'

'Well, Mahesh. Do you know anyone here who could help me?'

'What do you want?'

'Anyone who knew her – I just want to talk.'

Mahesh stepped forward and the inspector saw that he was casually careful about where he put his slippered feet. He held up an arm so that his elbow was facing Singh.

'She did this for me,' he said proudly.

Singh saw that there was a ragged scar where a wound had been carefully stitched up. It looked like a fat centipede, running from elbow to wrist.

'What happened?'

'I fell,' he said, looking down and failing to meet the inspector's eyes for the first time. The policeman sighed. Anyone who lied about the source of an injury, he knew from experience, had been injured by a loved one, by someone in a position of authority or in pursuit of an illegal activity. He looked at the skinny bright-eyed boy. Mahesh didn't look cowed which suggested that the third option was most likely.

'Ashu doctor stitched it up for me,' Mahesh added.

Singh had a sudden sense of how important Ashu's work at the slum had been. In these surroundings, if the cut hadn't been treated, Mahesh would have developed an infection which would have cost him the arm, if not his life.

'Where did she work?' he asked.

'Close by,' the boy said. 'Come, I will take you there.'

Singh followed in his wake and then did a little hop as a flurry of large rats, about the size of small cats, ran underfoot, whiskers quivering and long hairless tails trailing in the muck.

'Good to be careful,' said Mahesh. 'If rat is biting you, you will be very sick.'

A shudder ran through the stout frame of the policeman. He tried to remember if he'd ever seen a rat in Singapore. A few scrawny squirrels that looked a lot like rats and the occasional garden shrew – that was the sum of rodent life in his recent past. Inspector Singh, who prided himself on his familiarity with the dark fringes of society, realised that he'd been fooling himself. His Singaporean version was the Disney equivalent of the seedy side of life.

Mahesh led the way to a hut, about six feet square with a neatly swept floor, a stool and a small shelf on which sat a large white box marked with a red cross, an empty plastic water jug and a candle burnt halfway down.

'Needle and thread in there,' said the boy, pointing at the first-aid kit with the pride of someone identifying a treasure chest.

'So this was her clinic?'

There was a nod from Mahesh who was still gazing at the box in awe. He added as an afterthought, 'The man with the white coat will help us now.'

Singh's estimation of Sameer, previously compromised by the man's good looks and theatrical disposition, went up a notch.

After a moment's hesitation, Singh opened the first-aid kit. It was the only receptacle in the room. To his surprise, and interest, there was a thick file of papers sitting neatly on the top.

'What's this?' asked Singh.

'Doctor Amma, always writing and writing. About the sickness here.' Mahesh spoke with the indifference of the illiterate. He perked up. 'Always I was helping her – she couldn't manage her work without me, I think.'

Singh smiled at this claim to indispensability. The boy sounded like he meant it. Maybe it was even true. The inspector perched his large posterior carefully on the small stool, crossed his fingers figuratively, shifted his head so that the shadow from his turban did not fall over the file and began to read. It was a careful compilation of symptoms for an ailment that was rife within the slum, affecting children and adults both. As he followed the detail, it was apparent that the prevalence of the outbreak was increasing by the day. The final entry was just a few days before Ashu's disappearance, presumably the day she'd stopped working at the factory to prepare for her wedding.

On that last page, she'd written, 'Factory??' in large, angry red letters.

Mrs. Singh sat next to the mother of the deceased with her *dupatta* draped over her head as a mark of respect and mourning. The living room was stuffy although an old-fashioned, brown-panelled air-conditioning unit was huffing and puffing on the wall. There were too many people crammed within. The underlying smell of dried perspiration reminded her of her husband. She wondered where he was – traipsing around Mumbai stepping on people's toes most likely. She'd be lucky if she and her family were on speaking terms by the time he was done.

In the centre of the living-room carpet was a small table with a picture of Ashu in a frame. It was the photo that Singh had admired on the mantelpiece. A garland of flowers had been draped on the picture and a stick of incense created an olfactory exclusion zone around it. There were a few desultory chants of '*waheguru*' – the wonderful Lord – but none of the mourners seemed to have the heart for the traditional chants. It was hard to see the death of such a young thing as part of the inevitable cycle of life as dictated by a benevolent deity.

Mrs. Singh felt uncomfortable without the body. And she knew the rest of the mourners did too. They were there to bid farewell to Ashu but she was still lying in a hospital mortuary. The general feeling in the room, shared by Mrs. Singh, was that Ashu had taken her own life. Self-immolation was a peculiarly anticipatory gesture for someone who would eventually be cremated and her ashes scattered in a river. Mrs. Singh wondered whether the family would take the ashes to the Punjab or whether a river closer at hand would suffice. She knew that many Sikhs preferred to make the journey back to their homeland. Tara Singh seemed the type who would be a stickler for the more traditional practices. She tried to imagine for a moment what Singh would do when she died.

Probably chuck her ashes into the nearest monsoon drain and head to a coffee shop for a cold beer.

Tanvir Singh walked in, stopped impatiently at the door to receive the condolences of a few people and then came up to his mother.

'Ranjit has seen him. Have you?' whispered Jesvinder in an agitated tone.

'That fat man who pretends to be an investigator?'

Mrs. Singh winced. There were no prizes for guessing to whom Tanvir was referring. Also, she couldn't help but feel annoyed. Who was this young whippersnapper to criticise her husband? That was her task – and Superintendent Chen's.

'No, I haven't seen him yet,' continued Tanvir, 'and I don't want to.'

'Your grandfather has asked for his help,' cautioned his mother.

There was a sound very like a snort from the brother of the dead girl but any more articulate response was cut off by the entrance of another man. He walked into the living room wearing the full white of mourning and all eyes immediately focused on him. A quiet whisper ran through the room like a mild breeze through leaves. Mrs. Singh noticed that her cousin had gripped Tanvir's hand in a tight grip. With difficulty, Jesvinder Kaur got to her feet and with Tanvir in tow, she stepped forward.

'*Mata*,' said the stranger and hugged the old lady.

'Kirpal. We are so sorry this has happened.' Tanvir sounded genuinely regretful and the other man clasped his hands in response.

Mrs. Singh was staring openly now as was everyone else in

the room. So this was the young man Ashu had been destined to marry. The fine young MBA and pillar of society chosen by her grandfather for his favourite grandchild.

Kirpal was tall and broad-shouldered but not handsome like Tanvir. His beard was neatly trimmed and his full lips were pressed thin. His nose was too long and appeared to erupt from somewhere between his eyebrows. He seemed extremely put out but Mrs. Singh felt that there was some excuse for that. It was an uncomfortable situation – to be at the home of his dead fiancée when the general speculation was that she'd killed herself to avoid marrying him. It would be difficult for Kirpal to pretend to feel inconsolable. He had barely known the girl having met her only a few times and usually with family in tow.

'What do they think happened?' asked Kirpal in a low voice.

Mrs. Singh congratulated herself on her choice of seat. She was probably the only mourner in the room within hearing distance. She leaned forward while trying to look nonchalant. It was a pity she didn't have any shoelaces to tie.

'The police? Suicide,' said Tanvir bluntly.

'But why, Tanvir?'

'No one has any idea.'

Jesvinder was weeping quietly now, overwhelmed by the presence of the man who had been her future son-in-law. 'Whatever people are saying, I am sure that it had nothing to do with you.'

'Of course it had nothing to do with Kirpal,' said Tanvir bitingly. 'No one is suggesting otherwise.'

He was at the receiving end of a rueful glance from the

husband-that-was-to-be. 'That's not quite true. It seems that I'm suspected of cruelty, AIDS, a pre-existing wife, an army of children from prostitutes ... the gossip-mongers are having a field day.'

His remarks were greeted with silence.

Kirpal added bitterly, the first show of genuine emotion, 'It had nothing to do with me, I swear it. I would have been a good husband to her.'

Tanvir was sombre. 'We might never know why she did it.'

Mrs. Singh, still annoyed by his earlier remarks about the inspector, broke in loudly. 'Not to worry, I'm sure my husband will find the answer!'

'Who are you?' demanded Kirpal.

The manners of the next generation left much to be desired, decided Mrs. Singh.

'Tara Singh has asked my husband to investigate the death of Ashu Kaur,' she said, forgetting her earlier irritation that her husband had accepted the responsibility. Her statement immediately attracted the attention of the other mourners. A curly-haired young woman with tear-stained cheeks stared at her as if she had worn a colourful *salwar kameez* to the funeral house.

'He is a very important policeman from Singapore,' explained Jesvinder.

'What is there to investigate?' asked Tanvir. 'My sister, for reasons we will never know, has killed herself. What is the use of this investigation? It is best to let her rest in peace.'

Kirpal nodded his agreement and Mrs. Singh decided that his eyes were set too close together and his chin was weak.

'Surely Tara Baba knows best,' whispered the mother of the

girl. Neither of the men seconded this judgment and the inspector's wife had a distinct sensation that for these men at least, Tara Singh's influence had waned. In a feudal society, she would have expected them to be plotting a palace takeover. She knew that Tanvir worked for his grandfather. The old man probably had no idea that he was harbouring a viper in his bosom. She wondered whether Kirpal also worked for the Tara Singh conglomerate. It wouldn't surprise her. The abiding feature of Indian manhood was their desire to control their kin. Especially the womenfolk. Even so, Ashu's chosen method of escape had been extreme.

'I wouldn't worry about it,' said Tanvir. 'That fat fellow will soon give up his efforts and go back to Singapore where he belongs.'

'Actually, he never gives up,' said Mrs. Singh.

'But if she committed suicide . . .' Kirpal trailed off.

'Surely you want to know why?' demanded the inspector's wife.

Only Jesvinder nodded.

'Was there anyone else?' asked Kirpal, directing his question at Tanvir.

'Another boyfriend, you mean? That's what my husband suspects,' interjected Mrs. Singh, unwilling to be sidelined from the conversation.

Tanvir scowled but did not leap to his sister's defence. Perhaps he knew he was wasting his breath. It was what most people were thinking anyway.

'She could have just called it off,' said Kirpal.

'Would you have agreed?' asked Mrs. Singh.

'I would have had no choice.'

'But what about the dowry?'

'What about it?' asked Kirpal, his gaze fixed on Mrs. Singh, his expression forbidding.

Fools rush in, decided Mrs. Singh and threw down the gauntlet. 'I heard that your family needs the money badly. This marriage was your chance to recoup.'

'I would not have married a girl against her will.'

Mrs. Singh's flared nostrils gave away her doubts at this professed altruism.

'Tara Baba would have been furious if Ashu had a boyfriend,' said Jesvinder in an undertone.

'But surely he would have preferred to know the truth?' asked the inspector's wife.

Nobody responded to the question and Mrs. Singh was suddenly overwhelmed with pity for the dead girl, very much alone despite the family massed around her.

Nine

'That fat fellow', having failed in his effort to see Tyler to ask him about his quarrel with Ashu – he'd left the office for a meeting – was on his way to the headquarters of the Tara Singh empire close to the southern tip of Mumbai. Kuldeep had explained sheepishly that Tara Singh desired a progress report from the inspector.

They passed a fishing village which looked, to Singh's untrained eye, like a slum.

'This is where the terrorists are landing, Sardarji,' said the driver, pointing out of the window as if he was a tour guide.

There was a sandbagged police outpost next to the spot with a few bored khaki-clad coppers within. One of them was asleep with his head thrown back and mouth open. One didn't have to be particularly alert to shut the stable door, guessed Singh.

They reached their destination, a shiny building in a reflective glass sheath, and the inspector clambered out of the car. He carefully stepped around the sleeping figures of an extended family who were the same matted, grey colour as the pavements, and made his way past shiny gates and shiny guards to the elevator and was shown into a large circular office. The furnishings were modern except for an old antique desk that appeared to have been made from a carved, brass-studded palace door, now covered with a sheet of glass. The man himself sat behind it in an ergonomic black leather office chair. He wore a sleeveless dark tunic over a white shirt and looked extremely neat.

Tara Singh beckoned and the policeman hitched up his trousers and sat in the chair opposite him. He was suddenly conscious that his usually crisp white shirt had a sheen of Mumbai dust – he shuddered to imagine the origins of the dust in a country where seven hundred million people didn't have access to toilets.

'Have you discovered anything yet?'

Singh looked at the other man thoughtfully. He'd been summoned for this meeting. But that didn't mean the grand-father was going to dictate the conversation.

'I saw your grandson, Ranjit,' he replied.

'Well? What did he say?'

'That Ashu didn't believe in happy endings.'

'What's that supposed to mean?'

'That maybe she had a boyfriend. And committed suicide to avoid the marriage.'

'How dare you make such insinuations? Have you no respect for the dead?'

Singh folded his arms across his belly. Family members never realised that an investigator with 'respect for the dead' would never successfully resolve a case. He had to expect the worst, assume the worst, predict the worst – and then he might get to the root of a death.

'Did Ranjit *say* that she had a boyfriend?' Tara was looking for his favourite whipping boy.

Singh shook his head and wondered whether to mention Sameer. Not yet, he decided. He wanted to learn more about the family first. Besides, he wasn't ready to throw Sameer to the wolves. It would probably cost the young man his job at the factory if he told Tara Singh about his relationship with Ashu.

'What did Tanvir have to say?' asked Tara. 'He'd be able to give you some facts, not spout nonsense about *happy endings.*'

'Tanvir didn't turn up for his interview,' answered Singh, offering up the older brother as a sacrifice.

Tara's face darkened but he wasn't prepared to acknowledge that he might have been disobeyed by his preferred grandson. 'Something must have come up. Reschedule it.'

'I've just been to Bharat Chemicals,' said Singh. 'Met the boss – Tyler Junior. Tell me about him.'

'Oh? I don't see why you want to know about him.'

'Why don't you leave the investigating to me?'

Tara shrugged and continued. 'Provided by my joint venture partners from the US. But he isn't settling in very well.'

That was an understatement, thought Singh. 'Factory doing badly?'

'Actually, no. We've never been more profitable. A new line of face-whitening cream.'

'Tyler can't be that bad then . . .'

'Tanvir was in charge of business development,' said Tara, making it clear whom he thought was behind recent success.

'Anyway, I'm hoping to get Tyler out,' continued the industrialist. 'Replace him with an Indian. In fact, I was planning to appoint Ashu's fiancé, Kirpal, to the post after the wedding.'

'Had you told him?'

'Kirpal? I'd dropped a few hints – I still needed to discuss the matter further with the Americans.'

'They were reluctant?'

'Yes, Inspector Singh. The Americans only trust their own even when the person in question is an incompetent old fool sitting out his last few months in India.'

'Has there been any trouble at the factory?'

'Why in the world are we talking about that factory?'

'Just wondering if Ashu had ever complained about anything.'

'Why should she?' he asked. 'No one would give the granddaughter of Tara Singh anything to complain about.'

'She was investigating a pattern of illness in the slums next door.'

'What do you mean?'

'I found a file,' said Inspector Singh. 'She'd been recording the symptoms of patients at the slum. You're aware she did some medical work there?'

He nodded. 'I didn't approve – I thought it was too dangerous.'

'Her findings are interesting – there's been an increase in a core group of symptoms in the last few months – shivers, redness in the extremities, elevated heart-rate – that sort of thing.'

'Why are you telling me this?'

'There was a scribbled note at the end of the file. It suggested that Ashu thought the factory might be the source of the outbreak – that the factory was poisoning the slum dwellers.'

'That's nonsense!'

'Are you sure?'

'Of course. Have you seen those slums? The squalor – hardly any running water, raw sewage. There are a thousand reasons why those people might fall ill.'

Singh eyed the other man. Was he justifiably offended or unreasonably defensive? It was hard to tell. It was a serious allegation. But it wasn't being made by Singh but by this man's granddaughter. He remembered the piece of paper with the question – 'Factory??' In his considered opinion, Tara Singh was too quick to dismiss the possibility. If they'd been in Singapore, he'd have thrown an army of investigators at the place, established once and for all whether there was a nexus between the factory and the illness at the slum. He didn't have that option in India.

'Would Tyler have picked up on any leaks or spills or anything like that?'

'Of course.'

'I thought you said he was an "incompetent old fool"?'

Tara Singh's nostrils flared at having his words flung back at him but he didn't respond.

'So you're dismissing Ashu's suspicions out of hand?' demanded Singh.

The other man's turban bobbed up and down in agreement but he wasn't the sort to leave the initiative with anyone else. 'But enough of this sideshow,' snapped Tara. 'Do I need to remind you that you're supposed to find out what happened to my Ashu?' He closed his eyes. 'She was the best of them.'

'Your grandchildren have been fortunate to have you as their benefactor.'

'What choice did I have once their father had died?'

'I heard about what happened to him – it must have been a terrible time for your family.'

The response was unexpected. 'Do you think of yourself as an Indian, Inspector?'

'I suppose so. In Singapore, with so many different races living cheek to cheek, it's hard to forget your roots.'

'Outsiders think that all Indians are one big happy family. But within the country we know better.'

'What do you mean?' Tara Singh had the air of someone who was about to ride a hobby horse to death.

'Take the Moslems. Those that stayed after partition. Hindus call them "Pakistanis" even though they were born and bred here.'

'There are always tensions in societies with different religions,' agreed Singh.

Tara Singh continued as if he hadn't heard him. 'And the Dalits, the untouchables, the scheduled castes, whatever you want to call them. You think they're being invited to dinner by Brahmin families?'

Tara Singh's face had reddened and there was spittle on his bottom lip. He was clearly working himself into a passion.

'*And* we've got the Maoists, the Kashmiris, the Assamese, the communists and the Naxalites.'

'I guess, despite Indian economic success, some are still marginalised,' suggested Singh but he was wasting his breath. This was not a conversation, it was a monologue.

'And what about the Sikhs?'

The policeman from Singapore had been waiting for the gripes to get personal. He had noticed over the years that people with strong political views on what appeared to be a wide range of subjects usually had a single grievance at the root.

'Sikhs seem to have done quite well in India,' said the inspector provocatively, looking around the gleaming office with its panoramic views of the brown smog hanging over the city.

'Don't be fooled,' said Tara. 'This is just window dressing. There are Sikh figureheads everywhere including that Manmohan Singh. But if you look deeper, you will see the truth!'

'And what is that?' asked the inspector.

'We're second-class citizens. They deny us our rights in Punjab. What about water rights? What about Chandigarh? What about our language? They attack our places of worship and massacre our citizens.'

'The Golden Temple was housing separatists,' interjected Singh.

'They had *legitimate* political goals. Anyway, there was a slaughter of innocents as well. Later, the army stood by and let us be murdered – including my son – after Indira Gandhi was killed.'

'Do many Sikhs feel this way?'

'Some of the Sikhs are blind to our plight,' Tara admitted reluctantly. 'But we have to look out for *our* people – otherwise, who will do it?'

The policeman almost smiled. Tara Singh was echoing Mrs. Singh – just before they'd been fleeced by that taxi driver.

'It's not your passport that matters, Inspector, it's your blood.'

Singh felt sorry for Sameer Khan. It didn't seem likely that he would ever have been welcome into the bosom of the family. No cushy jobs within the Tara Singh empire for him, that was for sure.

He eyed the old man pensively, remembering Sameer Khan's insistence that Ashu had climbed into a car with a Sikh man after their rendezvous. He'd been certain it was a young man. Could he have been mistaken? Could it have been an elderly Sikh gentleman – one who was a package of prejudices like this one?

'Did you see Ashu after she left the house that day?' asked the policeman.

'See Ashu? What do you mean?'

'You know – out and about? Around Marine Drive maybe.'

'If I had, do you think I would have left her out there when she was supposed to be confined to the house?' He smacked the table with the palm of his hand. 'Don't you understand our traditions? It was after the *choora* ceremony!'

'I wasn't the one who crept out of the house,' pointed out the inspector.

Tara Singh subsided like a cake that had been taken out of

the oven too early. 'Just remember your responsibilities as a Sikh,' he muttered. 'Our people come first.'

Singh remembered the family on the pavement outside and the bright-eyed boy, Mahesh, in his orange shirt, who had hero-worshipped this man's granddaughter. He was suddenly angry. 'Perhaps there should be less talk in India about the plight of *our* people and more concern for the plight of *the* people – quite a few of them are still sleeping on the streets outside your office.'

Tara Singh was a man who preferred to have the last word. 'You foreigners,' he said. 'You don't understand India.'

Inspector Singh was quite convinced that only a good meal could cheer him up after such a tiresome encounter with Tara Singh. He debated going back to the Taj and then decided that he needed to be slightly more adventurous in his pursuit of a late lunch. Kuldeep was now going in circles, patiently negotiating the erratic traffic, waiting for the fat man to decide on his destination. Singh absent-mindedly noted the beautiful colonial-era buildings although the vast majority looked like they could use some work on the crumbling facades.

'Where are we?' he asked.

'Fort area, *saar*. Commercial district.'

'Where's a good place to eat?'

The car pulled up immediately and Singh stared at the various food vendors suspiciously. A hunchback in a white *dhoti* was crouched by a drain washing dirty dishes in a large steel basin. The water in it was the same colour as that in the drain. Although crowds of office workers were eating out of packets using their fingers, he didn't think his stomach was ready for any food from roadside stalls.

'No, no,' he said to the driver. 'I cannot eat in stalls.' He patted his stomach. 'I will get sick.'

Kuldeep looked horrified. 'Of course not, Sardarji. I mean Jimmy Boys'!'

'But I want Indian food.'

'Very good Parsi food, *saar*. Even Tara Singh is eating there sometimes.'

Singh followed the direction of his gaze and was comforted by the sight of a small café with awnings tucked into the corner of one of the lots.

He climbed out of the car. A group of wiry men in white Nehru caps were sorting individual tiffins onto a handcart. He could smell food. His salivary glands went into maximum production.

'What are they doing?'

'It is lunch for the office workers,' explained Kuldeep. 'They are collecting from the home and delivering to the offices.'

Singh looked around and noted that there were dozens of these carts, each tiffin labelled with some bizarre and incomprehensible code, being pushed around the area at high speed by the men. Home-cooked meals served fresh in the office at lunchtime, eh? These Indians definitely had some good ideas. He would drop a hint to the wife.

He made his way over to the restaurant, was shown to a table, sat down heavily and was pleased to spot a review taped to the wall that assured him this was the best place in Mumbai to try Parsi food, whatever that might be. He ordered the set lunch. He was hungry and it seemed to have a variety of dishes, all of which, in his hungry state, caused his mouth to water. Halfway through the meal, it was his eyes that were watering. All things being equal, the chef was not stinting on the chili. A whole fish, carefully wrapped in banana leaf, was particularly pungent.

'Are you enjoying your meal, *saar*?' asked a waiter.

He nodded and gulped down some water from a bottle, wishing he dared ask for ice.

A fried drumstick in eggy batter, spicy onion-filled salad and pulao rice with large chunks of mutton later, he was ready to sip his tea and consider his case.

In many ways it seemed cut and dried. There was the Moslem boyfriend, the arranged marriage and the strongly held political views of the patriarch. It all pointed to a young girl driven to despair and then extreme measures. The grandson, Ranjit, had been right. The old man was unlikely to have looked favourably on a relationship between his beloved granddaughter and Sameer Khan. But how did that square with the testimony of Sameer and Tara that Ashu was not the sort to kill herself, whatever the provocation? It tied in with his perception of the girl's character as well. Did someone who took her responsibilities in life so seriously, whether to her family or the underprivileged, just chuck it all in on a whim? And in such a terrible way?

His phone rang and he saw that it was his wife. His hand hovered over the device uncertainly. Did he really want to speak – well, listen – to his wife?

He held the receiver to his ear with his left hand. His right was still immersed in his food.

'What is it?'

'I'm with the family,' she whispered.

'I know – you said you were going there.'

'I'm hiding in the bathroom.'

Singh ears pricked up. What in the world was his wife up to?

'Harjeet, one of the aunties, just told me about a trust fund.'

'What?'

'We were talking about Ashu. Harjeet said that Ashu had a trust fund.'

'That's nice for her,' said Singh ironically.

'From the grandfather – only gets the money when she is thirty-five or when she gets married.'

'How much?'

'Three *crore* rupees.'

'In real money,' he demanded.

'Thirty million rupees.'

Wasn't that almost a million dollars? 'Lucky girl,' said Singh and then remembered the last time he'd seen her and winced.

'They say that's why the MBA was so keen. He's from a good family but I've heard from Harjeet that they're short of money because of business troubles.'

'Doesn't really help explain why Ashu killed herself,' said the inspector. 'Although it's very useful background information,' he added hastily. He didn't want to pour cold water on his wife's investigative efforts. After all, she was his spy in the family home.

'Might be a motive for murder?' she asked.

'Not for the MBA as he needed to marry her first to get his hands on the pot of gold.'

'Who inherits?' suggested Mrs. Singh.

'Well, the money had not passed to Ashu at the time of death so killing her wouldn't have left anyone rolling in it.' Singh was thinking hard, trying to see if there were any other angles but he was at a loss. Mostly, it seemed a good reason for a number of people to have wanted her alive not dead.

'I met Kirpal,' said his wife.

'Eh?'

'The MBA,' she snapped.

'Oh, what's he like?'

'Didn't like him.'

'Why not?'

There was a hesitation. 'I'm not sure. He said that he would never have gone through with the marriage if Ashu had been unwilling.'

'And you believed him?'

'He didn't deny that his family needed money . . .'

'But it does suggest that his fiancé was more valuable to him alive than dead,' remarked Singh. 'Tara Singh was going to offer him a good job at the factory where Ashu worked as well.'

He could almost sense Mrs. Singh's disappointment. For whatever reason, and notwithstanding his educational pedigree, his wife had not taken to the bridegroom. He'd have to interview Kirpal soon and decide if he agreed with his wife's assessment.

'Is that why you called?' Singh asked.

'Yes – but also to tell you that the body is coming back day after tomorrow afternoon.'

'Funeral next day?'

'Yes.'

'Impressive,' said Singh. 'Tara must have pulled some strings to get the autopsy done so quickly. I think we can assume it was a half-baked job.' He winced internally at his choice of words but his wife wasn't paying attention as usual. Besides, there was no question as to cause of death – or was there? – so what was the point in prolonging the process. He needed to speak to Patel and make sure there weren't any doubts – that Ashu hadn't been the victim of a premature funeral pyre to disguise some other cause of death.

'Is Tanvir there?' he asked, contemplating his next move.

'Yes.'

'Tell him to meet me at the Taj in an hour.'

'He won't like that,' she warned. 'He's telling everyone that he doesn't know why Tara asked you to look into this matter.'

'Too bad,' said the inspector.

There was an affirmative grunt from his wife. 'Have you found out anything?'

Singh debated his answer. Should he tell her about Sameer, let alone the file he'd found at the clinic? Maybe not – he wasn't sure whether she'd be able to keep the information under her *dupatta*.

'Nothing much.'

'Where are you now?' He suspected that she'd picked up on the telltale sounds of cutlery and crockery.

'Having lunch in Fort area.'

As always, Mrs Singh had the last word. 'How do you expect to find out anything if you only investigate in restaurants?'

*

Mrs. Singh exited the bathroom carefully and was disconcerted to find a young woman with a mass of curly hair standing directly outside the door. Had she been eavesdropping or was she merely in a hurry for the facilities?

'Mrs. Inspector Singh?'

'Yes,' agreed the policeman's wife although it was not a handle she'd heard previously.

'I am Ashu's friend, Farzana.'

Mrs. Singh noticed that the girl's eyes were red with crying and that her expression was anxious. She was restless and her gaze flickered up and down the narrow dark corridor that was lit only by a single lightbulb halfway down its length.

'I am sorry for your loss,' said Mrs. Singh. It was always awkward meeting people at funerals who had known and cared about the deceased. The majority, like her, were there as a mark of respect to the family and wouldn't have been able to pick the dead girl out of one of her husband's line-ups.

Farzana nodded acknowledgement but her mind was clearly on other things. 'I have some important information,' she whispered.

'What do you mean? What about?'

'About Ashu ... I need to tell someone but I'm afraid the family will be so angry. That Tanvir has a terrible temper. Even Ashu was afraid of him.'

Mrs. Singh hesitated. Did she really want to hear what this girl had to say? It sounded like trouble and trouble between family members was always to be avoided. Her curiosity quickly and unsurprisingly overwhelmed her caution. 'You can tell me,' she said. 'I can advise you what to do.'

Farzana nodded. 'That's why I thought I would ask

you – because you're a policeman's wife. I heard you say it earlier.'

Mrs. Singh realised that this was the young woman who had been staring at her in the living room after she'd made the announcement about Singh's role. A buxom, fair-skinned girl with smile lines etched around her mouth, she might have had a bubbly personality in less fraught circumstances. Ashu's friend looked the sort to be popular with matchmakers as well, assuming that she could cook and her family had deep pockets. Mrs. Singh warmed to her. 'I assist my husband with his work *all* the time,' she said reassuringly but untruthfully, hoping she conveyed the impression of being the power behind the throne.

'Ashu called me,' said Farzana abruptly. 'She called me and asked me to meet her at Marine Drive. The day she disappeared . . . died.'

'Why? Why was she leaving the house? She was not supposed to go out after the *choora* ceremony. Surely she knew that?'

'It was important,' said Farzana. 'She was meeting a . . . friend.'

Mrs. Singh's attention was caught by the hesitancy. 'What sort of friend?' she demanded.

'I promised never to say a word. She would kill me for telling,' wailed the girl.

'I think you're quite safe,' said Mrs. Singh dryly, and then wished that she didn't occasionally sound so much like her spouse.

'A boyfriend. She was going to meet a boyfriend.' So her annoying husband's first guess had been correct. There was

161

another man. Mrs. Singh felt a moment of sharp anger towards the dead girl who had thrown the conventions – which she herself had adhered to so faithfully – to the winds. And then she remembered the price Ashu had paid.

'She was going to run away with him?'

'No,' said Farzana. 'She was going to say goodbye. It was very sad.'

Mrs. Singh scowled at the young romantic. Was that a likely story? Did young girls with boyfriends return to the fold to do the right thing by the family?

'Why did she want you there anyway?' Mrs. Singh sounded cross but she wasn't sure what the object of her anger was – this friend who had kept a dead girl's secrets, the dead girl herself or this mysterious boyfriend?

'She wanted me to come back here with her. I was supposed to ring the doorbell and chat to all the relatives so that she could sneak in the back door.'

That made sense. Ashu would have tried to avoid trouble. 'So why are you telling me this?'

'Don't you understand? I spoke to her just before she left the house. She was all right. Not happy, of course. But not in despair. She'd made up her mind what she was going to do and she was going to do it.'

'What are you trying to say?'

'Ashu had a very strong character. There is just no way she killed herself!'

Singh, sitting in the back of Tara Singh's limo, was not amused to hear from his wife that the best friend of the dead girl had ranged herself on the side of the grandfather and boyfriend in

162

denying that Ashu would have committed suicide. Could they all be so wrong in their assessment of her character? He doubted it. This was a murder and he was determined to get to the bottom of it. Ashu – again the charred cadaver flashed into his mind – deserved that much at least.

The driver pulled up outside the hotel and Singh got out, still deep in thought. He hoped Tanvir would not stand him up this time. He was curious to hear what the brother had to say.

His attempts to get through security at the Taj were laborious. He turned out his pockets, stacked the contents into a cloth-lined basket, wandered through the metal detector at the entrance, set off wild beeps, discovered further coins hidden in his trouser lining – didn't everyone have holes in their pockets? – repeated the process a number of times and finally obtained entry just before one of the trigger-happy policemen decided that he was a Sikh separatist and shot him.

His reward for perseverance was to find ACP Patel lurking by the entrance. The Indian beamed like a spotlight when he saw Singh.

'What are you doing here?' asked Inspector Singh. He wasn't a fan of smiley faces that looked like emoticons. Besides, he was waiting for Tanvir. His manner had no effect on his counterpart who seized his hand and shook it violently.

'We are hearing that you are investigating death of Ashu Kaur.'

'The old man doesn't think it was suicide,' said Singh, deciding to be honest. It was a courtesy he could afford at this juncture. 'He . . . err, doesn't want to involve the local police till he's sure.'

There was a quick laugh. 'You are very tactful, Inspector Singh!'

That was something he was rarely accused of being.

'I don't blame him for not wanting the police involved,' continued Patel. 'Cats will be escaping from bag and running all over the place if we are launching an official investigation into death of Ashu Kaur.'

It seemed there was no need to wrap the truth in cotton wool for ACP Patel. He fully understood Tara Singh's motives in looking for freelance help, at least until they had something more solid to go on than an old man's hunch.

'Do *you* think it was suicide?'

Singh's response was cagey. 'Too early to tell.'

'Very well. You are keeping your cards close to your stomach – I am understanding that.' He gestured expansively with his arms. 'If you need any help from the Indian police, you just have to ask.'

'Really?'

'Of course it is depending on what you need,' said Patel, backtracking immediately.

'A bunch of policemen to go over the chemical works with a fine-tooth comb? Ashu suspected that the slum next door is being poisoned by the factory.'

Patel cleared his throat as if he was an election officer about to deliver bad news to a government candidate. 'Without evidence that would be a most impossible thing to do,' he explained.

'How will you get evidence if you don't look?'

'I am pefectly understanding your point,' said Patel. 'But Tara Singh and director general of police are good friends, you know what I'm saying?'

Singh scowled. He feared he was 'perfectly understanding' what Patel was telling him. The Indian police weren't going to go looking for trouble.

'So what do you want with me anyway?'

'Autopsy results have been released this morning,' answered Patel with an enthusiastic Indian head waggle.

'Cause of death?' asked Singh.

'The fire.'

'Not bumps on the head or bullet wounds?'

'Not a single thing like that.'

'Drugged?'

'Blood came up negative.'

'Well, that points to suicide,' said Singh and Patel nodded his agreement. Murder by fire was not the most practical method of getting rid of someone. Not impossible, just impractical.

'Unless the fire hid some trace of violence from the autopsy?'

Patel nodded his head again in cheerful concurrence. 'That is also possible. Especially flesh wounds!'

Singh scowled. Was this man going to acquiesce affably to every contradictory suggestion he put forward? Maybe that was the only way to get promoted in the Indian police force.

'So why are you here?' asked Singh. 'Shouldn't you be briefing Tara Singh?'

'Needing your advice.'

Singh's ears pricked up and he trained his turban on the other man as if it was a motion sensitive camera.

'What do you mean? What advice?'

'It is difficult situation – and you are family member and policeman ... also helping Tara Singh with this matter.'

'That bad, is it?'

The policeman's face drooped.

'Well, spit it out, man!'

There was a long pause while Patel pulled various unexpected faces as if he was suffering from severe indigestion. At last, he said, 'Ashu Kaur was pregnant.'

Ten

Singh, as plump as a bolster, sat on a lobby sofa and stared at the visitors to the hotel as if he was an undercover cop of limited abilities. The inspector was in a state of shock at Patel's news, but the Indian policeman sitting across from him was adamant. 'Autopsy is stating that dead girl was about ten weeks pregnant at time of death. So you see,' he concluded, 'that's why she killed herself. She is knowing it would become obvious soon.' Patel gestured with two hands to indicate a rounded belly which was not that far removed from his own.

'What about the wedding?' said Singh.

'Child is being born six months after marriage,' pointed out Patel.

'An unconvincing premmie,' agreed Singh. It would have been too late to pretend the baby had been fathered by a particularly virile MBA, not so soon after the marriage.

'Unless Kirpal Singh is father – in which case he cannot object to an early child, yes?' suggested Patel.

But Singh couldn't get his head around the hypothesis that the MBA was the delighted Dad. Surely it must have been Sameer? He tried to focus on the details of his conversation with the boyfriend, picturing the young man striding up and down like a beast of prey confined against its will. Sameer had been devastated by Ashu's death, but Singh had not picked up any hint that he had lost a child as well as a lover. Sameer would have been much more determined, and had far more leverage, to persuade her not to marry Kirpal, if he'd known. Which meant that either Singh had read the signs wrong – and this was not something the inspector ever admitted – or Ashu had kept the news of her child from her lover.

'That's why she was using the fire,' explained Patel, looking around warily for eavesdroppers. He was divulging society-pages gossip of the first order about one of Mumbai's leading families. 'Actually it is quite common. Girls are trying hard to hide pregnancy from family, you know?'

'Trying hard? If Ashu Kaur really did herself to death by fire just to hide the physical evidence of her condition that's a bit of an understatement, don't you think?'

And it hadn't worked. Singh suspected it hardly ever worked. Wouldn't Ashu, chemist and scientist, have known that? Or had she just been desperate – treated it as her last throw of the dice?

'Anyway now case is closed like a liquor shop next door to mosque,' Patel had said, wearily relieved. 'Definitely suicide.'

Singh tried to piece together the girl's movements to form a moving picture in his mind. She'd snuck out of the house at some yet-to-be determined time, rushed over to the factory – directly? – to have an altercation with the boss for the entertainment of Mrs. Bannerjee. Later in the day, she'd met her soon-to-be discarded lover on Marine Drive and then – if Sameer's testimony was true – been picked up by a young angry Sikh in a car. Where in the world had she found time to despair over her pregnancy, buy some kerosene, douse herself and then set herself alight? And hadn't he just come to the firm conclusion that he had a murder on his hands?

Singh's attention was drawn to the long-limbed stride of Tanvir Singh.

'You wished to question me?' asked Tanvir in clipped tones, scowling at Patel to indicate that he was surplus to requirements.

'Yup,' said Singh although truth be told, reeling from Patel's news, the favourite grandson was the last person he wanted to see.

Patel hauled himself out of the sofa and hurriedly shook both men vigorously by the hand. 'I'll be going now. We can . . . errr, discuss other matters later.'

Singh was tempted to shout 'coward' after his hastily retreating back. Instead, he led the way directly to his new 'office', the conference room on the first floor. Tanvir followed close behind, almost stepping on his heels in an effort to hurry the process.

'Making yourself comfortable, I see,' said Tanvir, looking around the room and at the freshly served coffee.

'Would you rather discuss family affairs in the lobby?'

'I'd rather not discuss family affairs at all.'

'Your grandfather's orders.'

'I told the old man he was making a mistake.'

'The old man? I see the respectful grandson thing is a bit of an act?'

'He's not on top of his game any more,' said Tanvir, raising an elegant eyebrow as if inviting Singh to dispute the point. 'This thing with Ashu is the final straw.'

'Because he doesn't believe it's suicide?'

'Why should we doubt the conclusion of the police?'

That was a fairly sanguine view from a man whom Singh suspected trusted no one's judgment but his own and who was not yet privy to the fresh information about his sister. He noted that Tanvir was looking at him thoughtfully, as if wondering whether to say something further. Whatever it was, he had second thoughts, because he fell silent again.

'So the empire will be yours soon?' asked Singh.

'I would expect to take over running the business when Tara Baba is ready to step down. I've been his right-hand man for a number of years now, learning the ropes.'

'So, do you have a trust fund?'

He shook his head. 'Only Ashu. Tara Baba thinks that men should make their own way in the world.'

'Do you agree?'

There was a sudden smile which revealed a personal charm which had hitherto been hidden from the tubby policeman. 'I wouldn't have said no.' He lifted his shoulders in a gesture of resignation. 'It's his money; he can do what he likes with it.'

'He paid for your studies in Canada and you work for him now ... doesn't sound much like making your "own way in the world" to me.'

'What's this got to do with Ashu's death?'

'Background,' said Singh – he suspected not very convincingly. He continued, 'What about her trust fund?'

'What about it?'

'Who gets the money?' Singh liked money motives.

'Ashu would only have received the money upon her marriage or at the age of thirty-five.'

'Thirty-five? Not twenty-one?'

'Tara Baba was quite old-fashioned. He wanted to believe that he would hand over the task of taking care of her to a good man.'

'And thirty-five was the *earliest* he was prepared to give up hope?'

'Tara Baba's been good to us – especially Ashu.' This was said with finality.

Singh considered the response. He supposed a trust fund with strings was better than none at all. 'But Tara Baba expects obedience in return and he's not a man you would like to cross?'

'What do you mean?'

'Ranjit said he wouldn't tolerate dissent in the ranks.'

'Ranjit? Ranjit doesn't know how to manage grandfather. Or anything else for that matter. He's a fool.'

'What about Ashu?'

'She was the favourite,' he said matter-of-factly.

'Never did anything to annoy him?'

'Not really – she was very loyal.'

'What if she'd had a boyfriend on the side – someone inappropriate – a Sikh without an MBA? Or not a Sikh?'

'She didn't,' retorted Tanvir.

'Try for a little imagination.'

'He wouldn't have been pleased.'

'So he was forcing Ashu to marry a man against her wishes?'

'Don't be ridiculous.'

'But she *had* a boyfriend on the side.'

'You have no idea what you're talking about.'

Singh pondered the possibility that this was true. It seemed incontrovertible that Ashu Kaur was not the sort to be bullied into an arranged marriage. All her menfolk were in agreement on that point. But it did seem probable that she might have agreed – before meeting Sameer – to an arranged marriage as a matter of gratitude and affection for her grandfather. But if it was a question of not upsetting the family, surely killing herself was rather worse than refusing to go through with a wedding? He had no idea where getting pregnant fitted into the whole scenario. He would have to ask his wife whether it would upset the family more to discover Ashu was pregnant or dead. It seemed a no-brainer to Singh but he knew that he'd never had a finger on the more conservative impulses of his people.

'I've met the boyfriend. Good-looking fellow. Easy to see why she fell for him.'

Tanvir's face was mottled and his fists clenched but his words were measured. 'Fine – you know about him? Keep the information to yourself.'

'How did *you* know?'

'She told me.'

'Because you're such a sympathetic character?'

'No, she wanted out of the marriage – was hoping for my support.'

'What did you say?'

'Nothing doing – it would have killed her grandfather, shamed the family.'

'Why would it be so bad?'

'You can ask that? He's a Moslem, for heaven's sake!'

'If she was the apple of his eye – wouldn't Tara have wanted her happiness?'

'He would have wanted the best for her – but that wouldn't have included marrying a Moslem,' said Tanvir, choosing his words with apparent care. 'Tara Baba is a Sikh nationalist.'

'Do you feel the same way?' asked Singh.

'No.'

'But your father was killed in anti-Sikh riots . . .'

'I haven't forgotten,' Tanvir said, his nostrils flaring slightly. 'My father – the family – we were just unlucky. Swept up in the unintended consequences of Gandhi's assasination.'

'You don't strike me as the type to turn the other cheek.'

'I'm not – if I knew who those men were who killed my father . . .' He didn't continue but Singh heard the anger in the low, vibrating voice.

The inspector watched as the other man made a visible effort to pull himself together. He continued in a more measured voice, 'It hasn't turned me into a Khalistani.'

'Khalistani?'

'What's the matter with you Sikhs from abroad? That's what the separatists want, right? A separate homeland for the Sikhs – which they call Khalistan.'

Singh knew that, of course. It was just disconcerting to meet anyone who believed that such an eventuality was possible or even desirable. He wondered whether Tara Singh's position was merely philosophical or whether he'd taken active steps to assist the separatist movement. In Singapore, Tamils had funded the Tigers in Sri Lanka even though many of them had never set foot in the country. Tara Singh had been more directly affected by government policy than most – it had cost him the life of his son. It wouldn't be entirely surprising if he had separatist sympathies.

'If you tell Tara Baba about that *kanjar*, it will kill him,' said Tanvir warningly.

The fellow was probably telling the truth as well, thought Singh tiredly. The old man was frail and the so-called betrayal by Ashu might well be too much for him. Unless, of course, contrary to any evidence revealed so far, he was a liberal old gentleman who didn't think considerations of religion should stand in the way of true love. Singh tugged on his beard as if it was a bell-rope. That would make a nice change. Certainly, he hadn't seen any signs of such progressive thinking in this extended family. He remembered Mrs. Singh and her unconcealed pleasure that the family had snared the MBA for Ashu. Most likely, Tara Baba was just a hairier version of his own wife.

'So what do you think happened to Ashu?'

'When I refused to help her, she panicked . . . killed herself.'

'You really believe that?'

'What other explanation could there be?'

'Someone murdered her?'

'Fairy tales.'

Tanvir was so sure it was suicide and he didn't even know about the pregnancy. Singh wondered whether to tell him. He understood Patel's reluctance to be the bearer of this particular item of bad news to the family. He felt exactly the same way. Shoot the messenger? He'd be hung, drawn and quartered and that would be nothing compared to what Tara Singh and his grandsons would do to the father of Ashu's child. Besides, he felt responsible for Ashu's good name. He was being sucked into his wife's family's eighteenth-century paradigm and it wasn't a pleasant view.

'Did you pick Ashu up the day she disappeared?' demanded Singh, changing the subject abruptly.

'I have no idea what you're talking about.'

'She met Sameer on Marine Drive when she left the house. That's why she went out.'

'It is difficult to believe that a sister of mine could be so lost to propriety.'

The inspector was suddenly reminded of his English literature classes as a teenager. The teacher dissecting Jane Austen while the boys looked bored and the girls swooned over Darcy. Certainly, there was enough pride and prejudice within this Sikh clan to write a number of sequels. Although Jane Austen had never felt the need to sully her books with premature death, or premature pregnancies for that matter.

'Sameer says someone pulled over. Ashu got in the car with him or them. Whoever it was might have been the last person to see her alive – might hold the answers.'

'It wasn't me.'

'The man wore a turban.'

'Well, that narrows it down to a few million Sikhs.'

Singh decided he'd love to pin a killing on this bastard, even that of his own sister. Tanvir would be slightly less smug once he'd been worked over in an Indian prison.

'What about your brother?'

'What about him?'

'Did he know about Sameer?'

'How would I know?'

'Would it have upset him if he knew?'

'Upset him so much that he doused my sister in kerosene and set her alight? I thought you said you'd *met* my brother?' Tanvir's eyebrows arched in disbelief. 'It sounds to me like you should ask this Sameer fellow your questions,' continued Tanvir when the policeman didn't respond. 'Don't you think it's just a bit convenient that he "saw" Ashu leave with a Sikh man? Otherwise, he would have been the last person who saw Ashu alive. Probably the jealous type.'

It was a fair point, thought Singh. But of the two of them, he felt much more sanguine about the honesty of the boyfriend than the brother.

'If grandfather is right and this was murder – I don't think you have to look any further than the Moslem,' insisted the brother.

If Tanvir couldn't persuade Tara Singh to ditch his conviction that the girl had been murdered, he'd at least identified a scapegoat, thought Singh.

The policeman remembered Sameer Khan's bruised face and cut knuckles and his assertion that the family was responsible.

'Did you assault him?'

'I have no idea what you're talking about.'

'Did you or some other *goondas* beat Khan up?' He looked the other man up and down. 'Well, I can see that you've not been in a fight recently so it must have been hired thugs. Very brave of you . . .'

'Why suspect me?'

'Because you have a motive *and* because you're precisely the

176

sort of young man who gets others to do his dirty work for him.'

'A pimp like that probably has quite a few enemies. You're not going to pin anything on me.'

That was probably the most truthful thing that Tanvir had said to him yet. Wherever one was in the world, it seemed that it was difficult to bring the rich and powerful to book. It was enough to turn anyone into a communist – as long as it didn't mean he had to share his cigarettes and beer. Singh remembered the passionate young man with the black eye and a willingness to take on Ashu's medical work. 'Sameer is worth a hundred of you,' he said.

'Why?' asked Tanvir snidely. 'Does he have a rich grand-father too?'

Eleven

'She was what?' Mrs. Singh's voice was as taut as a rubber band pulled to breaking point.

'Like I said,' replied her husband, sitting in the armchair by the window and watching his wife's reactions as if she was a murder suspect in a series of particularly grisly deaths.

'I don't believe you.'

'Disbelieve *me* by all means but it's in the autopsy report.'

'This is India – maybe they mixed up the bodies.'

The situation was serious if his wife was prepared to believe that her beloved India was capable of such an unfortunate bureaucratic error rather than accept that there might have been a bun in the wrong oven.

'I had a look at the report,' said Singh. 'The rest of it matched what I saw myself. There's no mistake. The girl was pregnant.'

'Have the police informed the family?'

'No – too afraid.'

'I don't blame them.'

'They want me to do it.'

She shook her head decisively. 'No.'

'Well, someone will have to tell them,' muttered the inspector.

'No wonder she killed herself . . .'

Singh looked at his wife with new respect. Mrs. Singh's knee-jerk responses were providing him useful insights.

'Being pregnant is a good enough reason to kill oneself?' Singh needed to be sure.

'Before marriage? Of course.'

'But Ashu was a *modern* girl.'

'Being a modern girl in India means wearing jeans in public – not having babies before marriage.'

The sarcasm was like a thick layer of sticky peanut butter on a slice of white bread. Singh cracked his knuckles together with frustration. It seemed that both his wife and Patel believed the pregnancy was conclusive of suicide. He still wasn't sure – couldn't get his head around a girl like Ashu taking such a way out. But those who had been certain that it wasn't suicide – the boyfriend, the grandfather and the best mate – none of them had known about the pregnancy. Or at least, he didn't think they'd known.

'So who was the father?'

'The MBA?' suggested Singh, largely to annoy his wife.

'Cannot be Kirpal. I saw him today,' said his wife. 'His reputation is destroyed; the dowry is lost . . . but not a child.'

'Maybe he didn't know?'

'Even so, if they had ... that sort of ... relationship, he would be more upset, I think.'

'I guess you're right.'

'So it must be the boyfriend,' insisted his wife.

'I don't think Sameer knew about the child,' said Singh in a sober tone. 'Should I tell him?'

'What's the use?' asked Mrs. Singh with a sudden outbreak of compassion. 'Too late now.'

'He's still a suspect,' pointed out the inspector. 'If he killed her out of jealousy – this knowledge might be enough to trigger a confession.' His mind balked at such crude tactics so he changed the subject quickly.

'What would Tara Singh and the brothers have done if they'd found out?'

'About the pregnancy? Disowned her.' The answer had the trajectory of a bullet.

'Are you sure?'

'Yes – unless they'd *already* disowned her for having a Moslem boyfriend.' She paused to contemplate the enormity of the situation. 'If she was having his child ...' Her voice disappeared into the recesses of her throat, the transgression too shocking for her to articulate.

'Sameer suggested that Ashu's death might have been an honour killing – because she had a Moslem boyfriend. And Tanvir certainly knew about Sameer – and had him beaten up as well, I believe.'

'Honour killing? That's a bit extreme, isn't it?' She would have raised her eyebrows if they hadn't been plucked into obscurity.

'Casting her out onto the street because of an untimely

pregnancy is perfectly understandable but killing her is beyond the pale?'

'When you put it that way . . .'

Singh brightened. 'So they wouldn't have disowned her over Sameer – or the child?'

'I meant you're right – probably the family killed her.'

When the phone rang, it was to inform Singh that a Mr. Khan was in the lobby waiting to see him. The fat man closed his eyes and leaned back in his chair like a fighter pilot subject to unbearable G-forces. Sameer Khan was possibly exactly the last person in the whole universe he wanted to see at that moment. What in the world was he supposed to say to him? Your girlfriend was pregnant with your baby, decided not to tell you in the hope she could pass it off as her soon-to-be husband's, realised that the maths didn't work and killed herself?

He rode the elevator down in silence and grunted in response to the attendant's cheery greeting. As he stepped out, he spotted Sameer immediately. It was almost impossible to miss the battered young man pacing up and down with his usual vigour. He raised a hand to acknowledge the policeman as Singh lumbered over.

'It's a bit late,' said Singh. He was wasting his time and he knew it. Sameer was completely indifferent to the convenience of others.

'Are there any developments?' he demanded.

'Is that why you came to see me?'

'What else? Do you think I care whether you're enjoying your stay in Mumbai?'

His voice was raised a fraction and Singh beckoned to him with a fleshy hand and led him to the bar overlooking the sea. It was a comfortable place reeking of old-world charm with elderly waiters dressed in white and fine china crockery. Singh chose a window alcove. The view was stunning – the setting sun seemed to have seeped into the waters of the horizon and the sea was alive with flames – but neither man noticed or cared.

Sameer's face was like a specially designed thermostat that measured impatience, the increased redness suggesting a reading well in the danger zone.

'Well,' he asked, 'have you discovered anything?'

'Like what?'

'Like that her family killed her?'

'Not yet,' said Singh. 'Even if it was true, it could be difficult to prove.'

'Not if you find the man in the turban who picked her up and shake the truth out of him.'

'Not my style,' said Singh. This was not the time to point out that Tanvir had suggested that the mysterious Sikh man was a convenient invention of the thwarted lover.

'Anything new at the chemical works?' asked Singh, changing the subject before Sameer decided to take matters into his own tightly clenched hands.

'Ashu was right – there's something very odd going on at the slum next door.'

'How do you know?'

'I've spent some time there – more and more people are turning up with those mysterious symptoms she was recording.'

'Which she thinks is caused by the factory?'

'Yes.'

'You're not so sure?'

For once the young man of absolute certainties looked doubtful. 'It could be anything, right?' It was almost as if he was seeking reassurance from Singh that his place of work wasn't causing the outbreak.

'Ashu went to see Tyler,' said Singh, 'just before coming to see you.'

'I know.'

'How did you find out?'

'She told me that morning . . .'

'What did she say about it?'

'Not much – that she'd gone to see Tyler – he'd denied everything.'

'Did she say that he threatened her?'

'What?' The exclamation caused other diners to turn around in surprise – this was a venue of low conversations and comfortable silences.

'Does that mean "no"?'

'She said he was angry,' he replied at last. 'And that I should be careful if I was going to sniff around . . . but no, I thought she was being a mother hen. I didn't sense danger.'

'Do you think Tyler is capable of violence?'

'That old fool?'

'Yes,' said Singh with gritted teeth. Why did the young always assume that the old were not capable of strong emotion or violent expression?

'I wouldn't have thought so . . .' muttered Sameer. 'But maybe if he felt cornered?'

Even old people might lash out if cornered like rats? It was not an unfair assessment of the American. Definitely not a risk-taker but someone who might have acted if he felt threatened.

'But surely she would have just gone to her grandfather if she really believed she was in danger?' asked Sameer. He didn't look pleased at the idea that the love of his life might have gone elsewhere for help but at least he was still thinking.

'It's a fair point,' agreed Singh.

'I still believe it was the brothers.'

'The apprehension of a murderer is not an act of faith,' growled the inspector, conveniently ignoring the occasions when he'd followed his gut rather than his head in identifying a killer. He glanced down at his overhanging stomach. Unfortunately, there were very few hints coming from his innards. There was nothing for it. Time to show his cards.

'The autopsy results are back,' he said by way of a preamble.

Sameer grimaced but didn't interrupt.

'Death was, in all likelihood, caused by fire. Any other trauma – bruises, cuts, that sort of thing – if it existed, was well disguised.'

'So there is nothing to rule out murder?'

'Or suicide,' said Singh bluntly.

'I've told you, I knew Ashu. She would never have taken her own life!'

'Well – there was one other finding in the autopsy report that might affect that conclusion.'

'What was that?' asked Sameer.

'Ashu was pregnant.'

Mahesh had bought some food from a vendor on the street and now he hurried back to the hut, holding his package carefully as he skipped across the puddles. The change jingled in his pocket and a small part of him realised what an unfamiliar sound that was to him. There had never been much spare cash in his short life. His heart was full to brimming, pride in his errand, delight at its source, and fear at the possible consequences of being found out. He felt almost light-headed at the conflicting emotions and stumbled over an exposed stone. Mahesh held the food bundle to his chest, feeling its warmth through the paper. He had money enough to go back for a second round but there was no way he was prepared to fail at any of the tasks set him, however trivial.

'Where are you going in such a hurry, Mahesh?'

He saw that the questioner was one of the men who lived in the slum with his wife and six children. He was not a popular man. A tough fellow who used his strength against his family. Mahesh felt his stomach turn and knew, with that insight of the emotionally aware, that it was because Raj reminded him of his father. Strong. Brutal. Terrifying.

'Didn't you hear me, boy?' Raj was on his feet now, looking menacing, and even from where he stood Mahesh could smell the alcohol fumes.

'On the way back to the hut,' he explained, rocking on the balls of his feet, ready to make a dash for it although Raj was blocking his path.

'Smells like a good dinner there,' said Raj.

'Not for me,' explained Mahesh nervously.

'Where did you get the money? I heard all the other boys are back at VT but not *you* ...'

Mahesh flushed at the implied criticism but didn't answer.

'What's your excuse now? You can't trail after that doctor woman any more, can you?'

The boy realised that it was possible to hate someone on a very brief acquaintance. But although his eyes blazed at the insult to Doctor Amma, he kept a firm hold of his temper. 'I have to go now,' he said awkwardly.

'What's the hurry?'

He didn't reply; bit his tongue, his cheek, his lip to keep from provoking the man further.

'How about you go but leave me some dinner? Think of it as a toll to pass my hut!' Raj cackled loudly at his own humour.

'It's for my mother,' he explained desperately. 'She has come from the village. She's not well. This food is for her.'

'Where'd you get the money?'

'Stole it,'said Mahesh boldly.

This provoked laughter. 'You'll go far, boy – all the way to prison.'

Raj tired of his sport and walked back into his hut but not before aiming a blow at Mahesh's ear. Mahesh dodged, he had years of practice after all, and ran past as fast as he could. He reached the hut and drew back the cloth door carefully. The woman inside looked worn and tired but she held out a welcoming hand and Mahesh placed the food gently into the outstretched palm. He knew that, whatever happened, he was not going to fail in his duty to protect her.

'I don't believe you.'

'It's the truth. I heard it from Patel himself and he said that he made sure that the information was double-checked.'

'There must be some mistake.' Sameer's mouth was wide open as if he intended to scream and shout but the words came out as quietly as a sigh. Singh wondered at the man's insistence. He'd expected him to be gutted at the information – who wouldn't be? His unborn child was dead. But this fervent denial? He was an intelligent young man. The fact of the matter was that Sameer had been careless or the protection had been faulty. Either way, the consequences were tragic.

Singh steepled his fingers and peered at Sameer over the apex. His wife's view was that sex before marriage was undesirable and unnecessary and to be frowned upon by all right-thinking members of society (like herself). Still, for Sameer and Ashu, in the throes of first love, blighted love, it must have been both a temptation and an affirmation of their feelings. *And look what happened* – he could almost hear his wife's snide tone, as if untimely death was the natural outcome of pre-marital sex.

'You don't understand.' Sameer's eyes were like dark tunnels into the recesses of a trouble mind.

'What don't I understand?' asked Singh, hoping the man wasn't going to talk about youth and first love and all those things that Singh had forgotten, if he'd ever known.

'I wasn't the father.'

'What did you say?'

'I wasn't the father. Ashu and I – we never, you know, we never . . .' he trailed off and buried his face in his hands, leaving a lardy inspector to stare at the top of his head with genuine, undisguised consternation.

Twelve

The next morning, Singh set out early. He hailed a cab – with AC – and directed it to Kirpal Singh's family home in Bandra. An hour later he was still sitting in traffic. How many crimes were solved in a city where setting out to question a suspect could take half the morning? And he didn't have a whole lot of time. Not with the funeral that afternoon. The inspector stared out of the window glumly and wondered whether he should have waited and cornered the young man at the ceremony. His wife would not have been amused but it would have saved him this particularly dull journey. The car inched forward a few yards and the driver said, 'Now we are moving, Sardarji!'

Singh's chin came to rest on his chest and his lips turned down at the corners. The fact of the matter was that he was spoilt. Singapore was such a pleasant place to hunt down murderers. It was easy to get around, hardly any traffic. The killers had nowhere to run, the island was so small. The air was clean and the trees green so his health didn't deteriorate as he pursued his vocation. He stared sadly at a dusty spindly tree surrounded by a protective cordon of railings. Here, even the trees were in prison. A sudden influx of auto rickshaws weaving between the cars was a source of relief rather than fear. It meant he was getting closer to Bandra. And sure enough, in ten minutes, the blue and white car drew up outside a large bungalow, hidden from the road by tall palms and a frangipani tree which was festooned in hot pink blossoms.

'This is house, Sardarji. I am waiting for you, yes?'

'Yes,' said Singh immediately.

'Very good, very good.' The man looked delighted and Singh supposed that the two-way fare was a bonus. It was a bonus for him as well. He didn't fancy trekking over cracked paving stones in the hot sun seeking a reliable driver who wasn't going to fleece him or murder him.

He turned to look at the whitewashed house. Cracks in the paint and plaster revealed concrete patches that reminded Singh of open bedsores. Crimson patterned balconies, red stone walls and, rather fetchingly, a red – or maybe rust-coloured – bicycle leaning against the front gate, gave the house a cheerful air. The windows were tall and thin and filled with the opaque glass that was still to be found in old-fashioned bathroom windows in Singapore. Freshly painted black metal grilles indicated to strangers that they were not welcome. A stone cutting on the wall suggested that the house had been built in the eighteen hundreds. It certainly had an air of dilapidated grandeur. Singh was prepared to believe his wife's gossip that Kirpal's family had pedigree but had fallen on hard times.

Singh walked up to the front door, noted more peeling paint and damp-stained crevices, found a shiny brass button and pushed at it firmly with a fat forefinger. He could see shadowy movement through the glass as if the residents had abandoned their corporeal forms in favour of a more wraith-like existence. There was the sound of numerous locks being snapped back and Kirpal Singh appeared on the stoop.

'Inspector Singh?' he asked, his tone polite but distant.

'That's me.'

'Please come in. Tara Baba asked me to speak to you.'

'Everyone dances to Tara Singh's tune,' agreed the policeman.

The tall man with the plump lips and dark eyes looked put out at the suggestion. 'Not at all,' he said. 'But I am happy to fall in with his wishes as a matter of courtesy.'

Singh paused to wonder why anyone would have thought this pedantic fellow was an appropriate husband for Ashu Kaur. A cat appeared at the door and Kirpal picked it up and stroked it gently. Perhaps she'd agreed because he was basically a nice guy. An arranged marriage must have felt like a real lottery to the independent-minded young woman.

'May I come in?' he asked pointedly and Kirpal moved aside with an air of reluctance.

'Is it true that Tara Baba doesn't think it was suicide?' asked Kirpal as Singh entered the living room which had a tiled black and white floor, heavy curtains, and leather sofas. Two standing lamps cast a gloomy light. Why didn't Kirpal just draw the curtains? The dislike of most Indians for natural light was a curious feature of the race. Perhaps they feared a darkening of their not-so-lily-white skin?

'Nope, he thinks it was *murder*.'

'I just can't believe that.'

Singh didn't bother to reply. Instead, he stared at a display cabinet housing various tarnished sporting trophies won by previous generations.

After a few long moments, Kirpal cleared his throat and glanced at his watch. Singh decided to take the hint.

'How close were you and Ashu?' he asked.

'Not very.'

'Give me details.'

'We met a couple of times before agreeing to the marriage. Tara Baba and my mother had already approved, of course.'

'And you decided to go ahead with it?'

'Yes.'

'Why?'

'What do you mean, why? She was young and beautiful, with a good job. There was nothing to find fault with.'

'Her expectations were good as well,' remarked Singh.

'What's that supposed to mean?'

'I hear your lot has fallen on hard times.'

'We are certainly not as well off as Tara Singh,' he said, without batting an eyelid. 'But I think you will find that most people thought it a good match.'

The haughtiness of pedigree, thought Singh admiringly. He wished he had some of that. Then Mrs. Singh would have known her place from the very beginning. She'd arrived demure and biddable but it wasn't long before her Stalinist tendencies had become apparent and now their home was run like a gulag with him, Inspector Singh of the Singapore Police, the sole prisoner.

Kirpal continued, 'We met a few times after the engagement to discuss wedding arrangements and so forth.'

'And you got along?'

'Very well.'

'So the news of her death must have come as a shock.'

'We were devastated, of course.'

'Who's "we"?' asked Singh rudely.

'My mother and me. My father is deceased.'

'Have to look elsewhere to restore the family fortunes, eh, now that Ashu's gone?'

There was a grimace but no immediate answer to the blatant provocation.

'I guess you were very disappointed to find out about Sameer.'

'Who's that?'

'You didn't know? The family didn't tell you?'

'Didn't know what?'

'That she was in love with a nice Moslem boy.'

'That's not true!' He pressed his lips together so firmly that they appeared bloodless.

'I guess when you found out you must have been really mad, huh?'

'I didn't know.'

'Angry enough to kill her?'

'I tell you, I didn't know!'

'What was it – a jealous rage because you really fancied her – or was it her dowry?'

'Don't be ridiculous!'

'So it was the family honour you were protecting then? A bit embarrassing really for you and your mother to be cast

193

aside for some outsider . . .' He leaned forward like an old woman with a juicy morsel of gossip. 'I have to tell you that Sameer is a real Bollywood leading man.'

Kirpal was shaking his head with the rhythm of a metronome.

'Might have been hard for mum to find you another bride – not when the first one ran straight into the arms of the first available alternative?'

'I can't believe you're saying these things.'

'Did you spot her with Sameer? Bundle her into your car? Take her somewhere and kill her? Was the fire to cover your tracks?'

'I think you're quite mad,' said Kirpal and he sounded as if he meant it.

Singh leaned forward, picked up a lemonade, gulped it down thirstily and slumped back in his armchair. Kirpal's elbows were on his knees which were bouncing up and down as if he was entertaining a small child with a 'horsy' ride.

'Did you know about the child when you did it?'

'What are you saying?'

'Ashu was pregnant with *your* child when she died . . .'

Singh realised he'd over-reached when Kirpal burst into genuine if somewhat tearful laughter. 'Now I know you're mad. How can Ashu be pregnant with my child when I've never ever been in her company alone?'

The coffin was a pine affair with gold-plated handles and a massive curved lid. Fortunately, it seemed to be airtight. Even Singh's sensitive nose for death could not pick up any unpleasant odours. Tara Singh sat next to it, upright like a crash-test dummy just before impact. Singh felt his heart go out to the old man. He remembered the cadaver, blackened by fire, lips drawn back and hair singed to the roots. And the intact earlobe with the glittering stone. If anything, that had emphasised the horror, reminding Singh that this had been a young creature with a fondness for coloured stones and the other accoutrements of youth – like first love.

His wife sidled up to him.

'What happens next?' he asked.

'Body leaves the house. We go to the *gurdwara* for prayers. Priests will do some last rites. Then the men go to the cremation grounds,' answered his wife.

Singh grimaced. He'd never been very good at funerals, preferring to skip them unless his wife issued a three-line whip. Mind you, weddings were worse. At least at funerals, his customary glum expression at family events looked appropriate. He suddenly remembered the funeral pyre of the senior Singh, the body perched on a pile of wood on a blackened cement platform. It had been his job to touch a lighted torch to the pyre and watch as the body of his father was engulfed in flames. At the time, overwhelmed with grief and shock, flinching from the incredible heat, he'd noticed that there was no smell of burning flesh. Just the richness of sandalwood and the mustiness of soot.

Earlier, his uncles had tied a turban around his head, indicating that, as the oldest son, he was now the head of the household. As if he could ever fill the shoes, or the turban, of that upright man with opinions as stiff as his starched trousers.

'So what did Kirpal say?' asked his wife in a penetrating whisper.

'That he wasn't the father.'

'Really? Then who?'

'That's what I'm wondering,' said Singh.

'You believed him?'

'I don't know what to believe,' admitted Singh.

'Must be Sameer,' she continued. 'Maybe too ashamed to tell the truth.'

The inspector remembered the shaking shoulders of Sameer Khan when he'd heard about the pregnancy. 'No, I don't think so,' he replied. He added provocatively, 'I don't think he's got anything to be ashamed of either.'

His wife's flared nostrils indicated what she thought of his morals but she didn't take him up on it. She was still reeling from the news that Sameer and Kirpal had both taken themselves out of the running.

'*Another* boyfriend?' he asked.

'Hard to imagine it.'

'I don't plan to try,' he retorted.

'Even when the matter is serious, you must play the fool.' Mrs. Singh retied her *dupatta* as if she was adjusting a noose. 'Ashu was a good girl . . .' she started and then lost her train of thought.

Singh didn't blame her. He still knew in his heart that Ashu was 'a good girl' – a scientist who helped out in the slums near her office – but he didn't use the same criteria to determine 'goodness' as his wife and her cronies. By their standards, the dead girl wasn't exactly an example to her peers. A Moslem boyfriend, pregnant, and now dead. It was enough to try the patience of the most liberal members of the Sikh community.

'It's not possible that she had *three* boyfriends,' said Mrs. Singh. 'So it *must* have been Sameer – or the MBA.'

'Well, it wasn't immaculate conception,' muttered her husband.

Their whispered conversation was put to an end by Tara Singh. He stood up and beckoned Singh imperiously, turning away as he did so. He was in no doubt that the policeman would treat his summons as an order, not an invitation. The inspector hurried in his direction, guiltily aware that his mind had been wandering all over the case. A subconscious effort, perhaps, to ignore the elephant in the room – or, in this case, the coffin on the carpet. Were he and his wife the only ones present who knew that there were two in that coffin?

He followed Tara Singh out onto the small balcony decorated with a few dusty potted plants. The old man looked him up and down with a pensive expression tinged with disappointment. Once again, the inspector was reminded of his own father. How many times had he seen that same look on his face? He straightened his back and squared his shoulders. He wasn't a recalcitrant teenager about to feel his father's belt any more. He didn't have to cower before the old man's hard-eyed gaze.

'Tanvir told me about that Moslem boy.'

So much for warning Singh that the information would have a deleterious effect on his grandfather's health. He'd probably hoped to provoke a heart attack and inherit, thought Singh.

'His name is Sameer Khan,' said Singh. He was tired of the attitude of his wife's family towards *that Moslem boy*.

'When were you planning to tell me?'

'Eventually,' responded Singh. 'Now didn't seem the right time.'

There was a silence between the men and Singh longed for a cigarette. It was like a physical ache. He would have turned his broad back on a cold beer and his wife's cooking for the rush of tobacco smoke into his lungs.

'When my son died, I brought up his children as if they were my own,' said Tara Singh.

'I'm sure they're very grateful.'

'Grateful? The girl discards everything she's been taught to have a relationship with an outsider? And Ranjit? He's a huge disappointment to me.'

'Tanvir?' asked Singh hopefully. He didn't like the fellow but maybe he was cut from Tara's cloth.

'Counting down the days to when he can light my funeral pyre.'

Three grandchildren. Three strikes.

'Ashu made a mistake in your eyes – I understand that,' said Singh. 'But she was still a very special girl.'

Tara turned to stare out over the city of twinkling lights and beggars.

'Just think how generous she was – helping out at the slum.'

He turned around to meet Singh's eyes. 'Did you find out anything further about the outbreak of disease?'

'Still looking into it,' replied Singh, not entirely accurately. The pregnancy had caused him to put all other leads on the back burner.

'You're wasting your time,' said Tara.

'What would you rather I did?'

'Prove that this Moslem boy killed Ashu!'

'Is that what you really believe?'

'Of course – he must have been in a jealous rage.'

'*He* thinks it was the family – some sort of honour killing.'

'What are you talking about?'

'One of you discovered the relationship between Ashu and Sameer and killed her to avenge the family honour.'

'Don't be absurd – you've been watching too many soap operas.'

Singh shifted uncomfortably. It did sound absurd to accuse anyone of a practice as archaic as honour killing. On the other hand, they'd been happy to countenance an arranged marriage which some would argue was also a trifle old-fashioned. He reminded himself that Ashu was dead and had last been seen with an unidentified man wearing a turban. And the family was adamant that Sameer Khan was unsuitable. How far were they prepared to go to punish such a transgression?

'Besides,' added Tara Singh, 'none of us knew about this Moslem.'

'That's not entirely accurate,' said Singh. 'Tanvir knew.'

Tanvir appeared like an apparition summoned by a witch doctor. Another young man, with the strong features of someone with Punjabi ancestry but without the turban, bangle and beard of Sikhdom, was by his side.

'This is my friend from Canada, Tara Baba. He wishes to pay his condolences.'

There was a tired nod in response. The old man was still standing ramrod straight but Singh could see the whites of his knuckles where he was grasping the head of his cane. The upright posture and air of command were an act of will, not of strength.

'I'm Jaswant Singh,' explained the man as he stepped into the halo of light from the single hanging lamp. 'I'm sorry for your loss.'

Singh tried to ignore the Sikh jokes from his schooldays that immediately popped into his head. How many Singhs does it take to change a light bulb? *Jas-want* Singh.

'You're from Canada?' inquired Tara.

'Yes, sir.'

'A lot of Sikhs have found their homes there.'

'Canada has a large Sikh population,' agreed Jaswant.

'Many of them have abandoned the old ways.'

Jaswant ran his hand over his clean-shaven jaw sheepishly. 'You're right, sir, but it is difficult sometimes to maintain the traditions in the West. I assure you that I have the interests of Sikhs close to my heart.'

'What are you doing in India?'

'Visiting friends and relatives – I have some business to take care of as well.'

For some reason, this last statement seemed to have an effect on Tanvir who slapped his friend on the back affectionately. 'Maybe we can work together sometime, *bro* – a joint venture between us,' he said.

The older men scowled simultaneously. The replacement of the traditional word 'bhai' meaning 'brother' with the American abbreviation had annoyed them both.

Cremations were not really his cup of tea, decided Singh. And looking around the very crowded room, he could see that there were others who felt the same way. Not his wife, who was in her element, her face the perfect combination of sorrow and interest that marked her down as a family member who had not known the deceased personally. The other women in the room would be able to read her expression and the status it conveyed. He wondered how his wife had achieved such expertise – years of practice while he'd been coming up with far-fetched excuses to avoid family gatherings?

As he watched, a young girl with a mass of curly hair sidled up to his wife. Mrs. Singh greeted her with the familiarity of previous acquaintance and he guessed that this was Farzana, the friend who had known about Sameer and been called to meet Ashu just before her death.

The American, Tyler Junior, arrived to pay his respects and now stood awkwardly with his back to a wall. He tried to look inconspicuous which was difficult as he was the tallest man present as well as the whitest.

Singh sauntered over. 'It's good of you to come here,' he said in a friendly tone which he did not feel.

'Have to do the right thing by Tara, I guess.'

'I'm sure he appreciates your thoughtfulness.'

There was a shrug of burly shoulders. 'How's the investigation going – any light at the end of the tunnel?'

'Of an oncoming train.'

'I heard you had a chat with the boyfriend.'

Singh almost smiled. The American could not resist embarking on a fishing expedition.

'Yup.'

'Did he have anything to say?'

'Nothing much.'

There was a pregnant pause which the inspector broke.

'How come you didn't tell me about Sameer and Ashu?'

'None of my business,' retorted Tyler. 'You seem to have found out anyway.'

'We have our methods,' Singh whispered, winking at the other man knowingly and was rewarded with a look that suggested Tyler had him pegged as the buffoon he was pretending to be.

'But,' he added, 'people should leave investigating to the professionals.'

'What do you mean?' The question was cursory, his interest in the answer minimal.

'Ashu was doing some poking around too.' Singh sniffed with disdain. 'What does she know about such things? You must have method and organisation. You can't just run around making allegations without proof.'

'What're you getting at?'

'She seemed to think there was something funny going on at the factory.'

'Like what for instance?'

'Don't really know – I'm not a scientist.'

'I *am* a scientist so perhaps you should run her theory by me.'

'People in the slums are falling ill.'

'That's hardly news.'

'Some strange symptoms – red lips and cheeks, erratic behaviour.'

'Could be anything.' The tone was dismissive. 'Cholera, dengue, malaria, rabies – you name it, they have it.'

'So you don't share Ashu's view that the outbreak of disease has something to do with the factory?' Singh had inched closer to the other man until he was glaring at him from a distance of a couple of feet.

'Of course not. How could that possibly be the case?'

'Leaking pipes, poisonous run-off, industrial sabotage?'

'You're being ridiculous.'

'Did Ashu ever raise the issue with you?'

'No way!'

'Not the morning of the day she disappeared?'

Tyler's light blue eyes stared at him with watery intensity. Singh knew he was trying to figure out what the policeman knew about that last altercation so helpfully reported by Mrs. Bannerjee.

His answer was succinct and to the point. 'No.'

'But she came to see you?'

'Might have done,' said Tyler at last, opting to hedge. 'A lot of people pop by during the day if they want to discuss something, report something, just have a chat.' He added rather desperately, 'I operate an open door policy with my staff.'

Singh gazed at him admiringly. 'I see – it must be difficult to distinguish between all those employees popping by to chew the cud and the granddaughter of the owner accusing you of industrial pollution on the morning of her disappearance and subsequent death.'

A telltale redness was spreading from the back of the man's neck up his cheeks. Caucasians were much more fun to question, decided Singh. Their colouring was so much more revealing. Not like Sikhs with their turbans and facial hair.

'I have no idea what you're talking about,' said Tyler.

'I have a witness' – where would investigators be without

prying secretaries? – 'who is prepared to testify that voices were raised at your meeting.'

'What are you trying to say?'

'That there is an unhappy nexus – for you – between the quarrel you had with her and the death of Ashu Kaur.'

'Are you accusing me of having something to do with Ashu's death?'

'Don't know about police methods in the United States,' remarked Singh, 'but where I come from a person last seen having an argument with someone who later turns up dead goes straight to the top of the list of suspects.'

'But Ashu committed suicide!'

'That's not what her grandfather believes … and I'm coming round to his point of view.'

'But that's just insane,' protested Tyler. 'Why would I kill her?'

'Because any evidence of negligence or malpractice at the site would have cost you that retirement package? You might even spend some time in an Indian prison. Not an experience that you'll enjoy – or survive. You have motives in spades.'

'You can't prove anything.'

'Not *yet*,' said Singh. 'But I'm working on it.'

'And if you spread any of these vicious unproven rumours – I'll sue you for slander.'

'I'm running scared,' agreed Singh amicably.

Tyler added with sudden insight, 'I'll bet your policemen bosses in Singapore don't know you're freelancing here in India – if you persist with this, I'll have your badge.'

'Wouldn't it be easier to just have me killed – like Ashu?' asked Singh and then took a hasty step back as the large

American looked as if he was willing to take up the suggestion on the spot.

He extricated himself from the encounter with Tyler by dint of hurrying over to his wife's side.

'Don't tell me you were investigating the death here?' was his wife's opening remark.

'I shan't tell you if you don't want me to,' agreed Singh, looking over his shoulder. Tyler had disappeared from view. Perhaps he'd decided to ditch the visit to the crematorium.

'Who was that man anyway?'

'Ashu's boss.'

'Do you suspect him?' she asked *sotto voce*.

'Not just him,' said Singh ruefully, wishing his turban didn't feel so tight. It was always a sign that he was developing a headache. No wonder, with all these potential killers in one room.

'What about that girl?' he asked, squeezing the back of his neck with thumb and index finger, trying to release the tension.

'What girl?'

'The one you were just speaking to.'

'Farzana – Ashu's friend. Ashu asked her to come to Marine Drive.'

'Yes, you told me.' Singh was impatient now. He wanted progress, not to re-hash old stories. 'Did she have anything to add?'

Mrs. Singh tugged at her *dupatta*. 'Just saying hello.'

Singh looked around and saw Farzana leave the room with Ranjit in tow. It reminded him that he hadn't asked the younger brother whether he'd known about Sameer. Ranjit's blanket denial might not be so effective now that Singh had a name. He hurried after them like a determined street vendor.

As he rounded a corner, he heard Ranjit's voice and slowed down.

'You can't tell. Please!'

'It doesn't seem right, keeping things from the police.' The girl was doubtful, uncertain.

'He's not really the police – just some fat guy my grandfather hired.' Singh grimaced. Was everyone in this family saying unpleasant things about him behind his back?

'Why don't you want anyone to know?'

'If Tara Baba found out that I'd kept this from him – well, you know what he's like.'

Singh picked up the hint of a sigh from Farzana – as if she was willing to accept his explanation but didn't like it. 'I guess Ashu wouldn't want me to get you into trouble,' she said. 'She always did her best to protect you from Tara Baba.'

'Thank you, Farzana. It means a lot to me.'

'What did Ashu say to you, anyway?' asked Farzana.

'That she was going through with the marriage ... that it was the right thing to do.'

'I just don't understand.' There was a note of profound pain in Farzana's voice.

'When I saw her, she was fine. Not happy, of course. But not ... suicidal. Typical Ashu really – stubborn and determined.'

There was a long silence and Singh wondered for a moment if they had left.

'I don't think she did it,' said Farzana, at last. 'Killed herself, I mean. Not her of all people.'

'Do you realise what you're saying? If she didn't do it ...' Ranjit's voice trailed off.

'I think someone murdered her.'

Whether she was going to identify any likely suspects was never to be known as Singh suddenly heard a cackle of voices behind him. Unwilling to be caught eavesdropping, he opened the nearest door and slipped in. It was a small, cluttered room with bright handloom bedspreads and towers of books. It smelt faintly of lavender. He guessed it had been Ashu's. He waited for the footsteps to pass and then scurried around the corner, determined to question the co-conspirators. Only Farzana was still there. She sat on a stool in the kitchen and sipped a glass of water, her expression despondent.

'Well then, young lady, I think it's time you and I had a chat.'

He wasn't entirely surprised when the glass slipped from her hand and shattered on the floor.

'Any developments?' asked Tanvir.

The two men had made their way through the throng of mourners and past the closed coffin to Tanvir's spartan room.

The Canadian shut the door carefully, pausing to listen for the click. He shook his head. 'Everything is ready. Nothing to do except wait.' He clenched and unclenched his fist. 'The hardest part.'

'It doesn't bother me – I've been waiting a long time. You must learn patience.'

Jaswant nodded and his expression was respectful. 'What about your grandfather?' he asked.

'What about him?'

'Surely he must feel the same way you do? Are you sure you don't want to rope him in?'

Tanvir shrugged, an elegant gesture. 'He makes the right noises – but I don't believe he has the courage to see something like this through.'

'He looks devastated about your sister.'

'Exactly – it is just as well that he has no part to play. He's a wreck right now.'

'And you? Ashu was your sister, after all.'

Tanvir looked discomfited for a moment. 'I'm all right.'

Jaswant gripped the other man by the shoulders with two large hands. 'Are you quite sure? There is no room for error. No room for personal tragedy. You know as well as I do that our mission can only succeed if we have one hundred per cent. commitment.'

Tanvir took a step back and Jaswant's hands fell to his sides. 'I'm all right, I told you. We have nothing to do except wait for the judgment.'

'So what did you find out?' Mrs. Singh spoke in a penetrating whisper.

'Ranjit,' said Singh. 'Farzana said that when she arrived at Marine Drive to meet Ashu, she was just in time to see her drive off in a car. With Ranjit.'

'Are we talking about the same person – the younger brother? Surely, she means Tanvir – or Kirpal?'

'She's quite sure.'

'Why didn't Farzana say anything earlier?'

'She was trying to protect him – for Ashu's sake. I heard him beg her to keep quiet about it.'

'Then why did she tell you?'

'I'm quite persuasive,' said Singh, his face forbidding. 'And,' he amended, 'she was willing to be persuaded.'

'I heard from Harjeet that Farzana is quite keen on Ranjit. But her family is not interested,' said Mrs. Singh.

'Are we still talking about the same person? Who could be keen on Ranjit? He looks like a stick with a beehive on the end!'

'Women are not so shallow,' was the tart response.

Singh leaned back against the wall and closed his eyes. He needed to think. For a death that might yet turn out to be suicide, there was no shortage of murder suspects. But Ranjit had not figured high on the list. Indeed, had not appeared on the list at all. He tried to remember his encounters with the young man: the worried fellow at his mother's elbow trying to keep the Singhs out when they had first arrived at the wedding house; the tearful man-child at the Taj, devastated by the loss of his sister. Neither manifestation had seemed out of character or suspicious. He'd not seemed that concerned about his sister's disappearance at first, worried about her reputation rather than her safety. But his grief had been genuine when the body was identified. Singh knew that this was not conclusive of innocence. Quite often the murderer was the loudest mourner at the funeral of the victim, guilt and anger adding to the emotional cauldron.

Looking around, he spotted Ranjit sitting next to his mother, his face a mask of sadness. There was no mistaking the honesty of the emotion. It was all there in the sallow face; the new lines, the hollow eyes. But Ranjit had withheld crucial information. He knew quite well that Singh, let alone

Tara and the rest of the family, would have wanted to know that he'd seen Ashu, been with her, the afternoon of her death. Try as he might, Singh could not find a single explanation for his reticence except a guilty conscience.

'Stop doing that,' whispered his wife.

'Doing what?'

'Staring at you-know-who!'

'Ranjit?'

'Yes. Everyone will think he did it.'

'Maybe he did do it,' responded Singh.

'Can't be,' was the response.

'Why not?'

'Mother says very gentle boy. Writes poetry.' She shuddered. For a woman who believed that all young Sikh men should pursue gainful employment and marriage with equal vigour, poetry was harder for her to understand than murder.

'For what would he do it anyway?'

'I don't know.' Surely not an honour killing by the young beanpole? There'd been no evidence that he shared the prejudices of his grandfather and brother. Wasn't he the quiet rebel who watched Bollywood movies with his sister and believed in happy endings?

'Why would he lie about seeing her?' he asked, giving himself a mental kicking for relying on his wife. Where would he turn next? A psychic?

'Something to hide. But maybe not murder.'

'Something to hide *but maybe not murder*? That about summed it up. And the only way he could find out was by cornering the young fool and beating it out of him – verbally of course. He stepped forward and his wife grabbed him by the arm.

'What?' he demanded.

'Not now,' she hissed and Singh realised that she was right. The cortege was about to leave the house. This was probably not the moment to confront Ranjit Singh about the death of his sister and the lies he had told.

Thirteen

Singh slipped out of the apartment and found a convenient but poorly lit stairwell around the corner from the heavy front door. The air was stale and he could smell piss but his need was urgent and not so easily thwarted. The inspector carefully extricated a packet from his trouser pocket, tapped one slim cigarette into his palm, slipped it between his thin upper lip and full lower lip, lit it with a cheap plastic lighter and inhaled deeply. The tobacco hit his lungs and he sighed with relief. The absence of cigarettes was affecting his investigative skills, he decided, crossing his eyes to admire the glowing orange tip of his cigarette. The usual cloud of smoke around his head, by obscuring his vision and clogging his nostrils, allowed him to turn his thoughts inwards and focus on the evidence. In its absence, he was just flailing around like a novice swimmer in the deep end.

Although, the crux of the matter was that he'd need more

than a single cigarette to work his way through this particular thicket of facts, truths, half-truths and lies. And there was still the very real possibility that a pregnant Ashu had killed herself. Singh scowled. Even if it was suicide, one of his suspects had probably driven her to it. But he'd get away scot free unless he'd been holding the match. The law was not a morality play.

Singh's phone vibrated in his pocket. He'd turned off the ring tone and now it felt as if he had a live lizard in his pocket. He extricated it gingerly and looked at the long Indian number with some puzzlement. He removed the cigarette from his mouth, tapped the ash onto the ground and held the small device to his ear with a beefy hand.

'Singh,' he said abruptly.

'ACP Patel here.'

What other bad news did the fellow have?

'Very glad to see that you are still with us in Mumbai, Inspector Singh.'

'Can't drag myself away.'

'Very good, very good.' Sarcasm was obviously wasted on ACP Patel.

'I have some information that I think you might be very pleased and interested in knowing.'

'Have I won the lottery?'

'I beg your pardon?'

'I'm sorry,' said Singh.

'Actually, to be very frank and honest, we are needing your help.'

'What is it?' asked Singh, warily. He couldn't think for a moment how he could be of assistance to the Indian police.

If they were going to nag him to disclose Ashu's pregnancy to Tara Singh they were wasting their breath.

'We have some news which is not at all good.'

Singh could almost hear Patel take a deep breath.

He continued, 'There's a fellow from Canada – Jaswant Singh. A friend of Tanvir. At university with him in Toronto.'

'He's here now, at the funeral house.'

'According to Canadian police, Jaswant Singh is also member of the Khalistan Liberation Front.'

'And who the hell are they?'

'Sikh separatists.'

'Everyone needs a hobby,' said Singh.

'Terrorists also.'

'Oh, I see,' said Singh, flippancy erased from his voice. 'That's not good news.'

'We are concerned that Jaswant Singh is here for *nefarious* purposes,' explained Patel.

Singh almost smiled. Did people actually have 'nefarious' purposes any more? Perhaps in India.

'Recently, KLF assassinated a few community leaders in Canada and Norway who were not at all sympathetic to their views,' continued the Indian. 'Organisation only has a few hundred members but quite effective at planning attacks. Maybe Jaswant has some intentions here.'

'Why don't you arrest him and ask him?'

'Better to see who his confederates are.'

The penny dropped. 'You suspect Tanvir?'

'Not at all, not at all.' Patel sounded positively panic-stricken at the suggestion.

Singh sucked on his cigarette as if he was mainlining oxygen. 'I get it – you do suspect Tanvir but you're afraid to get on the wrong side of Tara Singh if this turns out to be a storm in a teacup.'

'Very powerful man,' said Patel by way of agreement. He added defensively, 'Also, we want to know what they are planning ...'

That was actually credible. They might be able to pick Jaswant up and deport him to Canada to face whatever mild punishment was reserved for would-be terrorists but the reality was that they would be no further along in knowing whether he was in India with any actual scheme in mind and who his associates were. And it was the spider-web of fellow conspirators and the source of their finance that was of most interest to the authorities. Especially the latter. Without money, terrorists were just angry young men with an axe to grind. With money, the metaphorical axe became real and sharp and terrifying. He knew that very well – had learnt it the hard way – from his murder investigation in Bali after the bombings there.

'You think they might be planning an assassination?' he asked. 'Some Sikh leader?'

'Or something bigger,' muttered Patel. 'After Mumbai attacks, lot of chatter amongst Khalistani organisations – and rest as well.'

Singh knew that chatter meant the electronic conversations picked up by intelligence surveillance. The agencies monitored volume and content and tried to deduce the intentions and targets of the terrorists with varying success. It didn't surprise him that the Mumbai attacks had spawned copycats. If

215

publicity was the lifeblood of terrorists, the week-long siege of the hotel had been a massive transfusion.

'Why are you telling me all this?'

'You are still looking into death of Ashu Kaur? This morning you went to see Kirpal Singh?'

'Yes.' Impressive. They had their ears to the ground.

'So you can still be helping us,' Patel continued.

'How?'

'By keeping an eye on Tanvir.'

'I'm happy to keep an eye out for trouble,' agreed Singh, 'as long as you're not depending on me to foil some sort of terrorist attack.' He'd tried that once in his career – in Bali. It hadn't been fun.

'That is all we can ask, Inspector.'

'I was with Tanvir and his friend earlier,' added Singh, gazing down at the lighted end of his cigarette, clamped between index and middle finger. 'They seemed like good buddies ... Tanvir suggested that they should go into business – a joint venture – together some time.'

'No law against that.'

'Depends on the business, I suppose.' He paused to consider the matter. 'My advice – for what it's worth. Put a tail on both of them.'

'It shall be as you say,' agreed Patel and the inspector from Singapore didn't doubt that his head was waggling from side to side in that strange affirmative action of the Indian.

The inspector slipped his phone back in his pocket and sat down heavily on the stairs. He dropped his cigarette butt and crushed it underfoot. This suspicion about Tanvir was an unexpected and unwelcome development. Was Patel's story credible? It seemed unlikely that the scion of a wealthy Sikh family would be involved in any criminal activity. Perhaps he'd just been unlucky in his choice of friends while a student in Canada. It happened. Most of Singh's cohorts were now senior figures in government or running gargantuan public companies manufacturing plastic gizmos in China. It showed that one could never be too careful.

Even if it was true that this Jaswant Singh was a member of a fringe group prepared to use violent means to achieve their dubious ends, it was quite possible that he was merely using his friendship with Tanvir as cover for his own questionable activities. What better way to hide one's true intentions than to visit an old college mate with an impeccable background? Singh remembered with a wrenching feeling in his gut what had happened to the son of Tara and the father of Tanvir – murdered by a mob after the assassination of Indira Gandhi. He knew all too well that it was from exactly such roots that terrorist shoots appeared.

'What are you doing hiding here?'

'You almost gave me a heart attack,' growled Singh, scowling at his wife who was peering at him in the half-darkness, secretly glad that he'd stubbed out his cigarette.

She sniffed the air and grimaced. 'Don't tell me that you're smoking?'

'OK, I won't,' said the inspector. 'What do you want anyway? Can't a man have a bit of peace and quiet?'

'Here?'

There was no credible riposte. It really was a stinking, dank stairwell.

'We're leaving,' she said. 'Going to *gurdwara* and then the men to crematorium. Are you coming?'

Singh was immediately and profoundly reminded that he was investigating a death. Patel's call had been a sideshow. It was possible that there were terror plots afoot. But weren't there always? Especially if you were the gullible sort who believed the government and the security services when they insisted that the citizenry was in constant danger and needed their steady guiding hand at the helm, ideally unconstrained by such considerations as human rights and due process. The inspector exhaled sharply and the sound echoed down the stairwell.

'Do I have to come?'

'No,' she said unexpectedly.

Singh's expression filled with suspicion. 'Why not? You always say I have to come for everything!'

'It's a huge crowd – they won't even notice that you're not there.'

'There's always a huge crowd.'

She stared at him, blinking myopically. It was a rare treat when his wife was lost for words but Singh was too perturbed to kick back and enjoy it.

'Well?' he demanded.

'Too many people with too many secrets. I think someone murdered that girl.'

His shoulders slumped. 'Me too,' he agreed.

'Better if you spend your time looking for the killer – not attending funerals. Whoever it is must be punished.'

'I thought you didn't approve of my job.'

'Different when it's family.'

'Most murder victims have families.'

She nodded once. 'So you better hurry up and find this killer instead of hiding here smoking cigarettes.'

Mahesh didn't feel well. His heart was racing and his palms felt sweaty. He'd looked at himself in a piece of broken mirror earlier in the day and noticed that his lips and cheeks were flushed. And now, holding out his hands before him to gauge the tremors, he noticed that his fingertips were pink as well – as if he'd dipped them in a vat of paint. He stared down at his feet in the half-darkness, trying to decide if his toes, sticking out of his *chappels*, were a similar shade.

'Mahesh, what are you doing? You look unwell.'

The middle-aged woman, Janaki, had children enough of her own, eight at last count, but she was a kindly soul.

'Not feeling so good,' he admitted. 'Like the others . . .' His voice was a little slurred and the fear within him grew and spread and reached his shivering extremities.

Janaki looked worried. 'Doctor Amma asked me to look out for symptoms in my children. The pinkness especially. Do you have that?'

In response, Mahesh held out his hands so she could see the pink sheen for herself in the light cast by a fluorescent tube.

'What else?'

'Hands and legs shaking.'

He put a hand out to firm his stance against the nearest wall. The last thing he wanted to do was to keel over in all the filth.

'Do you think it is the rats?' asked Janaki. 'Or mosquitoes?

So many years I have lived here, never seen anything like this.'

'Doctor Amma said that it was something new – not the usual things. She was researching this disease. I was helping her.'

'And no cure,' said Janaki worriedly, sparing a quick glance for her sleeping children, a mass of tangled limbs, within her hut.

'No idea what is causing it,' he explained as if he was the adult and she the child. It was what Doctor Amma had told him. That it was difficult to find a cure, fashion a solution, because she had no idea what the ailment was.

'Has anyone got better?'

Mahesh's eyes were wide clear pools with dark centres of worry. 'Not yet. So far it is getting worse for everyone who has this pink disease.'

Mahesh knew better than the rest how widespread the illness was and how serious the symptoms of some of the early sufferers. That was because he'd been Doctor Amma's eyes and legs, going from hut to hut asking for information, checking the progress of those who were already ill to see if they were responding to any treatments, watching and recording in his head the deterioration in their conditions so that he could report back to the woman in the white coat. She would write down his findings, make notes of the date and time and name of the patient, and keep it all in the thick file. The file that the fat Sardarji had taken.

'Can I catch this thing from the sick ones?' he'd asked Ashu once.

'No sign of any common vector,' she had said and then

laughed and ruffled his hair at his mystified expression. 'The sick ones haven't been in contact with each other, nor worked the same sites. I don't think it is passed from person to person.'

'That's good, Doctor Amma. I wouldn't want to fall ill. Otherwise, how will I marry you when I'm older?'

Mahesh wondered if it was possible that she'd been wrong and he'd caught this illness helping her. Well, if that was the case, he clenched his jaw to convince himself that he meant it; it would have been worth it.

'We have to stop the degeneration before it becomes irreversible,' she had said to him and he'd nodded wisely. He'd no idea what she was talking about, of course, but it sounded like she was on top of things.

Unfortunately, Doctor Amma was not in a position to help him. What was he going to do? He didn't know and had to fight back tears. He couldn't go back to his village. His father would have no patience for a sickly creature. His mother couldn't protect him. The thought of his mother filled him with something close to panic. How was he to build a better life for her if he was unwell? He remembered the Sardarji who had daintily picked his way across the slum to the free clinic and been mesmerised by Doctor Amma's medical file. Maybe he would find out what was wrong in time to offer Mahesh some hope of salvation.

Mahesh made up his mind. If there was no cure – well, he knew what to do before he completely lost control of his arms and legs. It was a solution that no one could take away from him however poor and ill he was. It was his one personal freedom.

*

Sameer Khan was alone in the building except for the couple of security guards asleep at their post near the main entrance. He let himself into the laboratory using his cardkey and debated switching on a light. He decided against it – he didn't want to attract unnecessary attention. There were blinds on the window but he knew that the light would still be visible on the outside, thin strips indicating the presence of a nocturnal visitor. He already had a glib explanation for his presence on the tip of his tongue: unfinished work, deadlines, staying on the good side of the American boss. Most of his colleagues considered it a mark of status to have a non-Indian boss so they would appreciate his brown-nosing. Sameer's full lips twisted with derision. He didn't share their sycophantic views. He judged people as individuals. So he thought that Tyler Junior was a buffoon and he'd fallen in love with a Sikh girl.

A low hum in the room sounded like a swarm of sleepy mosquitoes. Probably, the air conditioning or the computers on stand-by, he surmised. He walked quickly to the nearest desktop, pulled up a chair and typed in his password, a tedious combination of letters and numbers. Many of his colleagues wrote down their passwords and taped it to their desks. The irony of a security arrangement that required more of the human brain than was practical. Sameer soon accessed the company database. He opened the files on the chemical compounds used at the plant and his shadowy, fine-print covered reflection showed his dismay. There were hundreds of items within the database. It would take him days – or nights – to get through it and he didn't have that kind of time. The situation was urgent. He'd been shown a newborn that morning with hands and feet gnarled and useless. It was the first time the disease had spread from mother to child through the womb. Prior to that, from Ashu's careful study, there had been no nexus between individuals except for the fact that they all lived in that particular slum next door to this particular factory.

It had been Ashu's suggestion, ill-received at the time, to research each substance used at the factory for possible poisoning side effects that matched the symptoms shown by residents of the slum. He intended, belatedly, to do as she had asked. For her. And for the slum dwellers whose plight was now his own.

Sameer began, for lack of any better ideas, alphabetically. 'Ammonia' was used in the manufacture of cleaning agents. He read with interest the toxicology reports on various websites and concluded that the common symptoms from exposure, irritation to the respiratory tract and eyes, didn't match. So much for that. He was soon immersed in his work, blinking rapidly from time to time to lubricate tired eyes, methodically going through the lists and products. After a few hours, he'd only just completed the 'A's and wasn't sure whether he'd missed something. Sameer straightened up in his chair, feeling the sharp bursts of pain as his spine elongated. He pulled back his shoulders as far as they would go – the pain was almost refreshing – and stood up. He needed a break. Maybe a short walk would clear his head.

Sameer sauntered over to the window, parted the blinds a crack and was surprised to see a large sedan pull up at the front gate. He watched with interest as the guards raised the barriers and saluted smartly. He recognised the silver four-wheel drive. It belonged to Tyler Junior, and he was very curious to know what he was doing at the plant so late in the evening. No one had ever accused the American of being a workaholic. He was usually the last one in and the first one out, counting down the days until his retirement. The car drew up under the porch.

Sameer decided to back a hunch and hurried down the corridor towards Tyler's office, a spacious room with all the modern accoutrements and a museum-quality collection of Moghul-era miniature art on the walls. The entrance was usually guarded by the ubiquitous Mrs. Bannerjee but she was long gone, hurrying home to cook dinner for her husband and children and regale them with the latest gossip from the office. He tried the door and was pleased to discover it was unlocked. Sameer walked around the desk, ears attuned for the slightest sound. There was nothing on the work surface except a computer and a photo in a heavy silver frame of Tyler, his spouse, who looked like a Stepford wife, and two over-weight teenage children. Sameer, thinking quickly, feeling reckless as the adrenaline surged through his body, ducked behind the leather couch in the corner. He was far from invisible to the observant but he would have wagered a large sum – if it hadn't been against his religion to do so – that Tyler Junior was not expecting company.

The inspector sat on the hotel bed, his back propped up against a pile of feather pillows and his feet bare. Papers were strewn across the bed so that at first glance it looked as if a hurricane had blown through the room and dispersed the contents despite the tubby paperweight in the middle.

Mrs. Singh had not come back from the expedition to the *gurdwara*, although, looking at the time, he suspected the cremation was over by now. Ashes to ashes, dust to dust. The Indians took the instructions literally.

Singh returned to his reading material, a glossy brochure that folded like a particularly annoying map, for the products of Bharat Chemicals. There were shiny pictures of a ribbon-cutting ceremony featuring a younger smiling Tara Singh, some gleaming steel tubes and men and women in white coats staring intently at colourful liquids in test tubes. A flowchart explained that the employee structure 'combined the best elements of East and West' – surly American management and cheap Indian labour, concluded Singh.

Products included various compounds with incomprehensible chemical names as well as some more ordinary sounding stuff like 'paint' and 'face-whitening cream'. The latter product had been behind the factory's improved finances, remembered Singh. It appeared that the sub-continental attachment to 'fair' skin had survived the nation's so-called modernisation and advancement into the nuclear age. The classifieds in the newspapers gleefully informed potential suitors that the available brides were 'fair'. Occasionally, they were apologetic – the girl was on the dark side – but insisted to would-be husbands that her other outstanding attributes would make up for this blight. Posters along the street had 'before' and 'after' pictures of various celebrities, speech bubbles informing passers-by that they owed their glittering movie careers to a lightening of skin tone rather than any acting talent. Having accidentally watched ten minutes of a head-waggling, hip-shaking, breast-jiggling extravaganza on television, the inspector wasn't surprised that thespian qualities were not at a premium. It was disheartening, however, to think that it was skin colour that was of paramount importance instead.

Singh wondered whether Ashu had objected to the manufacture of skin-whitening cream. He regretted not having known this girl in person. But as usual, he'd turned up at the death. And this time it had been unexpected – he hadn't come in his official capacity, forewarned of death, but as a layperson caught by surprise.

He sighed and a deep line appeared, bisecting his forehead. The careful perusal of the file he'd taken from the slum clinic had merely reaffirmed that some mysterious ailment was laying the dwellers low. He was no closer to discovering what it was or confirming that the source of the scourge was the chemical plant. He needed to speak to Ranjit but that would have to wait until morning. There was nothing for it. He was too keyed up to sleep although the idea of slumber certainly appealed. Singh reached for the remote control, found a news channel, clambered out of bed and padded to the fridge in his bare feet. He pulled the tab on his cold beer with a crooked index finger, enjoying the familiar snap and fizz. He had a deep swig, glanced at the news, turned over on his side and in a few moments had fallen into a deep dreamless sleep.

He was interrupted by a telephone ringing just as the faint light of a new day threw golden beams across the carpet from the not-fully drawn curtains. He saw with some dismay that it was his wife calling. She must have stayed the night at the funeral house. Singh picked up the phone reluctantly – why did she have to call him at dawn? – his eyes on the television which was showing the news. 'Hello,' he said into the phone.

'You better come here now.'

'What?' He wasn't sure whether he'd misheard or merely misunderstood.

'Something has happened.'

She was whispering, her voice dry and cracked, and he had to strain to make out her words.

'What is it? Why are you muttering?' He found himself shouting in compensation for her quiet tone. His eyes were still fixed on the television, reading the ticker tape more from habit than intent. It annoyed him, the stream of words at the bottom, usually without context, which still drew the eye with its almost hypnotic quality.

His wife was saying something but Singh's attention had been caught by the latest newsflash under 'Indian News'. He stared at it, hands growing clammy and heart-rate escalating. He realised after a few moments that he still held the phone and Mrs. Singh was twittering in his ear. This time he understood what she was saying. 'I'm coming,' he said bleakly. 'I'll be there as soon as I can.'

He glanced back at the screen. The ticker tape was rolling past again. 'The well-known industrialist and philanthropist, Tara Singh, was found dead this morning.'

Fourteen

'What happened?' demanded Singh. He was panting and out of breath. He'd had to fight his way through the throng of reporters downstairs. They had made a beeline for him – on the grounds he was a Sikh, he suspected – and therefore statistically more likely, at least in that building, to be related to Tara Singh. The inspector was jostled and shoved while palming newsmen off like a rugby player until he made it to the elevator. The security guard recognised him, waved him in and formed a one-man human barrier to the massed ranks of reporters.

A policeman at the door of the apartment refused to let him enter the premises. Singh, tugging at his beard in a fit of growing irritability, insisted that he be allowed to speak to his wife. This request was acceded to upon the revelation that he counted Assistant Commissioner Patel amongst his best friends. Singh shuddered. Name dropping – what would he stoop to next?

'He's dead,' said his wife at the door. She was dry-lipped with shock.

'I know. It was on the news.'

'Already?'

He nodded. The death of Tara Singh was always going to be big news. Especially in the week that his granddaughter had disappeared and been found dead.

'We don't know anything,' she whispered. 'The police are downstairs. In the carpark.' And in response to his querulous expression, 'The body was found in the carpark.'

'Where is everyone?' he asked, looking over her shoulder into the empty living room. Death was certainly thinning the ranks of the family but not to this extent. The last time he'd been here the premises had been crowded and brightly lit with a coffin as its focal point. He sighed – what was that expression? – it wouldn't be long before it was 'déjà vu all over again'.

'I don't know. In their rooms, I suppose. Police said to wait.'

'Who's here?'

'My cousin, Ranjit, Aunty Harjeet, I'm not sure who else.'

'What about Tanvir?'

'Must be here too. I haven't seen him.'

'Poor old Tara Singh,' said the inspector. He felt an overwhelming sense of pity for the wealthy industrialist who had not survived the death of his granddaughter by more than a few days. 'I guess the shock was too much for him.'

'What is the surprise of that?' asked his wife. 'Maybe if you'd found out what happened to Ashu, he would not have died.'

Was she really going to try and pin Tara's death on him? To think that he'd actually felt sorry for her just a few moments ago. He should have remembered that Mrs. Singh enjoyed finding new ways to blame him for events outside his control. He spun around on his heel. It was time to desert his wife and find the police. As far as Singh was concerned, Tara's death didn't change anything. He still needed to find out what had happened to Ashu even if the man who'd assigned him the job was dead. The inspector stopped mid-thought – he might have to conclude his investigation from somewhere other than his present luxurious abode. Singh mentally tested his enthusiasm for the case and discovered it was still intact. There was no way he was going to walk away until he'd bullied Ranjit into telling what he knew and made another effort to find out what was going on at the factory. The fat man rode a wave of smugness like a champion surfer. He wasn't half as shallow as his wife suspected.

Singh hurried down to the lobby and then crossed over to the elevator that served the carpark. The reporters were absent and a raised eyebrow at the security guard elicited a thumb pointed towards the main entrance. They'd been evicted apparently. To his annoyance, he saw that the carpark lift was 'out of service'. A cracked plastic sign indicated the stairs that led to the bowels of the building and Singh began his descent, rubbing the heel of his palm across his chest. If Tara had been required to do this journey in reverse, Singh wasn't surprised the old fellow had keeled over.

He opened the heavy door at the bottom and was confronted with a hive of activity. Bright lights had been erected, colourful tape randomly cordoned off areas, flashing lights indicated a phalanx of police cars and an ambulance lurked in the corner, back doors flung open to receive the dead. The two attendants leaning against the side of the vehicle looked bored – their role today limited to chauffeurs of the dead rather than first responders to the living.

Singh scanned the carpark. It could have been a policing scene from Singapore except for the preponderance of khaki over navy blue and the unexpectedly hirsute nature of the policemen. The inspector deduced that it was a quiet morning for crime in Mumbai by the large turnout of Indian policemen, handgun-obscuring pot bellies hanging over black belts.

'Inspector Singh, I knew that you would soon be turning up here like a bad apple.'

Did he mean a bad penny, wondered Singh, and did it really matter? Patel radiated the bonhomie of someone greeting an old friend at a cosy bar, several tankards of beer already safely downed.

'What's going on?' asked the inspector.

'Very shocking news.'

'Tara Singh?'

'Yes, a most important man – leading entrepreneur here in Mumbai. They are saying that president will be attending funeral.'

'I guess we all have to go sometime,' said Singh, wishing firstly that Patel didn't sound as status-conscious as Mrs. Singh and secondly that he didn't sound like a country singer.

The Indian led the way to a particularly crowded part of the basement carpark and the inspector assumed that he would soon be in a position to renew his acquaintance with Tara Singh. He felt a sharp pang of regret that he'd been unable to provide the old man with some closure by finding out what had happened to Ashu. But at least Tara had avoided knowledge of the inopportune pregnancy.

'But,' said Patel, 'no one should have to go in such a way, you know what I'm saying?'

Singh bit off the desire to say 'hardly ever' and nodded sagely instead. He said, 'I guess Ashu's death was the final straw.'

'What are you talking about?' asked Patel. 'You think deaths are connected?'

'Well, it's too much of a coincidence otherwise, isn't it?' He noted that Patel was looking sceptical and felt a frisson of irritation. Surely it was obvious that the trauma of attending his beloved granddaughter's funeral had been too much for Tara Singh? Did Indian policing methods shun deductive reasoning?

The Indian policeman waved away a few medics and coppers and, with the flourish of a circus ringmaster, invited Singh to have a look. Inspector Singh leaned forward, feeling slightly queasy. He didn't mind murder victims, he'd seen enough in his career to have developed an emotional immunity to the presence of violent death. It was death from natural causes that put him in mind of his own weak flesh and inevitable mortality.

He needn't have worried.

Tara Singh had been bludgeoned to death.

The weapon of choice seemed to have been his ivory-handled walking stick which lay next to the body. It was unfortunate that Sikh custom required that mourners be dressed in white because his clothes showed up the bloody stains with nauseating clarity. His face, however, was unmarked.

'I thought he'd had a heart attack,' said Singh.

It was all falling into place. He'd wondered why there was an officious policeman at the door to the flat. He'd assumed that the death of a man of Tara's stature called for a scattering of a police officers like confetti at a wedding.

'The family don't know it was murder yet,' explained Patel. 'Better for all to remain in complete pitch darkness.'

Singh tried to gather his thoughts that had scattered like chaff on a windy day. 'What happened?'

'Don't have much details. All cars are coming back from cremation. Driver dropped him near carpark elevator and drove off – or that's what he says.' Singh noticed for the first time that a middle-aged man was sitting with a blanket wrapped around his shoulders, occasionally shooting terrified glances in the direction of the huddle around the body.

'That's the driver?' he asked.

'Yes – but nothing was stolen – wallet, money, watch – and there is very much better times for drivers to be killing employers than when coming back from funerals. Also, he has worked for Tara Singh for twenty years.'

The inspector nodded in agreement. That sort of longevity of service was unlikely to end in hasty violent murder.

'Shortly after that,' continued Patel with a pontificatory air, 'someone is attacking Tara Singh and doing this.' He gestured at the body to make his point. 'Security guard found body this morning.'

'And he called the police?'

'Yes, a couple of hours ago. And then we informed family of the death.'

'Who did you tell?'

'Tanvir Singh.'

'It's already on the news,' remarked Singh.

'Indian police not at all good at keeping secrets.'

'The press doesn't seem to know that it's murder,' said Singh reassuringly.

The two men fell silent, the bloody exclamation mark to their conversation lying on the floor between them.

'So who do you think did this?' asked Singh, at last.

Patel's eyes widened with cherubic surprise. 'But that's why we are telling you all the facts, Inspector Singh. Maybe you can tell us who is murderer.'

'Me?'

'You have been investigating whole family!'

'That's true – but this could be anyone ... a business rival?' Even as he said it, he knew it was unlikely. The timing was too much of a coincidence and business rivals very rarely indulged in such uncontrolled violence. A paid hit man, a bullet or a well-aimed stab wound. Not this bloody mess.

'I hope one of the early blows killed him,' said Singh, not bothering to disguise his discomfort at the sight of the old man's corpse.

'Could be happening that way,' agreed Patel.

'He would have seen his killer ...'

'Yes.' Patel reached over and pulled back Tara's eyelids.

'What in the world are you doing?'

'Sometimes they are saying that image of killer is printed on eyeballs of dead man,' Patel explained, wiping his hands on his trousers.

Singh pressed his palms to his own retinas as if he was

destroying evidence. When he looked at Patel again, he found he was the subject of a suspicious stare.

'Killer would have had blood on him?' he asked, to change the subject.

'Maybe – not that much, I think. Most of bleeding under the clothes – blunt instrument trauma. Weapon is walking stick – so killer not so close to body.'

'Finger prints?'

'Wiped.'

Singh sighed. Was there a criminal out there who didn't know to wipe his prints?

'Anything else?' he asked. Investigators had to be careful never to make assumptions about the behaviour of killers, it was the first rule in the book – well, right after the unwritten one that said investigators shouldn't pull back eyelids to peer into the deceased's eyes.

Patel shook his head mournfully.

'So what are you going to do next?'

'The usual – first we are sending body for autopsy, interviewing family, waiting for crime scene results, searching premises of suspects . . .'

'Looking to see who benefits financially from the death?'

'Yes.'

'And checking into his business relationships?'

A slightly more dubious nod greeted this suggestion. Perhaps Patel didn't want to step on the toes of the Mumbai elite. Well, he was going to have to overcome his squeamish-ness. One of the Mumbai elite was lying at their feet, a puddle of his blood reflecting the fluorescent lights.

'Can I sit in on the interviews?'

'With our pleasure, Inspector Singh,' said Patel, most of his shiny square white teeth in evidence. 'To have someone of your seniority and experience assisting us would be a privilege.'

The policeman smiled back at his counterpart. One might quibble about the assistant commissioner's choice of words and investigative methodology but he had a welcoming air that was in marked contrast to the glowering mien of Superintendent Chen. Singh was prepared to put up with a few foibles for a dash of friendly respect.

'So where shall we begin?' He knew very well where he intended to start – and was prepared to insist if the man's choice let him down.

'Upstairs?' asked Patel.

'Upstairs,' agreed Singh.

They rode up in the elevator in silence, surrounded by houseboys carrying large buckets of water which slopped over the sides and made the floor slippery and unpleasant.

'Water lorry is coming,' explained Patel.

'What?'

'In Mumbai, water supply in pipes is not good. Pipes very old. Lot of leakages, theft, and water table is low.'

'So?'

Patel didn't seem in any way put out by Singh's taciturn response as water sloshed over his precious sneakers. 'So water truck is coming and households are collecting water in buckets for washing and cooking.'

Singh had noticed a few dusty lorries which announced themselves as water trucks in large colourful lettering down the sides. Slowly, he realised, his mental black and white picture of India was being coloured in with information. He would soon be a genuine expert on the country and its inhabitants, unlike his wife with her dodgy Internet sources. They stepped out of the lift and Singh was dismayed to see that he was trailing muddy tracks on the lobby floor.

'Not to worry – soon they will be cleaning it up,' said Patel reassuringly.

Yet another insight. Nothing ever worked in Mumbai but the process of cleaning up the inevitable mess provided jobs for many of the unskilled residents of the city. In a way, he was part of that process now. On the one hand, he was trailing dirty footprints for some poor soul to mop up. On the other hand, he was trying to clear up after two deaths.

'How come you got this case?' he asked Patel.

'Because I was so very involved in first phase,' explained the other man. Singh assumed that by 'first phase' he meant the death of Ashu although, as far as he was aware, all Patel had done was rubber-stamp the suicide theory.

'Also, Maharashtra police on high alert because of judgment today so police very, very busy,' continued Patel.

'Judgment?'

'Title case – Jama Masjid. Verdict is expected today at Mumbai High Court.'

Singh remembered his wife mentioning the case to him. 'Are you expecting trouble?' he asked.

'Not so much – but better to be very safe than extremely sorry. If everything is all right, I am thinking someone higher up will take over case of Tara Singh soon. He is very important entrepreneur, you know?'

'I know,' said Singh amicably. If he hadn't known, he would by now, the number of times Patel had reminded him that morning. The Indian policeman didn't seem to mind his potential demotion and Singh couldn't blame him. This was one of those high-profile cases which were a nightmare to the investigating cops with everyone – politicians, press and family – demanding answers but providing minimal cooperation.

'What sort of security operation are you mounting for judgment?'

'The usual – cordon off High Court.'

Singh nodded. The glorious old building that housed the courts and the sweaty lawyers in their colonial-era regalia was an obvious target.

'Also increased police presence at flash points, road blocks, surveillance of known trouble-makers, ban on mass text messaging,' continued Patel.

'Text messaging?'

'That is main way that trouble-makers are getting flash mobs together for riots,' explained Patel.

Singh chewed on his bottom lip thoughtfully. Technology had a lot to answer for. He gave himself a mental shake. Soon he would be longing for the 'good ol' days', a blissful time when men were men, women were in the kitchen and children showed their elders respect. It did beg the question though – how had the more tiresome elements of society begun riots before the era of mobile phones – carrier pigeons?

'Also, meetings between police and community leaders. Army on standby. Schools closed also.'

'Sounds like preparation for war,' remarked Singh, yet again forced to contemplate the difference between Singapore policing's idea of a tough day at the office, an outbreak of jay-walking perhaps, and the Indian equivalent.

'Sometimes it is *exactly* like war,' said Patel in a quiet voice and Singh had a sudden glimpse into the abyss.

When they reached the apartment there were two people in the living room. His wife and the MBA, Kirpal Singh. From his wife's expression, which would have curdled milk, he guessed that there had been a frigid silence between them rather than a conversational outpouring. Singh sat down and realised that his shirt buttons were on the verge of popping. His rich Indian diet had expanded his circumference, like a party balloon blown to maximum. The two occupants looked at him with an air of expectancy. He mentally agreed with his wife's earlier assessment of the MBA's chin. Kirpal would soon have found that he didn't wear the *churidar* in any house-hold involving Ashu.

Patel busied himself closing doors and then sat down next to Singh. Apparently, the living room was going to double as their interview venue.

'Inspector Singh, perhaps you can be introducing me?'

'This is my wife and the other is Kirpal Singh who was to have married Ashu Kaur today.'

The commissioner attempted to adopt a suitable expression for each introduction. With the former, he grinned and wag-gled his head to express delight at the privilege of meeting Inspector Singh's wife. With the latter, his face took on a lugubrious quality and he said, 'I'm sorry for your loss.'

'Is it true that Tara Baba is dead?' The tone was clipped and to the point. Kirpal wasn't there for commiserations.

'Yes, I am very sorry to say it is true.'

'That is very bad news,' said Mrs. Singh.

'Very bad and very sad news,' said Patel. 'Will you tell us what happened last night after the cremation?' he continued.

'We were there before sunset – at the cremation ghat. The usual prayers were read. Tanvir lit the flame as the oldest brother.'

'Did you head back here right away?' Singh was already butting in.

'No, Tara Baba wanted us at the *gurdwara* for a few more prayers.'

'And then?'

'People came back here in dribs and drabs.'

'How?'

'I took an AC cab.' Kirpal glared at Singh. 'What are all these questions about?'

'Answer them and you might find out eventually.'

'You were not driving?' interposed Patel.

'No, it was very late by then and I was tired. I came up here, sat with the family for a while and then Tanvir offered me a shower and a bed for the night which I accepted.'

'Were you surprised when Tara Singh didn't turn up?'

'We all were. I think Tanvir tried to call him but there was no answer on his mobile.'

Mrs. Singh nodded to signal her corroboration of this part of the story.

'In the end, everyone assumed that he'd gone home to bed,' continued Kirpal. 'That it had just been too much for him.' He added as an afterthought, 'And I guess it *was* too much for him.'

'Were you all together when you got back here?' continued Singh.

'I suppose so – there were a lot of comings and goings. Jesvinder *Mata* had a nap, I think. Tanvir was on the phone.'

'In other words, if someone had been absent for half an hour, no one would have been the wiser?'

'No,' agreed Kirpal. 'I wouldn't have noticed. Most people were lost in their own thoughts. We'd just come back from a cremation, after all.'

'Of your fiancée,' remarked Singh.

He was greeted with a pained look. 'You don't have to remind me.'

'I heard Tara Singh was going to make you boss of that chemical factory once Tyler Junior retired,' continued Singh.

He noticed that Patel was staring at him, presumably impressed by his intimate knowledge of the family. It was true that he'd picked up a lot of information in just a few days – but it hadn't rendered Ashu's death less inexplicable. And now there was another corpse. Were two murders in the same family the equivalent of lightning striking twice? Surely one family was unlikely to encompass a multitude of murderers or a multitude of enemies. Did that mean that Ashu had killed herself after all? Or was there a single murderer with some sort of grudge against the family? Singh wished that someone would stop the merry-go-round in his mind so he could clamber off.

'Yes, that was his plan,' said Kirpal. 'He was a very generous benefactor. In fact, he intended to go ahead with it despite Ashu's death.'

'Looks like you'll need to start job hunting.'

Patel, who was clearly not of the school of investigation that required gratuitous antagonism towards suspects, cleared his throat loudly to interrupt Singh. 'Thank you, that will be all.'

Kirpal didn't need any further encouragement. He rose to his feet quickly and asked, 'Can I go home?'

'Stick around for a bit longer,' ordered Singh and Patel nodded his agreement.

'Who is next?' asked Patel as Kirpal disappeared out of the room.

'Ranjit,' said Singh. 'I would very much like to have a chat with young Ranjit Singh.'

The assistant commissioner poked his head round the door and issued a curt command.

Singh looked down at the coffee table and noticed that an album had been placed on it. He flipped it open and saw that it was a record of Ashu, from black and white photos of a chubby-legged toddler, through posed studio photos of a serious-looking teenager. There was a blown-up picture of Ashu and the MBA standing side by side but not touching. Shortly after their official engagement, guessed Singh. The album must have been put out for mourners to peruse and remember. He turned the page and found the most recent shots, colour photos of the *choora* ceremony. The inspector couldn't help but smile – it was impossible not to warm to the long-suffering expression on Ashu's face as her relatives congregated around her. She'd obviously found family occasions as tedious as he did.

The rest of the album was empty. Singh stared down at the

empty clear-plastic slots and felt a profound sense of loss. These pages would remain forever empty now. No happy family, no children. Was that a bit sexist? No Nobel Prize for Chemistry, he amended.

A few moments later, Ranjit crept in like the ghost of Divalis past.

'You wanted to see me?'

'Sit down,' instructed Singh.

Ranjit complied with the absent-minded air of one who was used to being told what to do. Unlike the MBA, he didn't ask for confirmation that Tara was dead. But that, decided Singh, wasn't significant – not when the death was on the newswires.

'Why didn't you tell us about Ashu?'

'I don't understand ...'

'You've been lying to me since the beginning.'

'I don't know what you're talking about.'

'You saw her that afternoon – the day she disappeared – you picked her up in the car.'

The dilated irises would have been evidence enough that there were secrets here. 'Well?'

'I don't ... I don't know what you mean.'

'Liar!' The single word cracked like a whip and Ranjit jerked away as if he'd been hit.

'Better if you explain,' interjected Patel and Singh had to work hard not to scowl at the man. He was building the pressure on this young man but Patel was functioning like an escape valve.

'Nothing to explain,' snapped Singh. 'He saw his sister with Sameer Khan, realised it was a romantic assignation and killed her in some bizarre attempt to redeem the family honour.' He watched Ranjit carefully, noting the Adam's apple bobbing about like a boat on stormy seas. The boy was going to choke on his own saliva. He added pointedly, 'We have a witness.'

'I would never hurt Ashu.'

'Did you hope to get into your grandfather's good books? Show him that you too understood family pride?'

'You think I give a damn about the old man and his opinions?'

'Did you know about Sameer?' asked Patel.

'No. I wondered once or twice – just from things that Ashu let slip – whether she was entirely happy about the arranged marriage.'

'But you did see her that day?'

Ranjit hesitated and then nodded.

'What did she say when you picked her up?'

'That she was in love with Sameer – but that she'd decided to go through with the marriage to Kirpal.'

'Why?'

'To avoid the scandal – for the family's sake but especially my mother and grandfather. She met Sameer *after* she'd agreed to marry Kirpal, you see. And, of course, he was a Moslem.'

'Did you agree with her decision?' asked Singh.

'*I* said that she should run away with Sameer. I thought . . . I know it sounds corny . . . I thought love was more important than saving Tara Baba's face.'

He stood up suddenly and began pacing. This was not the angry prowl adopted so frequently by Sameer but the desperate strides of a tethered beast. 'That's why I didn't believe she'd come to any harm, you see? I thought she must have taken my advice!'

Singh was at his most sarcastic. 'You're trying to tell us that when you left her she was alive and well and when she disappeared you thought she'd headed for the hills with the love of her life.'

Ranjit met his eyes. 'Exactly,' he said.

'Why didn't you tell us you saw her that day?'

'When I thought she had run away – I didn't want to point Tara Baba in the right direction . . .'

'And later?'

'And later – I was afraid.'

'Of what are you afraid?' asked Patel.

'I knew everyone would be so angry that I hadn't mentioned it before. Tara Baba . . .' He trailed off and stared at the floor between his bony knees.

Singh felt like shaking the young fellow until his teeth rattled. He believed him though. This was a kid more afraid of his grandfather than of being accused of murder. Maybe he was innocent of everything except cowardice.

'Right – so if you didn't kill her – who do you think did?'

The hands were twisted together in a tight knot. 'I don't know,' he said. 'I don't know.'

'Maybe is suicide?' said Patel in an optimistic tone which was rewarded with three matching glares from the other occupants of the room.

'Where did she go after you picked her up?' asked Singh. He was even more puzzled now. 'Surely you brought her back here?'

A loud thumping on the front door interrupted any answer that Ranjit was about to provide.

Jesvinder hurried in with Tanvir and Kirpal.

'Who's that? What's going on?' demanded the heir. He looked worried and it was no wonder. The assault on the front door suggested that the Grim Reaper had arrived for another member of the clan.

'You appear to have a visitor,' said Singh. He was interested to see that all the suspects were tired – and nervous. Maybe it was the unexpected cacophony in a house that had been as hushed as a tomb. Ranjit was shaking with fright. He'd lost weight as well in just a few short days and looked like a human lollipop. Events had taken their toll.

'Isn't someone going to answer the door?'

'I'll get it,' said Tanvir. 'It'll probably turn out to be a carpet salesman.'

'Very keen on a sale, I guess,' said Singh.

'I have policeman at door,' said Patel.

Whether the words were a warning or a reassurance, Singh wasn't sure. The inhabitants seemed to take it as the latter because they all moved as one to the entrance. The door was flung wide open by Tanvir. His hand remained on the door handle, his body squared to prevent ingress.

Singh, peering over his shoulder, was taken aback to see Sameer Khan. The Moslem man put a hand on Tanvir's chest and unceremoniously shoved him into the apartment. Either because the attack was unexpected, or because he was a better talker than fighter, Tanvir stumbled backwards. Sameer strode into the room and looked around, taking in everyone's presence, including that of the uniformed Patel. To the inspector's amazement, a small boy trailed in after Sameer. He was wearing a bright orange shirt and looked wan except for his lips that were a bright pink as if he'd raided his sister's make-up box for a fancy-dress party.

'Mahesh?' asked Singh.

The boy saw the fat man and smiled in recognition but there was a quiver to his bottom lip that suggested his heart wasn't in it.

Tanvir's voice was raised and angry. 'How dare you come here? What the hell do you want?'

'Your grandfather,' retorted Sameer. 'I need to speak to Tara Singh.'

Singh noted that he was poised on the balls of his feet, ready for a fight.

'Who is this?' asked Jesvinder. A woman who had lost her daughter and father-in-law in the same week did not have the strength for the unexpected.

Seeing her and guessing who she must be, Sameer said in a stricken voice, 'I'm a friend of Ashu's.'

'Friend?' Tanvir spat the word out as if it was a fish bone that had been lodged in his throat.

'What's the matter, Tanvir? Why are you so angry?'

'This bastard brought dishonour to our family.'

'What do you mean . . . ?'

'I was in love with your daughter,' said Sameer. 'I wanted to marry her.'

Singh was interested to note that Kirpal was so pale his beard and moustache looked like they'd been slapped on with black paint. Singh almost felt sorry for him. He'd lost a lot this week – his bride, his dowry and his pride.

Kirpal whirled around to confront Tanvir. 'You knew about this fellow? But you were going to let me go through with the marriage?'

'She was prepared to forget about him and marry you.'

'How do you know that?' interrupted Singh.

'It was what I advised when she asked me – and she agreed.' He turned his attention to Kirpal. 'It meant nothing.'

'It meant everything!' Sameer's voice was low and throbbing with passion. Great, thought Singh. Heathcliff's back. Or maybe this time it was Romeo. Either way, the farce was threatening to dominate the play – and that wasn't acceptable in light of the growing pile of corpses.

'The family would never have allowed Ashu to marry you,' growled Tanvir.

'Yes, yes,' said Singh testily. 'We've heard all this before. I want to know what Sameer is doing here *now*?'

'I want to see Tara Singh. I want him to understand what he's done.'

'What *has* he done?' Singh hoped that none of the others would butt in and reveal that Tara Singh was lying dead on the basement carpark floor.

Sameer stepped back, put his arm around Mahesh and ushered him forward.

'Who is this boy?' asked Tanvir, his tone hostile.

'He lives in the slum next to the chemical factory.' It was Singh who answered.

'Yes, and he's not well,' said Sameer.

'I have no idea what you're doing here, what you're talking about or why you've brought a slum child to my home but I want you all out.'

Singh walked over to Tanvir until his stomach was almost touching the other man's. 'You're beginning to bore me, Tanvir. Your sister was investigating an outbreak of poisoning at the slum. I suggest that you be quiet or I'll have Patel here arrest you and let you cool your heels in a prison cell for a couple of days.'

Tanvir subsided suddenly. 'You're right. I'm sorry.'

Singh decided to ignore the reason for this unlikely capitulation. He bent down until he was eye-level with the boy. 'What's up with you, Mahesh?' He liked this kid with the air of sartorial elegance, the slicked-back hair and feisty attitude.

'My hands and legs are not so steady any more. Started yesterday.'

And his voice was slurring as well, realised Singh. The child had been fine just a couple of days ago. Was this the dreaded illness that Ashu had been recording? Suddenly, it had a human face. A thin young face that looked terrified.

'I know what's causing it,' said Sameer triumphantly, pushing his hair back from the high intelligent forehead.

Singh turned to him. This then was the denouement. 'Well, spit it out!'

'Mercury.'

'Mercury?' Singh considered the quicksilver liquid that shone like polished metal and pooled like blood. 'Are you sure?'

'I was looking into the symptoms of mercury poisoning most of last night. Everything fits.' Sameer gestured at Mahesh. 'Especially the pink lips and fingers.'

Mahesh held out his hands and spread his fingers so that they could all see the highlighted extremities.

'And the behaviour of the rats too,' added Sameer.

'Rats?' It was Jesvinder who whispered the question. The peculiarity of the subject matter had pierced her veil of misery.

'They've been acting strange.'

'Dancing,' explained Mahesh, grinning impetuously.

Singh decided to ignore this detour into performing animals. 'Mercury from the factory?' he asked.

'Yes.'

'That's just rubbish,' barked Tanvir. 'None of our products carry mercury.'

'Not officially,' said Sameer. 'That's why I couldn't find any compounds that matched the symptoms.'

'But?' asked Singh. There was clearly a 'but' here.

'But I now know that the factory's best-selling product – the skin-whitening cream – contains mercury,' replied Sameer.

Fifteen

'Adding mercury was illegal,' added Sameer. 'Someone pretty high up in the company – like Tara Singh – would have had to be behind it.'

'I have no idea what you're going on about,' said Tanvir in a biting tone, 'but you need to think hard before making accusations against my company.'

My company? The heir really wasn't letting the grass grow under his feet. His grandfather's body was barely cold.

'What are you going to do? Have me beaten up again?' demanded Sameer.

An expression of pure satisfaction crossed Tanvir's face as he looked at Sameer whose bruises had lost their purple intensity but were clearly of fairly recent origin. If Singh had ever been in any doubt, he was now certain that Tanvir was behind the attack on Sameer.

'How did you find out – about the mercury, I mean?' asked Singh.

'Last night, I was at the factory, researching the various compounds used on the production line.'

'Looking for a needle in a haystack,' muttered Tanvir.

Sameer didn't deny it. He just carried on with his tale in a determined manner, jaw thrust forward as if inviting contradiction. Or a punch.

'I wasn't having much success. Anyway, I heard a car pull up outside. I had a look and saw it was Tyler. I wasn't sure why he'd come to the factory so late at night but guessed – hoped – that it was something to do with the poisoning. Otherwise, why the secrecy? I decided to hide in his office to see what he was doing.' Sameer spoke as if spying on the boss in the middle of the night was par for the course for an employee at Bharat Chemicals.

'*Hide* in his office?' asked Singh.

'Yes, behind a couch.'

The inspector rolled his eyes at Patel. 'So what did he do? What did Tyler do?'

'Well, not very much that I could see – he just spent a long time at his computer.'

'And?' demanded Patel, unusually brief in his curiosity.

'And eventually he got up and left.'

'That's it?' asked Ranjit. 'That's all you've got?'

'Once he was gone – I had a look at his desktop. I thought I might be able to break into his computer.'

'That's password-protected,' pointed out Tanvir.

'The password was taped to his keyboard,' replied Sameer, grinning suddenly.

Singh looked at him with interest. This was Sameer's moment of triumph as far as the chemical poisoning was concerned. But that didn't change the fact that he'd just lost the woman he loved and, despite his denials, quite possibly a child too. He seemed remarkably cheerful in the circumstances, standing there, legs slightly apart, one careless and yet protective hand on Mahesh's shoulder. Was Mrs. Singh right? Were the affections of men that transient? Was Ashu already in the past or did revenge leaven sorrow? He would have to remember that prescription for future emergencies.

'And?' asked Patel.

'And there were some interesting insights into the chemical composition of our skin-whitening cream. When I realised there was mercury content, I did a bit more research. Symptoms of poisoning at the slum are similar to a catastrophe in Japan in the seventies.'

'There's no proof that any of it has leaked,' pointed out Singh.

'There will be though. I've made a report to the various municipal authorities. They can't ignore it now. I took blood and tissue samples from the residents and passed it to them. I think they will show elevated levels of mercury. And I had a look around the place – the stuff is leaking out of some old pipes into the ground *before* it gets to the containment and disposal tanks. It's possible that mercury vapour from the leaks is also being emitted through the air-conditioning ducts – the vents face out towards the dwellings. Probably a combination of these factors – and it's been going on for a while since the residents are showing chronic poisoning symptoms.'

'Will they get better?' asked Mrs. Singh, her eyes drawn to the small boy clutching Sameer's hand tightly.

Singh had a sudden insight into how lonely his childless

wife had been all these years while he furiously pursued murderers. The inspector focused his gaze on Mahesh. He was certainly a boy to tug at the heartstrings. The irrepressible smile, the combative air and now the shaking limbs.

'I hope so,' said Sameer, meeting her eyes and matching her worried expression. 'But it's too late for the children who've been *born* with deformities.' He reached into his pocket and flung a photo down on the table. It showed a mother holding a small baby. The mother's face was turned away, her head covered in what looked like a floral shawl, probably the end of her sari. The child's eyes were closed, he or she peacefully asleep, but one small hand stuck out of the swaddling cloth and it was twisted and gnarled like the limb of an ancient and arthritic man rather than a newborn. It was good to know there was hope for Mahesh but Singh's eyes were drawn to the unnatural horror of that small hand. The crooked limb beckoned to him, demanding his attention, defying him to look and be unmoved.

The inspector cleared his throat. 'None of this explains why you're here looking for Tara Singh.'

'I think he *knew*.'

'About the mercury?' The man had been an old-fashioned tyrant, but surely not irresponsible towards his fellow citizens? Besides, Singh had brought up Ashu's theories with him and he'd been dismissive. The policeman hadn't picked up any hint of a guilty conscience.

'I think he knew that the source of the outbreak was the factory and decided to keep quiet about it. After all, he must have okayed the addition of the mercury. He was looking at a long jail term if word got out.'

'How did *you* find out he knew?' asked Ranjit.

Singh immediately picked up on the slight emphasis. He turned to confront the young man. 'You believe the same thing?'

'I don't know what you're talking about.'

'You asked Sameer how *he* found out about the cover-up . . . but you weren't surprised about the accusation. Was it something Ashu said?'

'I just knew Tara Baba – what he was capable of doing – that's all,' mumbled Ranjit. 'If he thought adding mercury to skin-whitening cream would sell more tubs, he'd do it . . .'

'And you?' Singh addressed his question to Sameer.

'It had to be him – who else had the authority?' he replied.

'Is that what Ashu believed – that Tara Baba knew?' It was her mother with the question.

Sameer shuffled his feet uncomfortably. 'I don't know,' he answered at last.

Singh wondered about the hesitation. And what was the implication of Tara Singh knowing? Would he have killed his own granddaughter to stop her destroying his reputation, his empire? Surely it would have been best to accept the suicide theory if that was the case? Why ask Singh to look into the death if he himself was responsible?

'What about Tyler?' asked Singh.

'The police are looking for him.' Sameer added angrily, 'They can't find him. He's made a run for it – like Warren Anderson.'

Singh's expression of puzzlement provoked Sameer to snap, 'The CEO of Union Carbide – during the Bhopal disaster.'

The inspector nodded slowly, his mind whirring quicker than a high-speed fan.

'If Tyler is doing his very best to escape, it means he's more likely to be doing the mercury poisoning than Tara Singh.' It was Patel, trying, no doubt, to protect the reputation of a leading Indian entrepeneur.

'I doubt Tyler cared enough about the company to try and boost sales by illegal means,' said Singh. 'He was just waiting for his retirement.'

'He knew though – if it was on his computer,' said Sameer. 'And that's why he's gone …'

'So why are you wanting to see Tara Singh?' It was Patel with the question, directed at Sameer. It indicated that, of all those present including his Singaporean counterpart, he was the only one to whom the murder of Tara Singh was a priority.

'I want to show him what he's done!'

'He's dead,' said Jesvinder quietly.

'What?'

'Tara Baba is dead. He must have had a heart attack last night – after the cremation.' She turned to Patel for confirmation but the policeman was not looking at her. His eyes were scanning the occupants of the room, looking, guessed Singh, for a nervous twitch that signalled guilt.

Sameer's eyebrows were raised, his brow furrowed like a smallholding at harvest time. Was he acting? It was difficult to tell. None of the others were manifesting any sign of shock, but they knew, of course, that Tara was dead. That was not news. Only the manner of his death remained hidden.

Sameer sat down suddenly on the long sofa. His elbows

were resting on his thighs and his hands hanging down between his legs.

'Do you think Tara Baba had something to do with Ashu's death?' asked the inspector's wife. The words were squeezed past a constricted throat.

Singh felt a moment of sharp pride. That was the exact question at the exact moment that he would have chosen.

'What do you mean?' asked Jesvinder. The mother of the girl looked faint. There had been too many revelations, heaped upon tragedy, for her fragile state.

'If he knew about the poisoning and didn't do anything about it – well, he needed Ashu to keep his secret,' said the inspector.

'If she refused?' It was Patel with the question.

Singh's eyes were trained on Mahesh. For some reason, the boy was smiling – a mischievous, misplaced expression. He hoped it wasn't a symptom of further mercury-induced degeneration. But it didn't look like an involuntary facial spasm. Singh would have bet his last beer that there was real glee in the buck-toothed grin.

'If she refused, *I* believe he would have killed her,' said Ranjit, staring defiantly at his mother and brother.

'Ranjit, how can you say such a thing?' The voice of protest was from Jesvinder.

Tanvir walked over to his brother and grabbed him by his shirt front. 'Listen, you little fool. Just because Tara Baba knew *you* for a weakling and despised you – that's no reason to accuse him of murder.' He laughed but there was no humour in it. 'If we'd cremated *you* yesterday, Tara Baba might have been a credible suspect.'

'There's no need to be so cruel, Tanvir.'

The man turned to face his mother.

'*Mata*, he should not say such things about Tara Baba,' he explained.

'I agree, Tanvir. But we are still one family – what's left of us.'

Singh looked around at his wife's numerous relatives. He would have been lying to say that he was impressed. There was Jesvinder, her cousin, who had stood by while her daughter was railroaded into marriage. Jesvinder's son, Tanvir, grasping for power and wealth with greedy fingers, and her other boy, Ranjit, wearing a hairshirt of half-truths and lies. He had taken a fancy to Sameer but if he'd really loved the girl, he should have put his foot down and insisted on marriage. And wasn't he a trifle too cheerful for someone who had just lost 'everything'? Unless it was Kirpal who had slain the golden goose. Surely the MBA was not that much of a fool? And what about Tara Baba?

The fact remained that one of them had killed Ashu – or at the very least, driven her to her death.

Singh inched forward so that he was sitting on the edge of the seat. 'How *did* you know?' he demanded, reverting to his earlier question. The inspector was looking at Ranjit as he asked the question. 'About the cover-up?'

Patel was confused. 'You are speaking of the mercury poisoning?'

Singh nodded curtly but didn't take his eyes off Ranjit.

'She told me,' he said sullenly. 'That afternoon when I picked her up – Ashu told me. She didn't know it was mercury, of course – just that there was *something* poisoning the slum.'

'What made her think that Tara was hiding evidence?'

'She went to see Tyler Junior that morning. They had an argument.'

Singh nodded. He had Mrs. Bannerjee to thank for information on that quarrel.

'Tyler told her that Tara Baba *knew* that the factory was the likely cause of the outbreak at the settlement.' Ranjit laughed bitterly. 'Ashu was shocked. I told her it was nothing more or less than I would have expected of the old man.'

'She didn't tell me that!' exclaimed Sameer.

'Tara Baba wasn't your favourite person. She didn't want to give you any further reason to hate him until she got to the bottom of things.'

'What did she plan to do with the information that Tara Baba knew about the poisoning?' asked Singh.

'Confront him,' was the brief response. 'Give him an opportunity to explain.'

'And did she?'

'I think so.' Ranjit shrugged and the sharp points of his shoulders were etched against his t-shirt. 'I drove her to Tara Baba's office. She wouldn't let me come in with her. She said she'd speak to him – didn't want me there because I always put him in a bad mood. She told me to go home and wait – she'd tell me what happened the moment she could.' He paused for a moment and wiped a hand over his face.

'Well, carry on,' said Singh irritably.

'That was the last time I saw her ...'

'So you don't *know* for a fact that she ever saw him?'

'Of course she did!' shouted Ranjit, spittle running down his chin. 'She saw him and told him what she knew and he killed her. Surely that's obvious?'

There was a pause while they all absorbed the certainty of his belief that Tara Singh had killed his beloved grandaughter. Singh gritted his teeth so hard, he felt as if they might splinter into a thousand shards. He didn't buy it. The grandfather's pain at Ashu's death had been genuine. The policeman reminded himself that sorrow and guilt were not mutually exclusive.

'Well, I haven't got time to listen to my idiot brother make unfounded accusations against my grandfather or his business interests. I have an appointment with a friend so if you'll excuse me, I need to get going,' said Tanvir.

'No one is leaving the premises until I say so,' said Singh, propelling himself to his feet by dint of yanking on the armrests.

'And who left you in charge?' Tanvir was dismissive as he marched to the front door.

'Inspector Singh is very right,' interjected Patel. 'No one is leaving.'

Tanvir stopped in his tracks abruptly. 'And if I insist?'

'My man at front door will arrest you right away.'

'But why?' demanded Tanvir in a voice that suggested his control over his temper was tenuous at best. 'Why must I stay here? Even if this chemical poisoning nonsense is true, and I don't believe it, it has nothing to do with me.'

'Because,' explained the Indian policeman, 'Tara Singh was murdered!'

'I don't believe you,' whispered Tanvir.

Patel shrugged. 'It's not at all important what you believe.'

'How?' breathed Jesvinder.

'Clubbed to death with his own walking stick.'

'But ... who ... who did it?' Sameer stammered like a teenager on his first date.

'I have my suspicions,' said Singh.

'You think it has something to with Ashu's death?' asked Tanvir.

'How many enemies does your family have exactly?'

'But you don't even really know – whatever Ranjit says – that Ashu's death was murder.'

'That may be so – but I'm sure that someone of your sister's personality was highly unlikely to have killed herself – and in such a way – and I stand by that conclusion.'

'Anyway,' interrupted Patel quickly, 'we are most certainly having a murder now.'

Singh pulled a face. There was a certain irony that he'd been investigating a death for days without any concrete evidence that it had actually been a murder only to be offered a fresh body in these latter stages.

The fat man sank into a sofa and picked up the photo of the slum child again. He flipped open Ashu's album and looked at the chubby smiling black and white baby pictures of the heiress. In India, without any genuine social mobility, the conditions of birth pretty much determined the trajectory of each life. But the baby with the misshapen hand and the heiress's path had crossed in this most unlikely way. He turned the pages until he was staring at the most recent shot of Ashu – hand outstretched as the bangles were placed on her arm – and then turned his attention to the gnarled hand of the other. There would be no expensive, grandfather-funded wedding for this small child. He didn't need a crystal ball to read that into her future.

'Is that an album of Ashu?' asked Sameer, sitting down next to Singh. He stared at the picture of the *choora* ceremony and winced but otherwise didn't acknowledge that it was an occasion that could give him no pleasure.

The inspector looked at the photo for a while, contemplating the short and eventful life that had been Ashu's. Especially contemplating the end of it – by fire. In many ways, that was the single greatest impediment to a theory of murder – the manner of death. In the absence of narcotics in the blood stream and any visible evidence of a blow, it was hard to see why any murderer would have chosen such a method. Tara's death left no such doubt.

Suddenly, the inspector felt his veins contract with shock. He flicked through a few recent photos until there was a close-up of Ashu's face. He held the album up until it was almost touching his nose and his eyes were crossed with concentration. He stood up and stalked over to the mantelpiece, picking up the framed picture of Ashu on her graduation. He wasn't wrong but he couldn't believe he was right either. The fat man was filled with unusual self-doubt and he didn't like the feeling. It was like indigestion after a good curry. But the evidence of his eyes was difficult to contradict – there was exactly the same missing element in each of the photos of Ashu Kaur. And it undermined just about everything that he'd been led to believe about the case and the curious cadaver at the centre of it.

Sixteen

Singh buried his face in his hands. How could this be? The strain was starting to tell and he was hallucinating. That was the only possible explanation. He thought back to the events of the last few days commencing with their arrival at the wedding home only to discover that a girl was missing and culminating in the death of an old man in a parking lot. He looked up through bloodshot eyes at the protagonists in the room who were all staring at him with varying degrees of curiosity and fear.

'What's the matter?' asked his wife. 'You don't look well.'

'It's true – you are very pale,' agreed Jesvinder. 'Can we get you something? A drink?'

'Ate too much,' said Mrs. Singh severely. It was a statement, not a question.

The inspector wondered whether to put his sudden suspicion to them and then changed his mind immediately. He would be laughed out of the room. His wife would probably take a swing at him with her handbag. Jesvinder would inevitably faint and Patel might decide to release everyone else and arrest the policeman from Singapore on the grounds that he was a few sticks short of a bundle and had probably killed Tara Singh because he'd heard alien voices tell him to do so. The only ones who would not be surprised were those who already knew.

'Sameer, who do you think is responsible for Ashu's death?'

There was a pause while Sameer considered his answer, his eyes watchful.

'I've said from the beginning that I hold the family responsible for everything that has gone wrong.'

The plump protector of the people decided that Sameer deserved a medal for obfuscation.

'How about you, Mahesh?'

'Why are you asking me such a question, Sardarji?'

'Don't be ridiculous, Singh – what can the boy possibly know?' Sameer was quick to interrupt.

'He told me once that Ashu relied on him for her work...'

'You're right – that should give a ten-year-old real insight into her murder.' Sameer's voice dripped with sarcasm. 'Anyway, can't you see he's not well? You shouldn't be upsetting him.'

Singh nodded his great head although the boy didn't seem particularly bothered by his line of questioning.

'You're right, he's not well and I'm not feeling well either.'

Silence greeted this admission.

'I must go back to the hotel and lie down. My wife is right – I probably ate too much.'

'What?' exclaimed Patel. 'Now? But what about this very urgent investigation?'

264

'I have to go right now. I'm leaving the investigation in your good hands.' He was as good as his word, leaping to his feet with an unexpected nimbleness and hurrying towards the door.

A belated expression of relief crossed Patel's face. Perhaps when he agreed to Singh being in attendance, he hadn't expected such erratic behaviour as had been on display. Singh had reached the front door. 'Make sure no one leaves the house,' said the fat man. 'And confiscate their mobile phones.'

If Patel objected to being treated like a peon, he managed to hide it.

A few hands went to pockets protectively and Singh guessed it was where they kept their supposedly indispensable communication devices.

A phone beeped with impeccable timing and Patel looked sheepish as he retrieved it from his pocket. He read the message, his face growing sober.

'What is it?' asked Sameer.

'Jama mosque judgment is out.'

'And?' This was Tanvir.

Singh was surprised to see that his hands were clenching and unclenching in anticipation.

'Land awarded to Moslem parties.'

'All of it?' asked Tanvir.

Patel nodded curtly.

'There will be trouble,' was the response of the young man, his eyes gleaming prophetically.

'Do you want me to come with you?' It was Mrs. Singh, indifferent to court cases and land disputes, with the question. Belated wifely concern? More likely a determination to nag him all the way about his apparent lack of commitment to this murder inquiry.

'Err ... no. You stay here and keep your eye on things,' muttered Singh unconvincingly. He stopped at the door and turned back. 'But I'll take him,' he said and pointed at Mahesh.

'Mahesh? Why?' demanded Sameer, taking an antagonistic step forward and placing his body between that of Singh and the boy.

'No reason for him to be stuck indoors on a fine day like this with a bunch of murder suspects for company,' retorted Singh. 'I'll keep him safe.'

Mahesh shrugged and sauntered over, hands in his pockets.

'You'll come with me?' asked Singh.

'If you like, Sardarji. Maybe you'll need my help to get into the elevator,' and he blew out his cheeks in imitation of Singh's rotundity.

The inspector considered changing his mind and leaving the smart-mouthed kid behind but then relented. It was possible that he was going to be very useful indeed. He ushered Mahesh out ahead of him, ignoring the confused looks of his wife's family as they watched the policeman with the reputation for tenacity go back to his hotel room for a nap while they remained incarcerated in an apartment under suspicion of murder. Singh knew his behaviour was incomprehensible. But he had no choice but to play the maverick copper. They would understand when – *if*, he amended reluctantly – he returned with the identity of a murderer.

*

Fears of violence after the Jama mosque result had kept many people at home because the streets were strangely deserted and they maintained a good pace. Singh, cramped into the back of the taxi, gazed out of the window with unseeing eyes, his attention absorbed by his latest wild surmise.

'Is this the way to the hotel?' asked Mahesh.

'Nope.'

'Then where are we going?'

'Wait and see.'

The boy scowled at the policeman and Singh almost smiled. He would have made the perfect Indian parent, he decided. He knew exactly how to annoy small boys with half-answers.

'Could be trouble today,' ventured the driver, looking into his rear-view mirror and then nodding at the old dome and minaret of the Haji Ali mosque, glowing white against the turquoise sea.

Singh met his eyes, distracted for a moment from his internal struggles.

'What do you mean?'

'Jama mosque judgment. They are giving everything to the Moslems. It will be causing trouble.'

'Are you upset?' asked Singh, mildly curious.

'I am a Moslem, *saar*. I am not upset because justice is being done – but I am afraid.'

'Of the Hindus?'

'Of the troublemakers ...'

Singh nodded brusquely but sympathetically.

They reached the factory in less than half an hour and Singh handed over a generous fistful of rupees and was rewarded with a broad, gap-toothed smile.

'Why are we here?' demanded Mahesh but was again ignored by the policeman.

The guards at the main entrance to the factory recognised the inspector and immediately began raising the barrier. Singh put up a beefy hand to stop them and gestured with a pointed finger. He wasn't visiting Bharat Chemicals despite its mercury-laden skin-whitening cream and missing boss. He had other fish to fry.

This time he marched over the plank into the slum without hesitation, knowing from experience that it would hold his weight, ignoring the stagnant water underneath. He picked his way quickly and quietly through the huddle of huts, largely oblivious to the curious glances of the women and the mild hostility of the men. There were no children about and he hoped it didn't mean they had fallen ill too. He looked around to ensure that the boy who called this place home was following him.

'Where are we going?' asked Mahesh again, panting slightly and walking with a certain wary care as befitted someone with unsteady limbs.

'To the clinic,' said Singh, continuing to march ahead at a determined pace.

'No, no – there is no reason to go there, Sardarji!'

Singh smiled grimly as he recognised the note of panic in the high voice.

'Why not?'

'Nothing there to see. You have file already, yes? Better if you go to hotel and sleep. This slum is not right for you.'

'I'm feeling much better, thank you.'

Mahesh did not appear pleased by the news that the fat man had made a miraculous recovery. He accelerated until he'd scooted around the policeman and was blocking his path, a skinny immoveable object in the path of a bearded irresistible force. 'You wait here, Sardarji. I'll go ahead and check that the place is clean.'

'It was spotless the last time I visited.'

'You don't understand, my mother is there.'

'I would be delighted to meet her,' said Singh over his shoulder as he skirted around the boy and a filthy puddle as if he had all the time in the world for a social visit.

They had reached the hut. A drape substituting for a door prevented them from seeing in.

'She is not well. Please don't disturb her,' shouted Mahesh, pulling on the inspector's arm, trying with all his strength to keep the policeman from entering.

Singh pushed the curtain aside and noticed that his hands were shaking in anticipation.

A woman was within, sitting on a stool, surrounded by piles of paper. She looked up as they came in, her expression surprised but not fearful.

'Who are you?' she asked, the voice husky and low.

Singh stared at the wilful chin and the glossy hair. His eyes were drawn to the earlobes, bare and smooth. His mind flashed back to the charred corpse he had seen at the police station and he heard an echo of Tanvir Singh saying, 'Yes, that's my sister.'

Mahesh had followed him in and now he said, 'I'm sorry. I couldn't stop him coming here.'

'This lady looks a bit young to be your mother, Mahesh.'

'Who are you?' asked the girl again. Singh noticed for the first time that she was wan and tired. Her eyes were bloodshot and her lips were cracked as if she'd cried herself to the point of dehydration.

'I'm Inspector Singh of the Singapore police.'

Her eyes betrayed a hint of nervous recognition at the name.

'And you must be ...?'

'I'm Ashu Kaur,' she replied bluntly, shifting a pile of documents to the floor and standing up so that she was able to stare defiantly into his eyes.

Seventeen

'How did you know?'

'I saw the body that your brother identified. It was charred, unrecognisable – except for a ruby earring. Earlier today, I was looking through your photo album and I noticed that you never wore earrings.'

Singh shut his eyes tight. He and the Indian police had missed a trick. But the identification by Tanvir had been definitive – and it had thrown them all off the track. Who would have suspected the brother of lying?

Ashu nodded and tucked a strand behind her ear so that he could confirm the accuracy of his observation that her ears hadn't even been pierced. 'Never liked them,' she explained ruefully. 'It was a sort of – small – rebellion against what was expected of me as the dutiful Indian daughter.'

'And Mahesh here,' he patted the boy on the back, 'not to mention the boyfriend seemed less heartbroken than when I saw them last. Despite what my wife thinks about men, I didn't suspect either of them of being so flighty in their affections.'

'When I slipped back here to the slum, I revealed myself to them. I needed people I could trust.' She added defiantly, 'I love Sameer.'

'And yet you agreed to marry Kirpal.'

'I hadn't met Sameer at the time,' she said with a small smile. 'I wanted to make my grandfather happy.'

Singh nodded his head, remembering the grief-stricken young man he had first met and the cheerful fellow earlier that day. Now he understood the transformation. He had discovered that his dead love was alive and kicking.

'But you got cold feet in the end?'

'Of course not. I'd agreed to go through with it and I was prepared to do so.'

'Which explains why you're hiding out in a slum.'

'I have no choice,' she muttered, looking down at the dirt floor, refusing to meet his eyes.

There was enormous guilt here, realised Singh. This girl knew full well what she had put her family through. All of them, that is, except for the brother who had purposely and carefully misled the police and the family as to the identity of that corpse. What had Tanvir been thinking?

'How is my mother?' she asked.

'Devastated,' he said bluntly. He was not going to give this girl an easy ride. 'Why did you do it?'

Mahesh – he'd almost forgotten that Mahesh was with them – marched over to Ashu and turned to face Singh. 'Leave her alone,' he shouted.

'It's all right, Mahesh. He has a right to know – they all do.'

She straightened her back and brushed the tears away with the back of her hand. 'There is something poisoning the slum dwellers,' she said.

'I know,' said Singh. 'The mercury in the skin-whitening cream.'

Her eyes – brown pools filled with light – widened at his knowledge but she did not question him as to its origins. Maybe she guessed it was Sameer.

'I went to see Tyler Junior, the manager of the factory.'

'The day you disappeared?'

'That morning.' She continued, 'He laughed at me – said there was no proof and anyway, my *grandfather* knew about it and if he wasn't doing anything, I couldn't either.'

'You believed him?'

'No, not at first. But he insisted and I started to worry . . .'

'What did you do?'

'I had an appointment with Sameer. I didn't want to be late – I'd left my mobile charging at home when I snuck out so I couldn't call him.'

'On Marine Drive,' interjected Singh and she nodded.

'Ranjit spotted me – thank goodness it was him and not Tanvir.'

'He didn't seem to mind about the appearance of a Moslem boyfriend?'

'No, he was shocked at first. But when he heard my story he thought I should run away with Sameer – forget Tara Baba and the wedding. He said my happiness was more important.' She smiled, revealing small even white teeth and once again Singh remembered the burnt body on the trestle table and shuddered at the recollection. Unfortunately, he reminded himself, Ashu being alive just meant that some other poor lost soul was dead.

'And so you ran away?'

'Of course not – Ranjit was always a romantic. It was what most annoyed Tara Baba.' She shook her head firmly. 'No, I knew my responsibilities. But I explained to him about the sickness at the slum, told him I needed to confront my grandfather – I didn't know it was mercury at that point, of course, just that it was *something*. Ranjit dropped me near Tara Baba's office.'

'He didn't come with you?'

'He wanted to,' she said affectionately. 'But I knew that if he was there, I wouldn't be able to have a sensible conversation with Tara Baba. They really rubbed each other up the wrong way.'

'None of this explains why you've let your entire family think you're dead,' said Singh irritably.

She looked worried and the stubborn chin was thrust forward. Singh almost smiled. It was almost on the evidence of that chin alone that he'd been prepared to doubt the suicide theory. It seemed he'd been right about that, at least. Sadly, that had been the high point of this investigative episode. Since then, he'd been wandering around accusing all and sundry of the murder of this very-much-alive creature in front of him.

'So what did Tara say?' he demanded.

'I never saw him.'

'What?'

'I was walking across the parking lot when I heard the sound of a car speeding towards me. I turned around and just managed to jump out of the way. Someone was trying to run me over. I managed to duck behind a pillar and make it to the exit.' She spoke in a matter-of-fact tone which was almost convincing.

'Did you see who it was?'

'I only had a glimpse of the driver . . .'

'And?'

She sounded troubled, as if she'd questioned the accuracy of her fleeting memory for days. 'I thought I recognised him . . . as one of Tara Baba's drivers.'

'And so you decided your grandfather was trying to kill you.'

Singh managed to inject just the right amount of doubt to annoy Ashu.

'Of course not, not really,' she snapped. 'But Ranjit had been so sure that it was a credible story – about the cover-up by Tyler and Tara Baba, I mean. And I really did think I recognised the driver. I thought maybe Tyler had warned Tara Baba. Anyway, I panicked.'

'And decided to run away?'

'Just to avoid going home for a couple of days . . . to try and decide what to do next. Whether to go to the police about the outbreak at the slum. I didn't have any proof and Tara Baba is a powerful man.'

'You stayed with Sameer?'

She shook her head vigorously. 'No, he didn't know. I didn't dare tell him, you see. He was sure to confront Tara Baba. I told him I'd seen Tyler, nothing more.'

Singh contemplated the young hothead and nodded his agreement that this was an accurate assessment of the likely outcome.

'Where did you hide?'

'An old school friend – she's just moved into her own place from Delhi. I hadn't mentioned her to my family so I knew they wouldn't think of her.'

'And then?'

'And then, the following day I read in the newspapers that my body had been found, identified by a family member, a suspected suicide.' Her tone was as flat as a chapatti skillet. She'd clearly rehashed the developments in her own mind and still couldn't quite believe it had happened.

'It was Tanvir. Tanvir identified the body.'

'I thought it might have been Tara Baba, buying himself some time to hunt me down. I was so afraid ...' She met his gaze squarely. 'Could my brother have made a mistake?'

'He said it was the earring – he recognised the earring – that was how he claimed to know it was you. The body was charred beyond recognition otherwise.'

'So he lied.'

'Yes,' answered Singh, drooping jowls and hollow eyes enhancing his likeness to the Hush Puppy beagle.

'But why?'

'I don't know,' admitted the policeman from Singapore. He continued, 'I still don't understand why you stayed away. From what I've heard of your character, I'd have thought you'd relish turning up alive to confound Tanvir and confront Tara. Instead, you chose to destroy your mother.'

'It wasn't just about me, you see,' she said desperately. 'The slum dwellers were being poisoned. If I came back, if someone ... silenced me, who could they turn to? These people have no one.' She added more forcefully, 'This way – I had a chance to investigate without anyone being the wiser. And, of course, once I was back here, I had Sameer . . . and Mahesh' – she hugged the boy – 'to help me.'

Singh thought he understood why the girl had gone into hiding – a dangerous secret, an attempted murder and the false identification of a corpse by her own brother. That and the situation at the slum. It made sense. She wouldn't have known whom to trust, where she could turn. And – rightly or wrongly – an escape from her immediate nuptials must have seemed like a silver lining. So she was hiding here – with a ten-year-old boy to protect her.

'No exactly Happy Families, is it?' remarked Singh.

Tanvir could feel a vein throbbing in his forehead. The thump, thump counted out the seconds as he wasted his time kicking his heels in the apartment. Assistant Commissioner Patel had asked them a few desultory questions about motives and their whereabouts for the period when the police suspected that Tara Baba had been killed and then disappeared into a side room where he could be seen striding up and down with a mobile held to his ear. And the fat man? He'd gone back to the hotel for a nap. Tanvir made a promise to himself that the minute he was allowed to leave – and got his phone back – he would ring the Taj and explain that Tara Singh's estate was no longer prepared to foot the bill for the Singaporean's luxury sojourn. The lazy bastard would soon be on a plane back home once his special privileges were terminated.

Tanvir glanced around the room. He'd have started to pace – sitting still was driving him insane – but that ridiculous boyfriend of Ashu's was already marching up and down. They would constantly have to adjust their paths in that small room if he was on the move too. And that would be an affront to his dignity. He wondered for the thousandth time where Jaswant was, whether he'd reached the target. He stole a glance at the pile of mobile phones on the coffee table – what if Jaswant needed some last-minute advice and tried to call? The Jama mosque verdict had been interesting – granting all rights to one side. He had no idea what the legal rights and wrongs were and didn't really care. The key fact was that the result was perfect for their purposes. He couldn't have produced a better one if he'd written the damned thing himself. The situation was set up like an arrangement of dominoes – ready for him to flick the first tile and enjoy the well-planned sequential collapse. Except that he was stuck here and his plans might be thwarted by a couple of policemen, not by design but by accident.

His thoughts turned to his sister. He wondered where she was. He'd been convinced that she'd made off with Sameer, ignoring his advice that she abandon her illicit love and conform to the standards expected of her by her clan. It wouldn't have been the first time she'd ignored his counsel. Hence his surprise when the inspector had told him that the boyfriend was still at the chemical factory, mourning his dead love. Where in the world had Ashu gone on her own? Tanvir was fast coming to the conclusion that, although his identification of the body had been somewhat premature, some accident had befallen Ashu and she was actually dead. It had been a spur of the moment decision to identify that body as Ashu's. And it had worked too. The manhunt had been called off; the police had quietly let the matter drop. If Tara Baba hadn't asked the so-called sleuth from Singapore to investigate, he'd have had a clear run to the finish. Instead, he was incarcerated in the front room with this motley crew of characters. Tanvir bit the inside of his cheek to stop himself screaming with rage.

There would have been, might still be, a certain awkwardness when Ashu finally put in an appearance – he still didn't understand where she'd gone if it wasn't away with Sameer – but he would just insist that he'd made a mistake in his grief. He didn't doubt there would be hell to pay – but no one would think for a moment that he'd done it on purpose. What reason could he possibly have?

Jaswant looked at the curved access road to the Haji Ali mosque. It was low tide and passable. He could see the food sellers and beggars as well as numerous vendors of cheap brightly-coloured plastic junk designed to catch the eye of a population that was still largely deprived of the fruits of the Chinese merchandise-generating machine. He knew that if he went closer, he'd see the goats milling around and the crows hovering as well as the piles of rubbish washed up against the sea walls of the passage. The smell was excruciating even from where he stood. He had to work hard to avoid clamping a hand over his nostrils. Growing up in Canada just didn't prepare one for the olfactory assault that was India. But it wasn't the stench that was keeping him away from the mosque. A line of policemen – they reminded him of the carved wooden figures in table football – blocked the way, letting in the devout and the merely greedy one by one, occasionally looking into a plastic bag or rucksack. He noted that the effort was sporadic, they weren't searching everyone – but he couldn't afford to be unlucky. He wished Tanvir was with him. He needed the other man to tell him what to do. He was afraid that any decision he made would be the wrong one – and an opportunity of a lifetime would be wasted. The Haji Ali mosque had been the best option. They'd expected extra policing, of course – because of the judgment. But he would have been in the place long before the barricades if it hadn't been for the delay. He'd gone to Tanvir's apartment seeking advice only to find the place crawling with coppers. He'd legged it – watched the activity from across the road and then decided that there was to be no last-minute consultation with Tanvir. God only knew what the excitement was about – something to do with the dead sister? – but he couldn't risk drawing attention to himself. And when he'd tried to call, Tanvir's mobile had been switched off. A very curious development indeed in the countdown to zero hour. Jaswant spotted a passing Fiat taxi and raised his hand. It was time for plan B. The driver screeched to a halt, a broad grin on his face at the prospect of a fare on a day when the streets were quiet because of fears of violence after the Jama Masjid decision.

'I just don't understand why Tanvir would lie.' She could not keep the hurt from showing and Singh had a brief sense of how much she'd suffered in recent days.

'There was some advantage to him if you were thought to be *dead* – rather than missing. What could it have been?'

His question provoked a thoughtful nod 'You're right. That must be the key.'

'When we – my wife and I – arrived at your home, the family was debating whether to call the police.'

'Tara Baba wouldn't have liked that.'

'He asked me to look into your disappearance instead.'

'Freelance as a private eye?'

'Exactly,' said Singh. 'I advised contacting the Indian police but they were still concerned about keeping the story from coming out.'

'People might have noticed when I didn't turn up for the wedding,' she remarked pointedly.

'That's what I said,' agreed Singh. 'And then the call came that a body had been found,' he continued.

'And Tanvir said it was me ...'

'The police were convinced it was suicide. They were desperate to get shot of the matter.'

Singh remembered that she still did not know of Tara Singh's murder. Well, that was the ace up his sleeve. It was also a reminder that there was still a killer on the loose, albeit not of this girl.

'The police really thought it was suicide?'

'Yes, the method is quite common apparently – especially to hide a pregnancy.'

'The girl was pregnant?' Her voice reverberated with echoes of loss.

'Yes.'

'But fire wouldn't have hidden her condition.'

Singh gave himself a mental pat on the back. Ashu the scientist would not have made that mistake – just as he'd argued to the unimpressed Patel. Unfortunately, the policeman from India had merely been anxious to make the case go away.

Make the case go away.

'I've got it!' said Singh, slapping a fist into a palm. 'Tanvir didn't want the police searching for you or, for that matter, armies of private investigators, relatives and the odd available policeman from Singapore. He wanted "case closed" stamped on your file. He must have seen his chance when he saw the condition of the body ...' He stopped and fought the urge to run his fingernails through his facial hair. 'But you might have walked in the door at any moment – surely it was an absurdly risky thing to do?'

'He would have thought I'd run away with Sameer.'

'Tanvir knew about Sameer?' Singh needed corroboration although he'd heard the same thing from the brother earlier.

'Yes, I asked for his advice – he said I *had* to marry Kirpal – anything else would bring dishonour to the family.' When the inspector did not respond, she continued, 'But why did he want the whole thing to go away – knowing how much it would hurt my mother?'

Singh leaned against the wall and felt the wooden planks shift slightly. He straightened up in a hurry. He didn't want to fall into the gutter on the other side of this flimsy construct. 'He's up to something – something that only needs – needed – a few days ...'

'Why a few days?'

'He'd have expected you to turn up at some point – especially when you heard that you were "dead".'

Singh could almost feel the whirr of his brain turning like the dials on a Swiss watch. What was Tanvir up to that a few days of respite from a police investigation had been worth the risky step of identifying a convenient cadaver as that of his own sister? He remembered Patel's request that he keep an eye on Tanvir because his college friend had links with Khalistani terror groups.

What had Patel said – that the KLF were targeting leading Sikhs? Had there been a plot to murder Tara Singh? Was that why he needed a few more days without the big black boots of the police stomping all over his turf? The inspector couldn't quite make the picture fit. Tara Singh's killing had looked spontaneous – and angry. Not a calculated assasination – a murder pure and simple. Besides, whatever his level of activism, Tara Singh had been a separatist at heart – hardly the ideal target for members of a Khalistani group.

He pictured the scene at the apartment that morning – Tanvir desperate to leave. Tanvir acting out of character and subsiding when he'd threatened him with incarceration unless he quietened down. The heir had been genuinely upset when his mobile was taken. A man who needed time, his freedom and a phone. There were shades of the past here. When was the last time he'd met a man in a similar position? In Bali, it had been in Bali, Singh realised. 'I have an appointment with a friend.' Those were Tanvir's words. His friend Jaswant? Jaswant, a member of a terrorist cell according to Patel? Jaswant, with whom Tanvir had jokingly suggested a joint venture. What sort of joint venture?

'There will be violence.' The inspector had been struck by the prophetic note in Tanvir's voice. But then he'd dismissed it to pursue other thoughts. After all, it didn't take a rocket scientist to figure out that violence was possible, even likely.

Hindu against Moslem violence in revenge for the unfavourable decision of the court? Moslem against Hindu violence in reprisal? But what did a Khalistani gain?

'Unintended consequences' – that's what Tanvir had said when talking about the Gandhi assassination and the death of his father. A single event – and a country had gone up in flames.

What if there were *intended consequences*? A match to light that flame. On purpose. It would only take one or two for the whole city of Mumbai to turn into a conflagration. One or two matches – like Tanvir, or Jaswant. Could it be? He flinched from the thought, a skittish creature, reacting with fear.

'What is it?' asked Ashu, watching his face. 'What do you know?'

'I don't *know* anything.'

'What do you suspect?'

'The worst.'

Patel faced his suspects glumly. He'd be glad when this poisoned chalice was taken from him. He'd done what he could – asked them where they'd been when Tara Singh was killed, taken swabs of their hands although there'd been time enough to scrub away any traces of blood, and asked them as politely as he could whether any of them had a motive for killing an old man in such a brutal fashion. They'd cooperated after a fashion but made it clear that they thought he was barking up the wrong tree – the killer was most likely some desperado who'd beaten an old man for his wallet. He hadn't bothered to tell them that nothing had been stolen.

Tanvir Singh had stared gloomily into the distance, stopping periodically to throw an angry glance at the policeman and demand to be released or at least be given his mobile phone back. The assistant commissioner had been tempted to fall in with his wishes. It wouldn't do his career any good at all to be in the bad books of the new head of Tara Singh's business empire. Only that last wink from the fat cop from Singapore kept him from folding like a cheap map. Inspector Singh was up to something – and Patel was prepared to try and hang on a little longer to find out what it was. He just hoped that this reliance on the policeman from Singapore wasn't a career-ending decision.

His phone vibrated insistently in his pocket and Patel retrieved it quickly.

'Singh here – is that you, Patel?'

'Yes, yes – where are you?' He was whispering but the sibilant hiss carried around the room.

'At the slum next to Bharat Chemicals.'

'What are you doing there?'

'That's not important.'

'They want to be released.'

'Don't you dare let Tanvir Singh out of your sight!'

Patel had to move the phone a couple of inches away from his ear; the bellow had almost shattered his eardrum. He left the room hurriedly, escorted out by the hostile glares of his suspects.

'What's the matter?' he asked.

'You're right – Tanvir and that friend of his – Jaswant – are plotting something.'

'What do you mean – plotting something?'

'I think they plan to blow up a mosque or a temple – trigger some sort of outbreak of communal violence in Mumbai.'

Patel felt his knees give way and he sat down hurriedly on the arm of a chair.

'The Jama mosque judgment – if they trigger a violent aftermath between Hindus and Moslems, it will be a huge coup for the separatists,' continued Singh.

'I don't understand – why should Sikhs be interested in this judgment?'

'Don't you see? It's the ultimate revenge. Society in flames – but no one blaming the Sikhs this time around.'

'Oh my God . . .'

'It won't just be your God in this fight,' growled Singh.

'Are you quite sure, Singh? What is your evidence?'

'Just a gut feeling.' There was no time to convince Patel that Ashu was alive and well and that her brother had lied about it. The Indian policeman would certainly let the dogs out – but for him.

'How are you expecting me to act on a gut feeling? Do you know who we're talking about here? The heir to Tara Singh's empire!'

'You're the one who told me that Tanvir was up to nefarious purposes.'

'I said there was a *possibility* that his *friend* was up to something – that's not at all the same thing.' When there was no response, he continued, 'Tell me what you know, I can't just be taking your word for this.'

'Patel – if I told you the rest, you wouldn't believe me anyway. But hear me out – if I'm right, there's no time. The judgment is out. That's what they were waiting for. If Tanvir is planning anything, if they want to make it look as if any action was in reprisal for the judgment – well, it will have to be soon. Very soon.'

'But . . .'

'Don't you see? That's why he was so anxious to leave the apartment. So upset about his mobile phone. His grandfather is dead. His empire is crumbling – but he wants to meet a friend? Don't you remember – he apologised to me when I threatened him with a couple of days' jail to cool his heels? That was completely out of character. I'm telling you – I've been here before, believe me – there's a ticking bomb out there somewhere.'

Could he afford to ignore the possibility that the fat inspector was right? Patel sighed. He'd always hankered after an early retirement. It looked like he was going to get his wish. 'What do you suggest I do?' he asked.

'Did you put a tail on Jaswant?'

'Yes – as you suggested. I haven't even heard squeak of a mouse from him.'

'Call him – tell him to arrest the Canadian. We have to stop him before it's too late. And then ask Tanvir Singh what the hell he thinks he's doing. I'm on my way back.'

Patel hung up abruptly and pressed buttons with fingers that were stiff with shock. There was no answer from the young man who was supposed to be shadowing Jaswant Singh. He tried again and then again and finally heard a faint voice issue a greeting.

'Where is Jaswant?'

'Lost him, *saar*.'

'What do you mean, lost him?'

'Am following him to Haji Ali mosque. He is standing there for long time, just looking at it. Like a tourist,' he added helpfully. 'I thought he was going to visit. But then suddenly he jumped in taxi. By the time I am getting scooter, he is disappeared.'

'When did this happen?'

'About forty-five minutes ago, *saar*.'

Patel pressed a finger and thumb to his temples and terminated the call abruptly. They had lost the scent. And there was no way of picking up the trail of a single man in the teeming millions of Mumbai. Jaswant was on the loose – and his brief stop at the Haji Ali mosque had been instructive – and chilling.

The policeman's mouth thinned into a firm line. Tanvir might know something – and if that was the case, he would find a way of extracting it, heir to a business empire or otherwise. He marched back into the living room and yanked Tanvir to his feet by the collar of his shirt. This was no time for half measures.

'Where is Jaswant?'

'No idea,' replied Tanvir. 'Sight-seeing probably.'

'What are you up to?'

'Nothing.'

'Is it revenge for your father? Is that it?'

'I have no idea what you're talking about.'

Aunty Harjeet, she of the wandering eye and protective instincts, stormed over. 'Have you gone mad?' she demanded. The rest of the occupants were watching the scene – unable to fathom this turn of events.

'We know what you and Jaswant are planning!' shouted

Patel, spittle falling like a fine rain on the other man's face. He couldn't believe that his beloved Mumbai was on the verge of another atrocity. Hadn't the people suffered enough?

'Then you don't need my help,' replied Tanvir.

'What's the target?'

There was no response.

'What's the target?'

Again, he was met with silence. Patel slapped Tanvir across the mouth with the back of his hand. The grandson stumbled backwards but did not fall. He stuck out a tongue and ran it along his split lip.

'We will all taste blood tonight,' he whispered.

Patel turned to Jesvinder. 'Talk to him,' he begged. 'He and his confederates are planning a terrorist attack in Mumbai. They're going to blow up a mosque. Trigger reprisals by Hindus. There will be counter-attacks. The city will burn.'

'I don't believe you,' she whispered. She turned to her son. 'Tanvir?' she asked, voice shrouded in fear.

He shrugged, the careless gesture of a man who had long ago made up his mind. 'These people killed *Pita*, *Mata*. Don't you want them punished?'

'The men who killed him, my son. *Not* innocents.'

'There are no innocents, *Mata*. Only those who fight and those who stand and watch.' He drew himself straight and Patel saw the fanatical glint in his eye for the first time. 'I have decided to fight.'

'Fight?' Sameer had crossed the room in two strides and had Tanvir against a wall in a twinkling. 'You're just a coward and a murderer who gets others to do his dirty work for him.'

Tanvir's face took on a faraway look as if he was lost in

memory. '*Khoon ka badla khoon se lenge.*' He repeated, '*Khoon ka badla khoon se lenge,*' like a mantra.

Patel's phone beeped and saved him making the decision of whether to intervene or let Sameer try and extricate some information out of Tanvir. He looked down at the message from a colleague at headquarters. He felt his chest cage constrict. Two words – 'Watch TV'.

Patel scurried over to the corner and switched on the television, ignoring the bemused expressions on the faces of his suspects.

A familiar sight – Mumbai from the air – filled the screen. It was a wide-angle shot from a helicopter. And then the focus zoomed in on a scene of carnage; the all too familiar plumes of smoke, streaks of blood on the ground and walls and piles of slippers collected by bystanders after the dead and injured had been rushed to hospital.

The reporter at the scene appeared. 'Eyewitnesses are describing black and yellow non-AC cab which stopped on the road, blocking the traffic that usually streams past the Gol Mosque in Mumbai – the mosque in the middle of the road – on both sides. A rucksack was thrown out of the back window. The taxi drove away just as massive fireball erupted. It engulfed all cars around as well as building. Some witnesses claiming that taxi was caught up in explosion as well. Experts say that only a powerful explosive – like C4 – could have caused so much damage.' The announcer took a deep breath, glanced over his shoulder as if still unable to believe his eyes and continued, 'Speculation is that the explosives were part of the supply stolen from army depot earlier this month. Leaders have urged Mumbai residents not to draw hasty conclusions.'

The telecast was interrupted to show an interview with a Moslem community leader who was incandescent with rage. 'This is how Hindu majority has greeted decision of courts in Jama Masjid matter – with wickedness. We will show them the wrath of Allah for this desecration.'

The next shot was of the Chief Minister of Maharashtra begging people not to indulge in any reprisal activity until investigators had got to the root of matters.

When Patel turned away from the television, he was just in time to see the smile of satisfaction on Tanvir's face.

'I have avenged blood with blood.'

'We still have a murder to solve,' said Singh, rubbing a tired hand over his eyes. It had been an intense few hours. Tanvir Singh had been taken away and his room was being worked over by bomb disposal units and counter-terrorism agents. Singh's demands that he be allowed to speak to the heir about Tara Baba's death had been overruled. The terrorist attack took priority. Of Jaswant Singh, there was no sign. The inspector suspected that he had indeed been caught up in the blast. Certainly, pieces of at least one Fiat taxi had been found at the site. There did not appear to be any doubt that the two men had been involved in a plot to stir up trouble after the Jama mosque judgment and persuade the Hindu and Moslem communities to turn on each other. Bomb residue had been detected on Tanvir's hands – but not, as Singh pointed out to Patel, any trace of the old man's blood.

'Much better for all of us if Tanvir is killing Tara Singh,' said the assistant commissioner.

'Yes,' agreed Singh. 'Unfortunately wishful thinking is not the same thing as evidence.'

'You said that you had something to tell me that was very important?' asked Patel, alluding to Singh's opening remark when he had burst back into the apartment with Mahesh, only for their murder hunt to be overtaken by events.

'Yes.'

'What is it?'

To tell or not to tell, that was the question? At the last minute, he'd left Ashu behind at the slum. It was cruel to put Jesvinder through a few more hours of hell, compounded now by the arrest of her oldest son. But he had no choice unless he was to ignore the body in the basement carpark. Besides, a picture was starting to develop in the darkroom that was his mind, a series of stills punctuating the narrative at regular intervals, beginning with the photograph on the mantelpiece. Unfortunately, it was all conjecture, unaccompanied by proof. Which meant he needed the girl as bait, an inducement to honesty. Singh eyed the other policeman thoughtfully. He'd trust Patel with his life, but not necessarily with a secret. And if word got out that Ashu was alive – he'd lose all his leverage and a murder might yet go unsolved. Besides, what if Patel objected to Singh's tactics? After all, he was hamstrung by officialdom – unlike Singh who was, for once, a free agent. Patel's phone rang and pre-empted any need for immediate revelations. He held up a finger to silence the impatient inspector.

At last he hung up and turned to Singh. 'Tyler Junior,' he said. 'We've got him.'

'Where?'

'At the airport – trying to get a flight out.'

'Good work,' said Singh. 'Can we see him?'

'They're bringing him to the station.'

'All right. Let's go.' He paused and then continued, 'I need you to send a police car to the slum to pick someone up for me.'

'Who?'

'We'll let that be a surprise, shall we?'

'Very well, Inspector Singh, I shall be arranging it right this minute on the button.'

'Well then, let's get everyone together in a couple of hours,' said Singh, slapping his counterpart on the back. 'It won't hurt to let them cool their heels for a while longer.'

'So – what do you have to say for yourself?'

All the fight had gone out of the American. He was hunched in a small chair and his hair and clothes were dishevelled. Singh wondered if he'd been roughed up. He caught Patel's eye and guessed that he was wondering the same thing.

'We know about the mercury poisoning,' stated Singh.

'It wasn't my fault,' said Tyler, not meeting their eyes.

'It wasn't your fault that the factory under your supervision poisoned hundreds of people?' Singh took the picture of the baby with the gnarled hand and flung it on the small table between them. Tyler glanced up, saw the image and flinched.

'I didn't know,' he insisted. 'I swear it!'

'That's why you were at the airport? Fancied a holiday in the sun?'

'I meant I just found out – I knew the Indians would be

looking for a scapegoat so I legged it. You'd have done the same.'

'I wouldn't have poisoned an entire slum,' retorted the fat man.

'What do you mean you *just found out*?' asked Patel.

'Last night – I went in to do some research – at the factory. I was worried about the outbreak at the slum. Discovered the mercury.' Tyler looked up at Singh. His eyes were bloodshot, fine lines like country roads on a map. 'You have to believe me!'

'I don't because I *know* you're lying.'

'It's the truth, I swear it.'

'Ashu Kaur told you about her suspicions almost a week ago. You didn't deny it. Instead you threatened her.' As Tyler opened his mouth, gulping for air like a fish on land, Singh continued, 'And don't bother to pretend otherwise – you were overheard.' Let him think it was Mrs. Bannerjee. This was no time to let slip that the other participant to the conversation was alive and well.

The American buried his face in his hands.

Singh had to lean forward to hear Tyler's next words.

'I didn't have a choice. I swear – I didn't have a choice.'

'What do you mean?' Again, it was Patel, determined to have his say.

'He threatened me – told me that I would only leave India in a bodybag if I said anything . . .'

Singh nodded his large head. It made sense. A man as powerful as Tara Singh – his threats would have carried weight with the American. In a perfect world, Tyler Junior would have stood up to his boss and elected to do the right thing. But India was not a microcosm of a perfect world.

'We will need a statement,' said Patel, suddenly the officious policeman.

'Don't you see – I can't go on the record. He'll kill me.' Tyler Junior was almost as grey as the grimy walls behind him. Singh noted that his hands were balled into fists, knuckles bloodless with fear. He also noted the present tense. Had Tyler Junior killed Tara Singh? He had good reason. But Singh didn't think it was him. Tyler's solution had been to run – not murder. And now that he'd been caught, he was far too terrified to be watching his tenses.

'I wouldn't worry too much,' said Singh. 'Tara Singh isn't in a position to hurt anyone any more.'

Two hours later, 'on the button' as Patel might have said, the unhappy cast of characters was assembled in the living room once more. They stood or sat as was their inclination, hardly anyone bothering to look at Singh. Sameer Khan, Kirpal, Jesvinder, Ranjit and finally, Mahesh, grinning from ear to ear. His wife was present too but Singh doubted he'd be able to pin the murder on her. Perhaps one day, when he was the corpse.

Who was missing? Tara Singh, victim; Tyler Junior, demanding to see someone from the consulate; Tanvir Singh, under arrest for other crimes and Ashu Kaur, presumed dead by some of those present, excepting Sameer and Mahesh, but alive if not quite well after the stress of playing dead the last few days.

'Usually,' began Singh conversationally, 'when I have two related murders – of members of the same family, for instance – I assume that the killer is one and the same person.'

He had their attention. 'Despite what you see on TV, it's not that easy to kill someone – not in person, after looking at them in the eyes, not if you know them – maybe even love them. And so it makes sense to assume a single killer rather than a statistically unlikely collection of murderers.'

'But what motive do any of us have to kill either of them?' Kirpal was pleading for understanding. 'And,' he added, 'Ashu might have committed suicide. You don't know for sure that she didn't.'

'Actually, I do,' said Singh, a trifle smugly.

'But why?' whispered Jesvinder. 'Why would anyone do this to our family?'

'That's the question,' agreed Singh. 'Taking you in turn, it's easy to find a motive for one murder, but not both.' He glanced around the room, full pink lower lip thrust out in a thoughtful pout. 'Let's take Ashu's death, assuming for now that it *was* murder.'

He glanced at Sameer who was wearing a purposely fixed expression as if defying anyone to read the truth on his face.

'Sameer and Kirpal,' continued Singh, 'might both have killed Ashu in a jealous – of each other – rage, but then why kill Tara Singh?'

Kirpal, who had opened his mouth to protest indignantly, changed his mind.

'In fact, whatever Ashu did, I doubt that Kirpal would have slain the golden goose.'

The policeman was pleased to see that the MBA looked conflicted, pleased to be exonerated of murder but unhappy that it was on the basis of his greed.

'Jesvinder' – he smiled a little sadly – 'is, in my professional opinion, unlikely to have been involved in either murder. Ranjit? Well, he might have killed his sister in anger when he found her on Marine Drive with her Moslem boyfriend – an *honour* killing.' The policeman put up a heavy hand to prevent any interruption. 'But we know that he was a young romantic who actually encouraged her to elope with Sameer.'

'Tanvir?' suggested Mrs. Singh. The inspector nodded in her direction to acknowledge the suggestion. Like Patel, she was pushing this most convenient solution. They were all keen to chalk up a couple more to the mass murderer if it got them off the hook.

'Yes, it is possible to assume that someone with his inclinations would not have stood by and watched his sister carry on with a Moslem man. But we know now that he had more important matters on his mind.'

'What about Tyler?' asked Patel.

'To cover up what was happening at the factory?' Singh's eyebrows were raised high. 'Surely he would have depended on Tara Singh to keep his granddaughter quiet rather than adopt such a desperate measure as murder?'

'But that's everyone,' said Mrs. Singh, her shoulders slumped with disappointment.

'Except Tara,' interjected Ranjit. There was spittle on his chin and he looked exhausted but he was still prepared to fight his corner. 'You're forgetting that my grandfather killed my sister to protect his precious reputation.'

'Well, he didn't know about Sameer so he had no reason to kill her as a matter of so-called honour.'

'Not that! Don't you see – because she was going to spill the beans about the slum poisoning.'

'But then why is Tara Baba dead?' Harjeet barked the question at him as if she was questioning a fishmonger's prices at the market.

'A very good question,' said Singh. 'And one that suggests that he did not kill Ashu to cover up wrongdoing at the factory.'

'You're wrong,' said Ranjit desperately. 'I told you – she saw Tyler. He warned her away. She went to confront Tara Baba and died after that. He *must* have done it!'

'Unfortunately, it turns out that Tara Singh was in the dark about the poisonous leaks.'

'How could you possibly know that?'

Singh looked at the young man a little sadly. If things turned out the way he suspected, the young romantic was in for a nasty shock.

'Tyler told us.' It was Patel who answered the question. 'Tyler Junior said that Tara Baba didn't know ...'

'But that's not right,' insisted Ranjit. 'Tyler *told* Ashu that Tara Baba knew.'

'He was lying,' was the curt response from Patel.

Singh turned back to Ranjit. 'Tyler told Tanvir about the outbreak at the slum. Tanvir warned him to keep quiet about it. And if anyone came sniffing around, to make sure the buck stopped with Tara.'

The inspector didn't bother to describe Tyler's sarcastic laughter when he realised the policemen thought it was *Tara* he feared. Only their assurance that Tanvir had more important things to worry about than his inheritance and a threat from Patel to incarcerate Tyler with the dregs of Mumbai prison life had persuaded him to tell the truth. It was guesswork for the present – there was a long queue of people waiting to question Tanvir Singh – but Singh was fairly certain that Tanvir had arranged for mercury to be added to the skin-whitening cream, determined to make the product even more successful and indifferent to the risk to others.

'So Tanvir killed Ashu? But what about Tara Baba?'

All his suspects were leaning forward in their chairs now, waiting for his answer. He had their undivided attention.

'So let's turn to Tara's murder then . . .' It was like Cluedo, decided Singh. Who'd been in the library with a weapon at exactly the right moment?

'Well?' asked Sameer when Singh did not continue for a couple of moments.

'You might have killed Tara Singh, Sameer.'

'Why would I do that?'

'Because you believed he killed your beloved Ashu?'

'If I believed that, I might have killed him.'

'But he came over here to confront Tara about the mercury poisoning,' pointed out Mrs. Singh with the air of someone having to do her husband's dirty work.

'That's right,' said Singh. 'The behaviour of someone who did not know Tara was dead – unless of course it was a cunning attempt to pull wool over our eyes . . .'

'You're talking rubbish, old man.'

Singh paused to wonder why the young always believed that the epithet 'old' constituted an insult. It indicated a complete failure to appreciate the value of experience. This hot-headed young fool could certainly use a wiser head on his shoulders.

The doorbell rang before he could point this out to Sameer.

Singh clambered to his feet slowly. The moment of the denouement was nigh and he was nervous. This was a high stakes game and he wasn't above producing an ace from his sleeve. But would it be enough to win the hand?

'Patel,' he said politely. 'Would you escort our visitor in here?'

Jesvinder fainted. Her eyes rolled back into her head and she slumped to the ground. Sameer hurried to her side and gently carried her to the sofa where he laid her down. He spared a smile for Ashu but his underlying expression was filled with worry as she knelt down by the couch and hugged the reclining figure. He didn't like recent developments, guessed Singh.

'What's going on?' The question was from Ranjit. He had risen to his feet as if yanked upright by a puppeteer as his sister walked in but now stood with his eyes focused on the floor, refusing to look up at the apparition that was Ashu. A strange reaction for a brother who had just seen his sister rise from the dead?

Mahesh ran over to the girl and gave her a hug. 'I'm glad you are here, Doctor Amma,' he whispered.

'I'm glad to be home,' said Ashu, smiling a little through her tears, clasping her mother's hand tightly.

The inspector noted that Sameer was grimacing at her – trying to warn her that Singh had more conjuring tricks than a mere resurrection.

'Who is this?' demanded Patel, although Singh had spotted him turn to the mantelpiece to stare at the framed photograph and then back at Ashu again. He knew, but couldn't believe the evidence of his own eyes. His moustache was wriggling like a caterpillar as his mouth worked silently.

'Ahh, I see introductions are in order,' said Singh. 'Assistant Commissioner Patel, this is Ashu Kaur, previously presumed dead, granddaughter of Tara Singh, wife-to-be of Kirpal, sister of Ranjit and Tanvir, lover of Sameer ...'

He paused and looked around the room. This was the moment he had been waiting for but suddenly he was unsure whether to continue. Did he have the right to add to the trauma of those present? Especially Jesvinder? He remembered his recent case in Cambodia. He had weighed up justice against human heartbreak then, and regretted his decision almost every moment of every day. And now, that insidious choice was before him once more. Singh sighed. 'And Ashu's last role? *A murderer*, of course.'

'What?' 'What are you saying?' 'Have you gone quite mad?'

This must have been what the Tower of Babel sounded like, decided Singh, tempted to put his hands over his ears like a child.

Sameer marched up to him until they were toe to toe. 'What in hell are you talking about?' he demanded furiously. 'How dare you say such a thing?'

However, it was the accused killer – expression bewildered – who asked the most pertinent question. 'Who's dead?' said Ashu.

It was Mrs. Singh who answered. 'Your grandfather,' she said quietly. 'Tara Baba is dead.'

'Killed?' The voice was hollow with shock.

Patel glanced at Singh quickly. The inspector had no

difficulty in reading his mind – if this was the killer, she was a fine actress too.

Well, that was indubitably the case. Hadn't she played dead for almost a week?

'Yes,' answered Mrs. Singh, who seemed to have appointed herself spokesperson for the moment. 'The police say he was hit with his own walking stick.'

Ashu grasped the back of a chair for balance and whispered, 'But why would I want to hurt Tara Baba?'

Singh was ready for that. 'Because he was keeping you apart from Sameer, because he was poisoning the slum, because he was covering it up, because you suspected him of trying to kill you? Take your pick.'

'But I thought you said it was Tanvir?' said Mrs. Singh.

'I said that Tanvir had a good motive to kill Ashu,' corrected Singh. 'But as you can see, she's not actually dead.'

'Did Tanvir make a mistake?'

'With the identification? No, he did it on purpose.'

'But why?' Mrs. Singh's eyes and mouth made perfect circles of shock.

'He thought that she'd run away with Sameer – didn't want a manhunt until after the judgment so that nothing would interfere with his grand plans to turn Mumbai into a war zone.'

'I could never have harmed Tara Baba. I loved him,' whispered Ashu.

'I don't believe you,' said Singh in his most cutting tone. 'You killed him – an old man who loved you more than anyone. How could you do it?'

'No, I didn't – I swear it!'

'Such a pity you'll be gone again – arrested for the murder of your own flesh and blood – when your mother wakes up.' Singh knew that his words were causing pain but he gritted his teeth and persevered. 'It will be like you died twice for her now.'

Singh knew who had murdered Tara Singh, of course. Had known almost from the moment it transpired that Ashu was alive and therefore there was only one victim – and one killer – to be reckoned with. Tara Singh had been killed in a rage. The rage a brother might feel if he thought his beloved sister had been murdered. Callously done to death to preserve a dirty secret about tainted products at a factory. Not the older brother who only cared about honour and revenge but the younger one who already hated the old man for the years of humiliation he'd suffered at his hands.

Singh sighed. How was it that he so often felt sorry for the murderers he identified?

'Come, Ashu. It is time to go,' he said, refusing to acknowledge the bewilderment deepening to panic in her light eyes.

There was a strangled cry from across the room. The inspector turned to watch him – surely he would break now? Singh didn't believe, couldn't believe that his murderer would let another be taken in his place. On cue, Ranjit fell to his knees, sobbing as if his heart would break. A sapling felled, thought Singh sadly.

'I did it,' he sobbed. 'It wasn't Ashu, I swear. I killed Tara Baba.'

Epilogue

Patel, Mrs. Singh and the smug Singaporean inspector sat at a small table at Leopold's drinking large quantities of beer. Well, the policemen were drinking beer. Mrs. Singh was drinking a sour lime juice with a puckered mouth.

'But you knew it was Ranjit, isn't that so? You accused Ashu to trick him into confessing.' Patel's expression was of a man who intended to slam every stable door shut.

Singh nodded. 'I had to – there wasn't really any evidence against him, you see.'

'But how did *you* know?' asked Mrs. Singh, her tone suggesting that she expected him to confess to a lucky guess.

The inspector smiled. It appeared that her days of being a supportive wife had been numbered. Just as well, really. Singh was not one who liked unexpected changes in routine.

'He was always the most likely person to have killed Tara. He became convinced that Ashu hadn't committed suicide – I think Farzana's certainty that Ashu would never have done something like that was the final straw. He decided, based on what Ashu had told him about the factory, that his grandfather was responsible. It was the so-called death of Ashu that confused the issue for me. There was no way Ranjit would have harmed his sister. Once I realised that Ashu was alive ...'

Patel nodded energetically to acknowledge this insight – unlike Mrs. Singh, he was not stinting with praise.

Singh continued, 'Ranjit really hated the old man. Once he'd concluded that Tara murdered Ashu to protect his good name, well, there was always going to be trouble.'

'He says he confronted Tara that evening after cremation. Old man is mocking him for getting wrong end of pole. Ranjit is losing his temper ...' Patel trailed off as they both remembered the battered body of the frail old man.

'At least he was brave enough to confess when he thought you were going to lock his sister away,' said the inspector's wife tartly.

'Yes, he was,' agreed Singh, feeling sorry for the skinny young beanpole.

'But who *tried* to kill Ashu?' asked Mrs. Singh, who'd heard the whole story now from various sources but was struggling to turn the pieces into a complete picture. 'Who tried to run her over?'

'Tyler Junior arranged it,' said Singh. 'After he told her that Tara was aware of the problem at the factory to quieten her down. He knew she'd head straight to her grandfather to demand the truth from him. Tyler couldn't take that risk.' He continued, 'Tara Singh was an impossible fellow but he really did love his granddaughter.' There were nods of agreement all around.

The inspector paused to wonder how much Tara's nationalist rhetoric had influenced Tanvir growing up. Would he have become a killer anyway or had his grandfather watered the seeds of anger? There was blame enough to go around, that much was sure.

'We found that driver Ashu mentioned – the one she recognised as being Tara's employee – had been seconded to Bharat Chemicals,' said Patel. 'But Tyler is refusing to confess to this, of course,' added the Indian. 'He wants all the dollars and cents to stop with Tara or Tanvir.' The policeman looked glum at the thought that he wouldn't be able to pin attempted murder on Tyler Junior.

Singh winced at the mangling of yet another metaphor but then said bracingly, 'Don't look so depressed – you did solve the murder of Tara Singh.' Assistant Commissioner Patel had been lauded in the newspapers as the hero of the hour, solving a murder within twenty-four hours of the discovery of the body as well as apprehending the perpetrator of the Mumbai mosque attacks so rapidly.

The other man smiled his thanks.

'What about the dead girl?' asked Singh, his thoughts turning to the corpse that had sparked the murder investigation that wasn't.

'No one has come forward to claim body. No missing persons matching her description.'

Both men fell silent, aware that this Jane Doe – with no rich grandfather to demand answers – was destined to be a footnote in the annals of unsolved deaths.

Patel cleared his throat. 'How is your family, Mrs. Singh?'

'My poor cousin,' she muttered in response.

Jesvinder had awakened from her faint to discover she had regained a daughter but lost two sons. Sameer's solicitous behaviour towards her suggested that the numbers would soon change again. Mahesh had remained with them too, unwilling to leave his precious Doctor Amma and return to the slum. Ashu had assured Singh that she would take care of him, include him in the family, even help his mother escape from the brutal father. She owed him so much. A further evening up of the numbers of menfolk, thought Singh. And she had the money to do it now that Tara was dead and she was the last heir left standing.

'No husband and now no sons . . .' continued his wife.

It was time to change the subject, decided Singh – he needed to get away from a contemplation of his wife's enormous and conflicted family.

'Jaswant?' he asked, seeking an update on the terrorist investigation.

'We are finding his DNA at site of attack.'

Singh nodded – it was a sort of justice, he supposed.

'We have also managed to convince people that attack on Gol Mosque was by Sikh separatists, trying to cause very much trouble,' explained Patel.

Singh had seen the wall-to-wall coverage on television. 'So, there have been no reprisals for the attack? Their plan failed?'

Patel shifted uncomfortably in his seat. 'Well, no reprisals against Hindus or Moslems but a *gurdwara* was torched outside town and a few Sikhs were killed.'

Singh closed his eyes and contemplated the gloom within. Circles within circles. Would a child of one of these dead men – killed in a holy place – grow up with revenge on his mind like Tanvir Singh had done? It didn't bear thinking about.

The fat policeman from Singapore was pleased that his flight home was that evening. He would gladly fly over the rust and blue sea of slums and return to Singapore. Superintendent Chen had relented – no doubt the unsolved murder rate had spiked uncontrollably – and he was to be allowed back at his desk. He looked forward to having a smoke with only the usual amount of social opprobrium. In the meantime, there was only one thing for it. Inspector Singh stole a glance at his wife and then beckoned for a waiter. A beer would definitely help pass the time.

Also available in Shamini Flint's exciting series featuring one-of-a-kind Inspector Singh …

INSPECTOR SINGH INVESTIGATES: A MOST PECULIAR MALAYSIAN MURDER

Stop No. 1: Malaysia …

Inspector Singh is in a bad mood. He's been sent from his home in Singapore to Kuala Lumpur to solve a murder that has him stumped. Chelsea Liew – the famous Singaporean model – is on death row for the murder of her ex-husband. She swears she didn't do it, he *thinks* she didn't do it, but no matter how hard he tries to get to the bottom of things, he still arrives back at the same place – that Chelsea's husband was shot at point blank range, and that Chelsea had the best motivation to pull the trigger: he was taking her kids away from her.

Now Inspector Singh must pull out all the stops to crack a crime that could potentially free a beautiful and innocent woman and reunite a mother with her children. There's just one problem – the Malaysian police refuse to play ball …

978-0-7499-2975-6